Advance praise for *Fugue De*

"I've been a Stephen Mark Rainey fan for more than 30 years now, and there's good reason for that—he's a consummate storyteller who cares deeply about his craft. *Fugue Devil Resurgence* represents Rainey working at the top of his game and is cause for celebration. These stories frighten and dazzle, chill to the bone and linger. *Fugue Devil Resurgence* should be at the top of everyone's list this year!"

—Richard Chizmar
Publisher and editor of *Cemetery Dance*
Author of *Chasing the Boogeyman*
Gwendy's Magic Feather (with Stephen King)

"*Fugue Devil* is a modern masterpiece. The sense of place, the deceptively laid-back quality of the narrator's voice, the legend of the Fugue Devil itself, the familial disintegration, the feelings of alienation and guilt and helplessness, all combine to weave a genuinely scary story."

—Gary Braunbeck
Author of *In Silent Graves*
Prodigal Blues
Coffin County

"Stephen Mark Rainey is a master of stories featuring ordinary, recognizable, often flawed people who unwittingly or sometimes intentionally and defiantly encounter extraordinary, terrifying circumstances and creatures. The Fugue Devil is one of the scariest supernatural beings ever to grace fiction's pages.

Its legend precedes it: 'If you know about it, it knows about you. If you see it, it comes for you.' Rainey gives the reader glimpses of this monster, building the horror, page after page, until it hits the characters and the reader square in the face—and heart—with a clawed and bloody fist."

—Elizabeth Massie
Author of *Sineater*
Hell Gate
Madame Cruller's Couch and Other Dark and Bizarre Tales

FUGUE DEVIL

RESURGENCE

Also by Stephen Mark Rainey

Novels:
Balak
The Lebo Coven
Dark Shadows: Dreams of the Dark (with Elizabeth Massie)
The Nightmare Frontier
Blue Devil Island
The Monarchs
Young Blood: Evil Intentions (with Mat & Myron Smith)

Short Story Collections:
Fugue Devil & Other Weird Horrors
The Last Trumpet
Legends of the Night
Other Gods
The Gaki & Other Hungry Spirits

Novels in Elizabeth Massie's Ameri-Scares Series for Young Readers:
West Virginia: Lair of the Mothman
Michigan: The Dragon of Lake Superior
Ohio: Fear the Grassman!
New Hampshire: Ghosts from the Skies
Georgia: The Haunting of Tate's Mill

Anthologies Edited:
Deathrealms
Song of Cthulhu
Evermore (with James Robert Smith)

Audio Drama Scripts
Dark Shadows: The Path of Fate
Dark Shadows: Curse of the Pharoah
Dark Shadows: Blood Dance

Black Raven Books

Be mighty afeared!
All the best.

FUGUE DEVIL
RESURGENCE

STEPHEN MARK RAINEY

FIRST EDITION

Cover illustrations copyright © 2022 by Daniele Serra

www.stephenmarkrainey.com/

ISBN 9781948594479

This book is dedicated to the memory of my brother, Alan "Phred" Rainey. May your music, art, life, and love grace the heavens now and forever.

Table of Contents

Introduction

The Devil in the Dream

It was a youthful night horror—the most intense I've ever had—that would eventually give birth to "Fugue Devil." I was 12 or 13 years old when that terrifying dream occurred, and I still recall its details more clearly than most waking memories. In it, the titular beast haunted the woods behind my family's house (which, since my mom's passing some time ago, I now own and hope to keep for the duration of this life).

These woods are not very large; maybe a dozen or so acres that create a buffer between streets in the neighborhood. In the spring and summer, though, when the woods are in full bloom, they feel like a massive forest because you can't see the houses that, in reality, aren't very far away.

To this day, I call those "The Fugue Devil's Woods." They're quite beautiful, really, and I've always loved wandering among them. I still do, frequently. But even now, at night, when I gaze into their deep, impenetrable shadows, a little chill comes rushing back.

I can't say that I believe in any sort of spirit world; however, if spirit beings should exist in whatever fashion, I can't help but think the one that inspired such a traumatic experience must still linger in those woods.

The dream came in three phases, each of which culminated in the appearance of the Fugue Devil itself. With each of its manifestations, I woke in a cold sweat—a peculiar sensation I had never experienced before and never have since.

After the first two frightful jolts into consciousness, I fell back to sleep, only for the dream to continue where it had left off. The Fugue Devil's final appearance woke me just as dawn began to brighten the sky. And that was all she wrote for that night's sleep.

The adolescent Mark was most enamored of monster movies (as is the adult Mark, I will readily confess), and I religiously collected copies of *Famous Monsters of Filmland*, *Castle of Frankenstein*, *The Monster Times*, and other publications that showcased my favorite cinematic horrors.

Back then, the black-and-white chillers of the 1930s through the 1960s were most prevalent, and the beastly main characters from *The Creature from the Black Lagoon*, *Curse (Night) of the Demon*, *The She-Creature*, and others of that ilk emblazoned themselves in my impressionable little brain (as much from images in the monster magazines as from the movies themselves; had my parents known this, I certainly wouldn't have so many of those old issues tucked away in the vault today).

It's safe to say the Fugue Devil was an amalgamation of those critters that unnerved me so in my impressionable youth.

I began writing professionally in the mid-1980s, and for several years, I struggled with how to turn that nightmare into some kind of coherent story. In 1991, I figured it out, and thus wrote the novelette, "Fugue Devil," roughly 20 years after experiencing the dream. The story's theme, characters, and plot diverge radically from the dream itself, but the creature's main appearances are all in there. They *had* to be.

Later in the 1990s, I experienced another nightmare featuring the Fugue Devil. It certainly wasn't as traumatic as the original, but unlike so many dreams, it had a solid, lucid plot. Clearly, it sprang from some of my most significant life experiences at that time, and I was able to write the dream as the sequel to "Fugue Devil" (titled "The Devil's Eye") almost exactly as it had unfolded in my subconscious.

During my early years as a writer, I developed certain continuities among stories—settings, characters, themes— and the Fugue Devil novelettes fit very nicely into the continuity I had begun with the tale "Threnody" (1986), which also appears in this collection.

It has been 30 years since the publication of my first fiction collection, *Fugue Devil & Other Weird Horrors* (Macabre Ink, 1992), now long out of print. When the proprietor of Black Raven Books asked whether I might be interested in compiling a new fiction collection as something of a 30th anniversary celebration of "Fugue Devil," you can bet I enthusiastically agreed.

So, here it is: the Fugue Devil's *Resurgence*, featuring three of what I consider my most essential tales—"Fugue Devil," "Threnody," and "The Devil's Eye"—along with a number of others that span the three-plus decades of my career. Several of these have been published in other magazines and anthologies, and a few are being presented here for the first time. I hope you enjoy the lot, and that they might even scare the pants off you.

(Bear in mind, I cannot be held responsible for your pants.)

Go forth, and be greatly afeared.

—Stephen Mark Rainey
12/12/21, Greensboro, NC

Fugue Devil

1991

I was fifteen years old when I first came to Beckham, Virginia, to live. My dad had been hired as an English professor at the local junior college, after years of applying at countless other, larger colleges and universities. We moved from Atlanta, where he had taught middle school, in the fall of 1974, just in time for me to enroll as a freshman at Beckham High.

Being city-bred, I wasn't sure how I would take to relocating to a mountain community of barely a thousand people—not counting the six hundred or so college students who took up residence during the academic year. I was afraid I would end up stuck in some gloomy old farmhouse, miles from the nearest neighbors—who would all be backwoods rednecks and Ku Klux Klansmen anyway—with my parents and older sister the only company I would ever see outside of school.

I was half-right. Beck-Hi, as it was commonly known, did have its share of long-haired dopeheads, junior bigots, and teachers whose eyes betrayed their hatred of the few

5

black children in their classrooms, but on the whole, the school—and the town—seemed to follow the example of the college in embracing more progressive social attitudes.

Our house was indeed off the beaten track, but a few kids lived within walking distance, and the miles of unbroken woodland offered me an opportunity for exploration and adventure unlike any I could have imagined in Atlanta.

That was the year I learned about the Fugue Devil.

Ronnie Neely told me about it one day while riding home on the school bus. He lived about a mile past my place, and being kind of lonely out there, he took to me immediately upon learning how close my house was. He became my first and best friend in my new hometown.

I remember that afternoon well: We had been talking about the kinds of music we listened to; I was partial to good old rock and roll, "Radar Love" by Golden Earring being my favorite at the time. Ronnie was a country boy and loved bluegrass. His father had been an accomplished fiddler, so he told me.

"You know, my dad used to know an old man up on Copper Peak, out toward Aiken Mill," he said. "He was a musician who worshipped the devil. Dad said you could hear horrible sounds coming from up there on Halloween and on the Witches' Sabbath. He played the fiddle to call up demons and stuff. They say there's this one called the

Fugue Devil, and since the old man woke it up, it comes out every seventeen years looking for souls."

"Really? Who was the old man?"

"People don't speak his name. And nobody goes up on Copper Peak anymore. I guess he's probably dead now, and in hell."

"Cool."

"Sherry Wilson's dad saw it one time. That's what made him blind."

My heart leaped at the mention of her name. "Sherry's dad is blind?"

"Shoot yeah. She'll tell you about it, if you ask her."

Sherry Wilson. She was a slim, golden-haired beauty with wide brown eyes and perfect legs, a ninth-grader who had captured my notice from Day One in school. I had never spoken to her, but how I wanted to meet her! She lived up on Mount Signal, a humpbacked ridge a mile or so north of my house.

From my backyard, the mountain looked like a big tortoise shell, and at night I could even see the lights from Sherry's house. Frequently, I would gaze up there and imagine she was looking down at my house, dreaming about me the way I did about her, sharing our unspoken love across the distance.

Now, maybe I came into manhood late or something, I don't know. All my friends in Atlanta had been going out with girls for quite a while, and some of them had even gotten laid. I had always been more interested in model airplanes and playing baseball, and I guess there were even whispers that I must have been queer.

But when we arrived in Beckham, my hormones suddenly caught up with me and drowned me with an insatiable desire for this winsome lass. Now, to hear that her dad had seen a demon, and it had blinded him... I had to meet her.

"You know her pretty well?" I asked.

"Kinda," Ronnie said. "I can introduce you, if you want."

"You like her?"

"Well, yeah, I like her, but not like...you know. It's Stephanie Asberry for me, man."

"Ah. Okay."

Ronnie was tall and bony, with longish red hair. He lit up a Winchester little cigar—the driver never cared if people smoked as long as they sat in the back of the bus—and offered one to me. I ended up nearly coughing my lungs out because he didn't tell me it was best not to inhale them.

"Don't light up in front of Sherry," he said. "She doesn't like men who smoke."

I nodded. That was important information. My stop was next. I stood up and gave Ronnie a wave. "See you tomorrow, huh?"

"Yeah. Be cool."

The bus groaned to a halt, and the rear doors hissed open. I jumped out into the chilly mountain air, noticing that the sun had already dipped beyond the ridge to the west. Far to the northwest, I could see the tip of Copper Peak towering above the forest. Straight ahead of me, Mt. Signal rose like a huge castle for the queen who lived at its summit. Her bus would probably be dropping her off about now.

I hurried up the long gravel driveway to my house. Smoke was pouring from the chimney. My mom had probably built a fire, even though it hadn't gotten that cold yet. How I would have loved to sit next to a fire with my arms wrapped around Sherry, maybe under a fur blanket, seeing her eyes filled with longing for me. We'd kiss, and she'd whisper, "I love you, Mike."

Yeah. That's how it would be.

My sister Tammy was seventeen. She had starting smoking pot before we left Atlanta, and was always trying to turn me on to it. I wouldn't do it. Most days after school, instead of taking the bus home with me, she would catch a ride with some other seniors and go over to the college. I guessed she was looking for connections now that she was in a new town. She would even meet up with Dad and ride home with him some evenings, stoned out of her mind. My parents knew—they *had* to have—but they never said anything. They wanted to pretend that it wasn't happening.

Dinner at our house had become a tense thing, a gathering of family around an utterly silent table, except for the sound of flatware clanking. Tammy seemed to enjoy knowing that she could have such a profound effect on everyone. That night, her eyes were glassy and red while we ate. You could smell the reefer on her.

When I was younger, my dad had been a stern man. With Tammy, he seemed to have turned into a pansy. I couldn't understand what it meant.

My mom had made coffee, and when dinner was over, she asked, "Tammy, would you pour us a cup, please?"

Tammy nodded and rose to get the coffee pot. She poured Dad's first. It went straight into his empty salad bowl.

"Oh, shit," she whispered. Then she burst into silly laughter. "Sorry about that!"

I started to laugh in spite of myself. Then, to my surprise, my father reached over the table and smacked me across the face. "That wasn't funny, son, so I suggest you can the laughtrack." He gave Tammy a scowl, but then turned his attention back to me. "You'd better go to your room."

"Dad, I didn't do anything."

"Go."

I gave Mom a pleading look, but she just shook her head, sighed, and averted her eyes.

Adults have their quirks, and I knew my parents had their share. I could understand their reluctance to confront Tammy about her extracurricular activities. But I could not understand them taking their frustrations out on me. It just wasn't like them.

I did as I was told without a word. As I left, I heard a chair scrape the floor, and I looked back to see Mom getting up to leave the room.

Dad gave Tammy a harsh glare. Her face grew about five miles long, and she poured his coffee for him. I stopped in the hallway just out of their sight, peering around the corner to watch them. Tammy sat down next to him.

"You haven't told her, have you?" Dad whispered.

"No, of course not. She's probably figured it out by now, though."

"Look, Tammy, I swore it would never happen again. You know I'm sorry for it. What do I have to do to convince you?"

"You didn't have to do that to Mike."

"It's no big deal. He'll get over it."

"Yeah, sure. Like I'm sure you're not going to touch him...the wrong way?"

"Now you look here," he said, raising his voice dangerously. "I know what you think about me after what I did. But Tammy, we have to work it out and come back together. How long are you going to put us all through this?"

She glared defiantly back at him. "As long as I feel like it, Dad. Because I don't think you're really very sorry about it."

"You're wrong about that."

"I don't think so."

"God, Tammy, if your mother ever finds out...if anybody ever finds out..."

"I know. It's the end of your life as you know it." She slid her chair back and rose from the table. I ducked out of sight and headed for the stairs to my room. I stomped my feet as hard as I could, not caring if I shook the house or broke the floorboards.

I finally understood it all. Yes, naïve little me, I saw exactly what had happened. Dad had molested Tammy, and she'd agreed to keep it quiet—for a price. Somehow, I didn't exactly feel sorry for her. Mom must have suspected *something*, though she probably thought it was just about drugs. The only thing I didn't know was how long this had been going on. In the city, I'd heard about this kind of thing; it had happened to some of my classmates. But it couldn't happen in my family. Not mine.

I shut my bedroom door, turned on the radio, and lay back on the bed, not knowing whom to hate, whom to feel sorry for, whom to turn to for help. Blue Swede began chanting, "Ooka, ooka, ookachaka, ooka, ooka, ooka-chaka...

"I can't stop this feeling deep inside of me..."

It was dark as sin in the backyard. In Atlanta, streetlights had burned outside my windows all night long. I reached over and switched off my lamp, gazing out toward the black forest, the mountain looming over my house, the tiny lights up there where my precious queen lived. What was she doing now? Having dinner? Doing her homework? And her parents—did she and her dad ever—

Christ!

Sherry's dad couldn't even see what she looked like.

An early autumn wind sighed through the trees, rustling the leaves that had begun to gather in the yard. It was a lonely sound, melancholy and bitter. Why did it sound like the music my heart made—a dirge that drowned the song on the radio? How could my family, my normal, decent, Christian family, ever sink into the kind of depravity that you only heard about in the ugliest of stories?

I lay in the dark for hours, hoping Dad would come and tell me I was wrong, that I was stupid for even thinking such things. I tried to convince myself that I had jumped to conclusions, that somehow I had just misread everything I had seen and heard. But I knew I had not.

As I finally began drifting off to sleep, my door opened softly. The light from the hall burned into my eyes, so that I couldn't tell who was standing just outside. I expected it to be my father.

It was Tammy. She came in and laid something on my nightstand, then turned and disappeared without a word, closing the door noiselessly. I gaped after her for a moment, not quite sure I was really awake.

I turned on my lamp and looked to see what she had left me.

It was a hand-rolled cigarette—a joint. And a butane lighter.

I started to crush the joint in my hand, but then I stopped. Instead, I opened my nightstand drawer, placed the items inside, and covered them with some notebook paper.

Maybe it was time to see what it was all about.

"Mike...this is Sherry Wilson."

She stood next to Ronnie, giving me a tentative smile. Her hair was full and wavy, not flat and lifeless like so many of the other girls'. She wore a medium length gray jumper over a red, longsleeved knit top, her long legs crossed demurely as she leaned against the wall. She held a stack of books in one hand.

"So," I said, careful not to trip over my tongue, "you wanna sit with Ronnie and me at lunch?"

She shrugged. "Sure, I guess so."

Her soft voice held only the barest hint of a southern accent, even though she'd lived in Beckham all her life. She turned to accompany us to the cafeteria, her tight-fitting top revealing a figure that was just beginning to turn glorious.

"Where are you from, Mike?"

"Atlanta."

"Mike wants to know about the Fugue Devil," Ronnie interjected. I felt my face go red.

"So, you've heard about it?"

"Ronnie told me."

"Bad news. It's dangerous to know about the Fugue Devil."

"Dangerous? How come?"

"Because if you know about it, it knows about you."

"Get out of here."

She gave me a stern glare. "I'm quite serious."

Needless to say, I didn't believe there could be such a thing, but I was intrigued by the story—and by what she might have to say about her father.

We entered the lunchroom and got in line. Sherry waved to several of her friends gathered in a corner. They looked in our direction and giggled.

"This is the year it's supposed to come," she said. "Every seventeen years it flies up from hell in search of souls. If you know about it, it knows about you. And if you see it, it will come for you."

"Every seventeen years," Ronnie said. "Like the locusts."

"At midnight of the autumn equinox it appears. Everybody from Beckham to Aiken Mill stays inside and closes up their houses on that night. Sometimes it just goes away. Sometimes it doesn't."

"Sounds like an old folk tale," I said. "Kinda like the St. Simons Island lights, in Georgia, or the headless ghost that wanders down the Gainesville Midland tracks at certain times of the year."

"Yeah," Sherry said. "But the Fugue Devil is real."

"Tell him about your dad."

"Well," she said, drawing out the word dramatically. "We don't much like to talk about that."

"So what, nobody else is listening," Ronnie said. "Go on, tell him."

"Daddy only told the story once, when I was very small. But I remember it because it scared him to tell it. He didn't used to believe in the demon. So on that night, seventeen years ago, he looked out the window at midnight. And there it was, coming through the trees toward our house. It was so terrifying, Daddy's eyes just couldn't take it. He went blind, and he's been that way ever since. He won't talk about it with anybody, so if you meet him, don't ever ask him. He doesn't like me talking about it, either."

"But you do because it makes you special," Ronnie said with a mock sneer.

Sherry punched him in the arm. Hard.

"But that doesn't sound like it took his soul or anything," I said.

"He thinks it did, in some way," she said mysteriously. "It has its own methods that we don't understand."

"So, how does this thing know how to find you...if you know about it?"

"It has a giant bloodhound. It sniffs you out."

"A giant bloodhound. Right."

"It's true."

She looked like she meant it. Her father must have really told her a whopper to explain his blindness, I thought. It seemed like carrying a tall tale a little too far.

We got our lunch and went to sit down. We ended up next to a bunch of Sherry's friends, so other than small talk, we hardly got to say anything else to each other. But my eyes remained glued to her, my efforts to be cool and dignified failing dismally.

Her every move was graceful, full of self-assurance. Even the way she lifted the forkfuls of mystery meat to her mouth was elegant. Once in a while, our eyes met, and my heart would flutter. I couldn't read her expressions, but I had never been able to read girls anyway—as if anyone ever has.

To emphasize that point, when the bell rang, my sister came into the cafeteria for the next lunch period. She saw me as I was dumping the leftovers from my tray into the garbage can, and she walked by to say hi. I didn't even want to look at her, much less speak. I guess she had figured out that I knew what had happened with Dad and her. "Mike, you don't understand anything. Don't be mad at me."

I didn't answer. I slid my tray through the slot in the wall, where an anonymous pair of hands grabbed it and pulled it out of sight.

"This doesn't concern you, Mike, see? Nothing between us has changed. How about you just let Dad and me work it out, all right?"

I shook my head and started to leave. She grabbed me by the arm.

"Don't go away mad, Mike. You don't understand."

I finally turned around and looked her in the eye. She wasn't stoned, but she looked tired.

"What I understand," I said, just loudly enough for people nearby to hear, "is that Dad molested you, and you're trying to pay him back. But all you're doing is digging yourself in deeper. You could have gotten help. You could have even come to me. But you've decided to blackmail him, so you can do whatever you want. What about Mom, Tammy? You don't give a damn about her, or me, or anybody but yourself. You make me as sick as he does."

Her look of contempt only confirmed what I already knew. I turned and left, feeling that the devil was indeed real and living in my house.

"This weekend is the equinox," Ronnie said, blowing the smoke from his Winchester. "The night of the Fugue Devil."

The bus bumped down Route 2 with Ronnie and me the last passengers left. Somehow, the story of the Fugue Devil had lost some of its charm.

"Nice," I said. "You going to board up your house?"

"No, but Mom and Dad will be in bed early with all the curtains closed."

"What about you?"

"I reckon I'll just be asleep."

"You know...I was kind of thinking about going out to watch for it."

"Huh?"

"I mean, it only comes around every seventeen years. We weren't even born the last time it came, and we'll be old by the next time. I want to get a look at it."

Ronnie stared at me with big, surprised eyes. "You serious?"

I leaned over to him and asked, "You ever get high before?"

"Not really. But I've drunk moonshine. You're in the moonshine capital of the world, you know."

"I got some grass. You want to smoke it with me?"

"When?"

"Tomorrow night. At midnight."

He whistled. "You don't believe in the Fugue Devil, do you?"

"Hell, I don't know. But I guess I'll find out tomorrow night."

He shook his head dubiously. "Have you ever got high?"

"Nope. This'll be the first time."

"Damn, man. I don't know." Ronnie's face was pale. Was it fear of trying drugs for the first time, or was it something else?

"C'mon, let's do it. You in?"

The bus slowed down and shuddered to a stop in front of my house. I stood up and grabbed my books. Ronnie stared at me thoughtfully for a long moment.

"If you see it," he said at last, "it will come for you."

"Hell, I want to see its dog."

He laughed sharply, then gave me a resigned shake of his head. "Okay. I'm in."

Satisfaction exploded in my chest. I could barely believe what I was scheming.

"So, come to my house before midnight. Knock on my window if I'm not already outside, and we'll go out to Mr. Miller's field. It's just up the ridge a little ways."

The doors opened, and I hopped out. As the bus rumbled away, I waved to Ronnie. He leaned out the window, peering after me, still shaking his head.

"Don't chicken out on me, man!" I called to him.

"I'll be there!"

I looked toward my house. Mom's car was parked in the driveway. I didn't want to talk to her, though I knew I would have to. She had barely spoken this morning before I had left for school. I knew she must be angry and ashamed, her feelings too private to divulge to anyone else. What if I told her what I knew? Would it make it easier for her or hurt her all the more?

She was sitting in the living room when I came in, listening to an Al Martino record. "Daddy's Little Girl." She didn't look up.

"Hi, Mom."

"Hey."

I couldn't do it. She obviously had guessed everything, and there was nothing I could say to her, not now. She still wore her housecoat, and her eyes had a dim, faraway look. I couldn't bring myself to intrude. She would have to make the first move.

The night of the equinox, I went to my room right after dinner—another grim, silent affair—and did my homework. My father had apologized for hitting me and punishing me, but he had said and done nothing to explain himself. He just looked uncomfortable, as if he wanted to tell me something but it wouldn't come out. I didn't know how to feel about him anymore. I kind of hated him, but in a way, I pitied him. I knew that as long as this wall of failed deception divided our family, there would be no chance for reconciliation.

Tammy had gone out to the college. About nine o'clock, I heard my parents' voices drifting down the hall from the living room. They were raised in anger, and I gathered that the dam had finally burst. I couldn't make out what they were saying, but I wasn't about to creep from my room to try and listen. I focused on my math paper, forcing myself to keep my mind on the value of x.

"I didn't mean for it to happen!"

"But it did. How many times?"

Their voices were growing clearer. I heard a door slam. They had gone outside.

"So what's it going to be, Emily?"

"I'm going to Martha's."

The car started, and tires spat gravel. So. Mom was leaving. She hadn't even come to tell me goodbye, or that she would be back soon, or that everything would work out in the end. That was what Mom and Dad had always stood for. Things working out.

Now I was going to be alone in the house with my dad. Did she not even care about that?

I crossed the room and looked out my window that faced the driveway. I saw the headlights of Mom's car turn up the road toward Beckham. In a moment, she was gone.

The back door slammed again, and I heard heavy footsteps approaching my room. I quickly sat down at my desk, hunched over my paper. The door opened.

"Mike, your mom's gone to visit her sister in Roanoke. I don't know when she'll be back."

"Okay."

"I'm going to grade some papers. Please don't disturb me for the rest of the evening, all right?"

"Sure, Dad."

"Good night."

"'Night."

He closed my door, and his footsteps retreated down the hall. I heard his bedroom door close. Something fell to the floor with a crash. Mom's jewelry box. After that, I didn't hear anything from the other end of the house until I went to the bathroom around ten o'clock.

A low noise came from behind Dad's door. I detoured from the bathroom and softly made my way down the hall. Before reaching the end, I could tell that the sound was muffled sobbing. My dad was crying.

Back in my room, I opened my drawer and took out the joint Tammy had given me. Just looking at it scared me, yet it fascinated me. Was this how my sister fought back? Was she so ashamed that she couldn't talk to anyone, only drag herself down with drugs and wild behavior? I was still hurt and mad as hell at her, but I wanted to understand. Maybe this was the means.

In a couple of hours, I would be going out with Ronnie to look for a devil. I didn't think I even believed in it, but all the same, I was nervous. Combined with the anticipation of getting high for the first time in my life, the anxiety set my stomach fluttering. My hands and feet were cold, going on numb. All my overwhelmed senses cried out for release.

I lay down on my bed, feeling sorry for my mother, hating my father, and not knowing what to think about my sister. And I dreaded what I was about to do.

Oh, Sherry, I need you so.

I turned to peer out the window toward her house. I could see the lights up on the mountain, twinkling like little stars. At eleven o'clock, they went out.

Ronnie showed up at twenty minutes till midnight. I had already put on my coat and gone outside to wait for him. My father had cried himself to sleep, I guessed. There hadn't been a sound in the house for over an hour.

"This is it, man," he said. "I think we're crazy."

"You scared?"

"Naw, man. Well...actually...how about you?"

"Kinda."

"Yeah." He lit a Winchester and gave me one.

We headed out of my yard, into the woods leading up and around Mt. Signal, toward Mr. Miller's field, about half a mile distant. Fortunately, we both had brought flashlights, for beneath the trees, the darkness was impenetrable. Our footsteps crunched and crackled in the dry leaves. Far in the distance, the cries of whippoorwills and barred owls echoed like mournful choirs.

"You got the stuff?"

"Yep."

"You don't suppose we'll have a bad trip or anything, do you?"

"I don't think so. Not if we keep our shit together," I said, nearly biting my tongue when I thought of Tammy and the depths to which she had sunk. In reality, I had no idea how the pot would affect me. But I did know one thing: I was going to prove myself stronger than the pot, stronger than my mom, stronger than my sister. And certainly stronger than my dad.

We made our way through the limbs that slapped at our faces and clothes. Every now and again, I would peer up at the mountain's summit, trying to catch a glimpse of Sherry's house, but there were too many trees in the way.

"Talk to Sherry anymore?"

"Not really," I said. "I sure wish she was here now, though. Except that she probably wouldn't go for the pot, huh?"

"I doubt it. But I wish Stephanie was here, too. We could double-date."

"That'd be something, wouldn't it?"

"You know, we could even swap dates, just for shits and giggles." Ronnie paused and smiled real big. "Actually, I'd just end up with both of them, and you'd be all alone out in the cold."

"You're sick."

"But it's a good kind of sick."

I laughed. The cool night air felt wonderful, revitalizing. Out here with Ronnie, it was like I could almost forget everything that had happened. Even Mom's leaving didn't seem quite so bad. Tomorrow, things would work out. Tonight, I had me a devil to watch.

Ahead, I could see a break in the trees and a wide, misty gray space beyond. To our right, the small white shape of Mr. Miller's farmhouse nestled in a shallow valley, pale smoke rolling from its chimney. All the lights were off. We waded into the tall grass and made our way up the hill to a circular mound about twenty feet in diameter.

A few dark shrubs grew around its sloping sides. We cleared a space at the top and sat down, facing northwest. Copper Peak rose above the ridge before us. To the left, out in the distance, a scant few lights burned in Beckham. The college lay farther south, beyond our line of sight.

I reached into my pocket and pulled out the joint. I held it up for Ronnie to see.

"Ready to burn it?"

"Yeah," he said. "What time is it?"

"A couple of minutes till."

"Do it."

I placed the joint between my lips, flicked the lighter, and touched it to the tip. I sucked in a deep lungful of sweet-tasting smoke. I had heard you were supposed to hold it in; but the smoke seemed to expand inside my chest, and a second later, I coughed it out in a big gray cloud.

Ronnie took the joint from me and puffed tentatively. Then he drew in a long breath. He also coughed it up immediately.

I tried again, and this time I was able to hold the smoke in longer. My throat burned, but the sensation was not unpleasant. When I blew the smoke out, a sudden dizziness nearly sent me reeling.

We passed the joint back and forth several times, each drag of smoke making me feel more lightheaded. I noticed an almost subliminal humming sound rising around me. When I looked at my feet, they seemed to be a mile away. My body felt anchored to the ground, while the rest of me—my spirit—floated freely, looking down.

"Jesus," Ronnie whispered. "I feel weird."

"Yeah. It's kind of neat."

"Look at the stars."

I peered at the sky. A few thin clouds drifted past a brilliant star field, and a three-quarter moon hovered above the ridge. The chilly breeze that swirled down the slopes was just shy of uncomfortable.

Out toward Copper Peak, I glimpsed a flicker of light. My eyes turned toward it but were slow to focus. Making my body obey my commands took a supreme act of will. The joint, almost gone now, came back for a final drag. I sucked the smoke in and tossed the roach into the tall grass.

"What the hell's that?" Ronnie asked, pointing to the northwest.

The light I had seen on Copper Peak was now rising into the sky, a tiny golden globe heading for the heavens. As it ascended, it began to zoom back and forth across the sky in a zigzag pattern. It moved quickly, soundlessly, and within a matter of seconds, it reached a zenith directly over our heads.

"My God...that's it!" Ronnie whispered.

"You're full of shit."

"LOOK AT IT!"

I had to struggle to keep my eyes on the ball of light. But now I could see that it was trailing sparks, and in its heart, something dark was taking form. I saw a pattern of limbs emerge, like a distorted fetus within a fiery amniotic sac. A distinct figure was beginning to take shape—something with arms and legs, and there was something else up there with it.

"I don't believe it," I said.

"Is it the grass, man? Is it making us see things?"

"You don't hallucinate from grass. I mean, I don't think so. But we're both seeing the same thing."

"Christ. Do you know what this means?"

"It means it's real. Man, it's real!"

"It means we're dead, Higgins. We're fucking dead!"

The brilliant shape disappeared over the ridge behind us. I could see a wispy trail of black smoke, like the remnants of some nonsensical skywriting. Within moments, the smoke had dissipated in the breeze. We had only our memories as evidence we had seen anything at all.

"If you know about it, it knows about you," Ronnie said. "And if you see it, it will come for you."

Without a word, we simultaneously turned and galloped down the hill toward the woods. My feet kicked the earth, seemingly hundreds of feet below, my head swimming in a murky pool of unreality. As I ran, I forgot where I was; I knew only that I had to run, to hide, to escape.

When we reached the woods, we tore through the tree limbs as if they were shadows, ignoring the cuts and lashes we received. I may have tripped and fallen, perhaps more than once, but I remembered nothing more until I saw the moonlit roof of my house in the distance.

We hurtled into the yard, gasping and panting. Our eyes scanned the sky, the woods, and our ears strained to catch the slightest hint of movement anywhere around us.

"It's out there, Mike. What are we going to do?"

"How can we make it leave us alone?"

"There is no way."

I swore under my breath. I had gotten us into this, led Ronnie to what must be certain death. But he had told me about the thing. *He* was the one who started it all in the first place.

As if he knew what I was thinking, he began to whine, "Why the hell did Sherry have to tell me about it? Damn bitch! Why did she have to tell me?"

That was too much. I could accept the responsibility for what we had done, but I would not allow him to blame Sherry. I leaped at him, shoving him roughly to the ground. "You leave her out of this. It wasn't her fault."

"If she hadn't told us about it, we'd never have gone out there."

"We could have chosen not to go. We could have kept on believing it was just a story."

"Bullshit. If you know about it...you look for it."

I realized he was right. The temptation of such a tale was simply too great. "How many other people might have seen it?"

"I don't know," Ronnie groaned, dragging himself from the ground. "People just don't talk about it. They try to forget, so people like us won't look for it."

"Too fucking late," I said. "What are we going to do?"

"I gotta get home."

"We better stay together. You can't take off alone."

"You'll let me stay here tonight?"

"Hell, yeah."

"Let's get inside, then."

We turned and trotted up to the back door. I was about to open it when I heard a rumble and saw lights coming up the driveway. It took a moment for me to realize it was a car.

It was Tammy coming home in Dad's LTD. She parked beneath the balcony over the turnaround, switched off the engine, and opened the door to climb out.

Suddenly, I heard a heavy crunching sound in the woods on the other side of the driveway. A slow, deliberate tread approached the house, accompanied by a low snuffling sound. My heart slammed into overdrive.

Tammy shut off the headlights, which plunged the driveway into almost total darkness. The crunching sounds drew nearer.

"Tammy, turn the lights back on!" I cried. "No, get up here! Hurry! Just get the hell up here!"

"What are you yelling about?"

Ronnie joined in, "Just hurry! Come on!"

She began climbing the steps. I looked past her into the woods, toward the source of the heavy footsteps. High above the ground, a pair of glowing, golden eyes stared at me from the cover of the trees. They moved back and forth slowly, as if sizing me up.

I screamed. A moment later, Ronnie saw them. He screamed too.

"Jesus Christ, what's wrong with you?" Tammy asked as she reached the top of the stairs. "Are you nuts?"

"It's out there!" Ronnie cried. "It's seen us!"

"What are you talking about?"

My tongue was frozen. I gaped stupidly at Tammy, unable to explain. The footsteps began to recede into the woods. She must have heard them because she turned around. But the thing was gone.

The back door opened, and there stood my father, still dressed but disheveled. He flipped on the porch light, which illuminated the driveway to the edge of the woods. I stared into their depths, searching for any movement. There was none.

"What's going on out here?"

"I just got home," Tammy said. "They were out here yelling."

"I thought you were in bed," Dad said to me.

"I...I couldn't sleep."

"Ronnie, what are you doing here? You've got to go home, son."

"Mike said I could spend the night."

"Mike didn't ask. I don't know what you young men think you're doing, but you won't be doing it here tonight. Mike, inside. Ronnie, you get on home."

His face turned ashen. "I don't...I can't..."

"Do your folks know you're out this late?"

"No, sir."

"Then I suggest you get moving."

"What if...could you take me home?"

"No, I could not. You apparently got here on your own. You may leave the same way."

Dad gripped me by the shoulder and gave me a tug. "Let's go."

I raised a hand toward Ronnie, but Dad slapped it away and pulled me by the arm into the kitchen. I struggled free and nearly sent my fist right into his face; somehow, I restrained myself.

Tammy came inside after me, and Dad closed the door. I saw Ronnie peering in through the window with pleading eyes. He looked back into the darkness, then at me.

"Dad, there's something..."

"Get to bed, Mike. It's too late for this crap. We'll talk tomorrow."

"But..."

"Go."

The command was final. He locked and deadbolted the door, then turned and stalked out of the kitchen and down the hall to his room. Tammy gave me a long, icy stare, her hands on her hips. I leaped for the back door and fumbled with the lock, but I could already see that Ronnie was gone.

I hurried to the kitchen window and looked out at the front yard. In the moonlight, I could see him racing down the hill toward the road. He looked back once, but I doubt he saw me. He rounded the corner at the bottom of our driveway and turned left without breaking stride. I had never seen anyone move so fast.

I felt Tammy's eyes boring into the back of my head. I watched the retreating figure disappear beyond the trees at the end of the yard. He had nearly a mile to run. I stared out the window long after he was gone.

My sister did not hear me when I whispered, "I loved you, Ronnie."

Brilliant daylight was streaming into my eyes when I next opened them. I didn't remember falling asleep. I was lying on my bed, still dressed. It all came flooding back: going out to Mr. Miller's field with Ronnie, smoking the joint, seeing the light in the sky, and then...those golden eyes peering at me from the woods.

Ronnie. He had run home by himself.

It had to have been the pot. Some kind of bad trip. *Tammy!* She knew how pot affected you. She had been smoking for a year or more now.

I slid off the bed and hurried to the kitchen. The clock over the table read eight-forty-two. The house was quiet. Too quiet.

"Tammy?" I called. My voice echoed emptily through the house. I glanced out the back door and saw Dad's car was gone. He must have already gone out on his errands, like he always did. Like when we all loved each other, and everything was simple and sweet, and Saturday mornings meant cartoons and playtime, with no worries, and...

Mom. She was at my aunt Martha's. I had to call her.

I went to the living room phone and dialed the number. It rang once...twice...three times. No answer. I slammed the phone down. Where the hell could they be? I was home alone. *Completely* alone. Vulnerable.

"Oh, shit."

I was just about to go back to the kitchen when the phone rang. I spun around and grabbed it up. "Hello?"

"Mike? This is Julia Neely, Ron's mother. He wouldn't happen to be over there, would he?"

A cold iron fist grabbed me and stole my breath. It took a moment to stammer, "No...no, ma'am. He isn't here."

"He was gone when we got up this morning. We saw him when he went to bed last night. But he doesn't usually get up early on weekends. Did he say anything to you about what he might be doing today?"

"No, Mrs. Neely," I said, not knowing what else to tell her. "He isn't here."

"I'm worried about him. His bike is still here, so he didn't go off riding."

My voice was about to fail me. All I could do was breathe into the receiver.

"If you see him, please tell him to hurry home."

"Okay."

"Thank you, Mike."

"Yes, ma'am."

I dropped the receiver into its cradle, feeling like I had just told the most horrible lie of my entire life. My hands were shaking.

Jesus Christ. It had gotten Ronnie

There was no other possibility. He had raced for home with the devil literally at his heels. I tried to think rationally. Maybe he had fallen and hurt himself along the way. What if he were lying in a ditch somewhere with a broken leg or something? He could need help. Wasn't that the most logical explanation?

But I had seen the thing in the sky.

Even under the influence of the marijuana, I knew I had not imagined or hallucinated the monster. Ronnie had seen it too. We both heard it in the woods near the house.

Where was it now? Did it lurk somewhere nearby, waiting to catch me alone?

Like now?

Sherry. She would know.

I opened the drawer where we kept the phone book and looked up the listing for Wilson. I didn't know her dad's first name, and there were five Wilsons in town. I knew she lived on Rural Route 7. There...Wilson, Kirby C. I quickly dialed the number.

It was her voice that answered, "Hello?"

"Sherry? It's me, Mike Higgins."

"Hi, Mike." Her voice sounded cautious.

"Sherry, last night...Ronnie and me went out to Mr. Miller's field. We saw the Fugue Devil. I think it got him."

"You saw it?"

"Yeah."

"And Ronnie?"

"He ran home, not long after midnight. The thing was near my house. I saw it. And Ronnie's mom called this morning and said he was gone."

"Oh, God."

"What am I going to do? What can I do?"

"What do you mean? You know about it, it knows about you. And you saw it, so..."

"There's got to be some way to stop it."

"No. There isn't."

"Well, when does it come? How long does it stay?"

"I don't know. As long as it takes."

"Who else knows about it? Somebody must know something about it."

"Nobody that does will admit it."

"You did!"

There was a long silence. "Mike, don't you understand? I didn't believe it, either. I always thought it was just some story my dad told me."

"It isn't. I saw it. I swear I did."

"I know."

"You do?"

"My mom just talked to one of her friends. Some kids from the college have disappeared. I guess they heard about the Fugue Devil and drove up to Copper Peak last night. The cops found their car this morning, empty."

"Maybe they're okay, somewhere..."

"No, Mike. There was blood. Lots of it."

Not knowing anything else to do, I locked myself in my room. I had thought of taking my bike out and riding toward Ronnie's house, to see if I could find him. But I was too afraid to go out on my own.

I sweated and fidgeted, actually praying that my dad would get home so I wouldn't have to be alone in the big, silent house. Every creak of floorboards settling, every rustle in the yard sent cold chills up and down my spine. I had never been so terrified in my life.

Just after eleven, I heard Dad's car in the driveway. I ran out to meet him, overcome with relief. He got out and began unloading several bags of groceries from the trunk.

"Hey, Mike, come give me a hand with these."

I went down and took a couple of the sacks. Dad looked weak and beaten. Standing close to him, I found myself feeling dirty, as if the ugliness inside him tainted the air around him. But, for the moment, it was a discomfort I was willing to suffer.

"Where's your sister?"

"I don't know. She was gone when I got up."

"She must have gone to the college with those damned friends of hers." He didn't hide the disgust in his voice. And I could scarcely conceal my disdain for his hypocrisy.

I turned to go up the stairs, which were lined by a dense row of evergreen trees. On the other side, I heard something moving in the woods. A low grunt, like a dog snuffling, came from the hillside beyond the yard. My heart skipped a beat and I froze.

Animals often came out of the woods. It was just an animal. Through the evergreens, I caught a glimpse of something moving in the backyard, and I halted on the steps, my heart going to my throat.

Dad came up behind me. "Get a move on, son. These bags are heavy."

Reluctantly, I proceeded up the stairs. At the top, I stepped aside and let him pass. I turned and peered into the backyard, up the hill into the woods.

I didn't see it until it moved. A pair of huge, black eyes were staring at me. Cavernous nostrils flared as if to catch my scent. Bluish splotches covered its dull gray back and sides. A stiletto-like tail pointed rigidly from its hind end.

It was a monstrous hound the size of a horse, standing between two thick pines on tall, muscular legs. Even worse, though, behind it, something was moving, pushing its way through the tree branches. Leaves cascaded over the monstrous dog. Then a huge silhouette on two legs materialized beside it.

The thing that had taken Ronnie.

I barely caught a glimpse of two deep-set golden eyes staring at me before I spun around, dropping my sacks of groceries. Glass shattered. I shoved my way past Dad, knocking one of the bags from his arms. But as I pushed the door to the kitchen open, something tugged at my collar. I frantically turned around, fists flailing blindly.

The blow caught my dad squarely in the jaw. His remaining bag pitched over the railing to smash on the driveway below. His look of shock lasted only a second. Then he charged at me with an angry snarl.

"You little shit! What the hell's wrong with you?"

The fists that pummeled me, if stronger, would have knocked me cold. I raised an arm in a vain attempt to defend myself, but a blow to my solar plexus drove the wind out of my lungs. I went down, gasping for breath.

"You want another one? Huh?"

I saw his foot draw back for a kick. I managed to croak, "Something...out back. Out back!"

He hesitated. I pulled myself toward the door, out of his immediate reach. He looked at me in bewilderment.

"What are you talking about?"

"There's something in the backyard. It's after me."

He took a couple of uncertain steps back. He peered around the corner of the house. "There's nothing there."

I should have known it. Dad didn't know about the Fugue Devil. It certainly would not show itself to him.

I whispered, "It was...an animal. Some kind of animal."

He stared at me with puzzled contempt. "God damn, son."

"I'm sorry...I didn't mean to hit you."

His expression softened, and he peered down at the ruined groceries. He looked as if he were about to break down.

"That took all my money," he whispered.

I began to cry. He seemed to draw up something inside, and he came to me, extending a hand to help me up. I suddenly wanted to tell him everything, to admit what I had done, to be his little boy again. I fell into his arms, and there was a strength in his embrace that I hadn't felt in a long time.

"I'm sorry too, son."

There was no ugliness radiating from him now. For the moment, I could almost believe he was the same dad I had known as a child: a strong, protective, loving man untouched by whatever disease or evil had worked its way into his heart. I felt safe, even when I heard heavy, crunching footsteps retreating into the depths of the woods.

A minute later, a car pulled into the driveway, followed by a chorus of female voices bidding their farewells. Tammy was coming home.

And Dad left me standing there to cry alone.

After that, I expected Dad to come to me, to repent, to bring Mom home, to make us a family again. I just wanted things to be put right, to feel safe. As a family, we could overcome the evil I had brought upon myself.

But late that afternoon, my mom called and talked to Dad. I heard him say something from time to time, but mostly he just listened. At last, when he hung up, he came to my room and said, "Your mom is getting a lawyer and says she wants to have me brought up on charges. She's going to be coming to take you and Tammy away."

My heart sank. Everything familiar, everything I had ever known and loved was being stripped away. And, outside, there lurked a devil. It was waiting for me.

"What's going to happen?" I asked.

"I don't know. We probably won't be seeing much of each other."

"Where will we go?"

"All that will have to be worked out."

"Dad," I said, feeling tears coming on again, "I don't want this to happen."

He stared at me for a long time. I couldn't tell what was going on behind those clouded eyes. At last, he said, "Maybe it's for the better."

Then he turned and went out. His footsteps shuffled down the hall to his room. I heard his door close gently. I went to my desk and picked up my radio. It shattered into a thousand pieces with a resounding crash as it struck the wall.

Somehow, I had survived the previous night. I remembered Sherry's words: "Sometimes it goes away...sometimes it doesn't..."

As long as it takes, she had said.

I knew it wasn't going away. It was going to stay until it did to me whatever it had done to poor Ronnie.

Ronnie. He acted tough, but he was just a funny kid, sensitive and mild. Gone. God, how horrible it must have been. He had known the thing was after him. I remembered the pleading look he had given me through the window just before he took off running.

He had tried to blame Sherry for revealing a lethal secret; he had *needed* to blame somebody. But Sherry hadn't even believed in it herself. *Was* she to blame? If she had never told us, Ronnie would still be alive, and I might have a chance to see my family reconcile. *Why the hell hadn't she known what would happen?*

Deep down, I knew better. I had to put aside all blame. *I had led Ronnie to his death. I had condemned myself to an unknown but surely awful fate.*

Me, myself, and I.

I stared out the window into the pure blackness. It took several moments for my eyes to pick out the tiny lights at the top of the mountain. I was seized by the deepest, most bitter melancholy I had ever known. My heart wept like a sweet violin. There was so much love in me with no channel, no release. Such unresolved love could only turn to misery. My sobs wracked my entire body.

Through my tears, I saw the lights at Sherry's house go out. But a moment later they came on again. And then...off.

Something was intermittently blocking my view of her house.

Something coming down the mountain

Oh, God...this was it.

I left my room and went down the hall to my parents' room. My father sat on the bed with a stack of papers at his side. He held a red pen in one hand.

"What is it, Mike?"

"Dad...there is this thing, it's called the Fugue Devil. It was called up from hell, and now, every seventeen years, it comes out to take souls. If you know about it, it knows about you. And if you see it, it will come for you."

"What in God's name are you babbling about?"

"It killed Ronnie last night. When you sent him away, it got him. It got some other people, too, from the college. Maybe they were students of yours."

Dad stood up. "What the hell kind of story is this? What's the point?"

"The point is, Dad, that now you know about it. And I wouldn't be at all surprised if you see it tonight."

I had willingly accepted the slap across the face and the sentence of bedroom imprisonment until my mother came to pick up Tammy and me the next day. I locked my door, turned out the lights, and knelt on the floor next to my bed to pray. I knew I had only minutes of life left, if that.

But for hours, nothing happened. Dad went to bed around midnight, I guess. I heard him brush his teeth and go to the bathroom. Tammy had gone out somewhere, as usual. I actually wished to hear the thing coming for me, to get it over with. My heart could not withstand such furious pounding, drawn out for so long. Surely, I was being toyed with.

Then, just after one o'clock in the morning: A *thump* came from the basement. Then a heavy creak. At last, it was in the house. By now, I felt I would welcome death. It would be the release I ached for. But when I heard the heavy creak on the steps, I realized I was wrong. Terror flooded my veins, and a new desire to stay alive seized me with unexpected intensity. But there was no chance, no hope. The Fugue Devil collected souls.

Something was scraping the paneled walls, something hard and sharp. The floor groaned beneath an immense weight. And from outside my window came the snuffling sound I had heard before in the woods. The contents of my stomach rose to my throat. Blood rushed through my ears like the banshee scream of jet engines.

It was in the hall now. Boards popped and screeched as the heavy steps approached my door. I heard a strange buzzing sound, like a swarm of bees, rising and falling rhythmically. *Its breath!*

The door handle turned. I could barely see the rectangle of blackness expanding as the door slowly opened, revealing a huge, vague shape: something tall, broad, hunched in the hallway. A pair of golden eyes blazed at me from near the ceiling. And as it crossed the threshold, the true shape of the thing began to crystallize.

The Fugue Devil had the head of a wolf, with five bony horns protruding like a crown atop its skull. The massive body looked to be covered with reflective scales or plates, like armor. Its arms were long and muscular, manlike, but ending in talons resembling an eagle's. On its back, a pair of gold wings arched over its shoulders, half-folded like a bat's. From its bristly throat, it emitted a low, grating buzz, which rose to a thunderous rumble.

No...I did *not* want to be taken by this thing! It was so tall it had to lean forward so its head would clear the ceiling. It bent even lower to regard me with undisguised malevolence, tilting its head oddly, as if it *recognized* me.

No wonder Sherry's dad had gone blind.

"Please," I whispered. "Go away."

Its canine jaws spread in a wicked parody of a smile. I felt the temperature in the room rising. The smell of scorched flesh assailed my nostrils.

"Don't take me, please," I sobbed. "Please."

I heard the sound of huge paws thumping across the yard outside, moving toward the other end of the house. The sniffing came from near my dad's window.

"Take him. Take my dad. Leave me alone. Please. Please!" The word came out as a screech.

The Fugue Devil stared at me with those brilliant eyes. I could see that they had depth—as if they were merely lenses that revealed some new and infinitely remote and dark dimension. There was in that gaze something more than intelligence. I began to realize that this beastlike horror was merely a physical manifestation of something else entirely: a horrifying shell to clothe a deeper, spiritual force that came from somewhere far, far beyond the little mortal world that I knew. I was not so much terrified now as humbled. I was looking at a mere symptom of consummate evil.

A talon rose toward my face. The scream I longed to release hung in my throat. All that came out was a whimper: "Not me. Please...not me."

A searing heat swept over my body. I closed my eyes. This had to be death. Yet, after a moment, the sensation passed. The air cooled quickly.

When I opened my eyes, the room was empty. But I could hear the thumping of the devil's footsteps out in the hall, heading away from my room. A door creaked. The footsteps stopped.

And the screaming began. The buzzing rose in a wavering harmony. A sharp, agonized wail was cut short by a quick ripping sound, like wet newspaper being shredded. A few moist gasps followed, then another shrill scream. It died slowly this time, ending with a muted rattle, as if something were stuck in my father's throat.

I remained perched on the edge of my bed, unable to move. I heard a rough scraping sound, then the splintering of wood. The rhythmic thumping began outside the house, and leaves rustled in accompaniment as the thing returned to the woods. The sniffing and snorting of the hound faded, as did the footsteps moments later.

After a minute or two more, I realized I could hear a faint hissing sound, wavering unsteadily, from the far end of the house. It was an agonized, weak sound: my father's tortured breathing. Life somehow remained in his body. I went to my door to listen. The sound was desperate, futile, blended with intermittent sobs.

Within a minute, the breathing stopped.

And then, I heard the downstairs door slam and footsteps coming up from the garage. Tammy. I kept silent, waiting to see what she was going to do. Her footsteps went down the hall, toward her room, then on to the bathroom. Then they stopped. I heard her voice call softly, "Dad?"

A moment later, her horrified shrieks filled the house, and I collapsed on the floor. I gathered a lungful of air, and my misery erupted in a howl that went on and on, until my vocal cords simply failed.

That was seventeen years ago.

At first, my sister and my mother thought I had murdered him. But when the police came, they absolved me immediately, for he had been killed by something incredibly large and powerful; in fact, the coroner went so far as to say that it would have taken a crazed bear to inflict the kind of damage my father's body suffered.

The killing remains unsolved, as do the disappearances of Ronnie Neely and the college students whose car was found on Copper Peak. The official report theorizes that all were victims of some wild animal, never minding the fact that no physical evidence was ever found—no hair, no saliva, not *anything*—to implicate a bear. And I, of course, could offer no explanation.

My sister and mother eventually recovered from the shock; Tammy, in particular, seemed to take the death remarkably well. While they never had any inkling of what had killed my father, they always seemed to have an intuitive understanding that his death had been a part of something much bigger than a random act of violence.

Mom grieved for a long time, I know; as much for having lost my dad to his worst side during his last months as for his actual death. But she never talked to me about her feelings. Her suffering remained hers alone, which forced me to be forever an observer to what became a crippling, withering battle for her sanity.

She won out in the end.

I, however, have carried the burden of my guilt for these years with no relief, keeping it locked inside myself, much as my mother did with her grief. While the thing that tore my father limb from limb was not of my making, the bargain I made with it makes me as guilty as if I had killed him myself. And I have never learned to forgive.

Sherry Wilson told me the Fugue Devil was a collector of souls, and I believe she was right in more ways than she knew. While it may have destroyed my father, it placed a lien on my own soul as everlasting as the death it brought to its other victims.

For seventeen years, I have wondered if Sherry's father also made some bargain with the demon, to exchange his sight for his life. It is a subject I would like to have broached with him, had he not taken his family to another state shortly after the night my father was killed. I never saw Sherry again.

So, in the ensuing years, my struggle for my heart and soul has taken me through doctors and clergymen, an institution, and countless prescription drugs, all of which have been as effective as sugar water against cancer. For since that night, I have been completely mute; after that final scream, my tongue was frozen for all time.

I cannot talk of the world, of love, of hate, of people and their affairs; I read it as a cruel joke, for my ability to use a pen is unhampered. Yet it is a story I have refused—until now—to commit to paper.

Last night was the equinox.

It was with great deliberation that I made the decision to leave the meager existence I have managed to eke out in Atlanta over the past few years and return to Beckham. I resolved to own up to my sin and repay in full the lien on my soul with my life.

I intended to go back to Mr. Miller's field, the place where the Fugue Devil made its first appearance to me, and to make sure that I was there at midnight to witness its next arrival.

So that is precisely what I did. I arrived there well before time, remembering in fullest detail every step I had taken with Ronnie on that night long ago. Old Mr. Miller still lives in his house in that shallow valley. I made a place for myself on the small knoll in the middle of his field and sat down to watch the sky. The stars were clear.

At midnight, I was struck blind. Just as my tongue prohibited me from speaking of that horror, now my sight was taken from me, denying me the glimpse I needed to draw the beast back to me. At a minute past, my eyesight was restored—just in time to see the last vestiges of black smoke in the sky like demonic skywriting.

The Fugue Devil proved itself the master engineer. I don't understand the strange laws that govern the spirit world whence it comes, or the conditions that allow its interaction with us at the specified time every seventeen years. I know only that I am condemned yet again, and that for the beast itself, my father's death must take on a whole new sweetness, trapped as it is within my memory.

So, my story is here, like a road map to this world for the thing on the other side, for now the reader has dangerous knowledge.

The Fugue Devil will appear again at its prescribed time, in the prescribed place.

If you know about the Fugue Devil, it knows about you.

And if you see it...

Threnody

1986

I never knew my father's father. My parents had been city dwellers since long before I was born, though before them, all our generations since the early eighteenth century were native to the Appalachian Mountains of Virginia. Grandfather lived in the old house atop Copper Peak, which my father's family members had inhabited since their arrival in this land.

I had never been to the place before, though over the course of my life, the stories birthed there, the pictures, and my dad's related memories had combined to create a mental image that I came to find was not far off the mark in reality.

Grandfather was dead and buried now. His house and property were destined to be sold, a fact that somehow did not rest well with me. My parents' attitude that the place had outlasted its value, practical or otherwise, seemed almost peculiar, as my dad had lived there through his adolescence and generally reflected on those days with some degree of affection.

Still, his reluctance to talk much about his family hinted at what I sometimes took to be shame. The reasons for this I never questioned; but I now found myself fantasizing about what life in the mountains must have been like in those simpler but more physically rigorous days, and what family secrets might lurk within the shadows of the ancient dwelling. Over two centuries of history had been viewed from its windows.

Few people, even those who live among them, consider the Appalachian Mountains mysterious or oppressive. Unlike the Rockies, or the wilds of Canada, the Appalachians do not harbor many grave threats to man. There are few dangerous animals, the weather is usually moderate, and pockets of population are generally never too few or far between.

However, as with all wild terrain, there are corners left that men seldom travel. Copper Peak lies in the western arm of Virginia, amid a range of treacherously steep, densely wooded ridges. The nearest town to our family place is twelve miles away; a little hamlet called Barren Creek that nestles in the valley between Copper Peak, Thunder Knob, and Mount Signal.

There is only one road on Copper Peak; it leads from the house to the highway into town. In the last ten years, it has fallen into disuse as my grandfather's health precluded him traveling even those miles into Barren Creek. I have never quite understood how he existed. I know he did have a hired man to deliver food and other necessities once a week, and to bring his mail from the Barren Creek post office, but I cannot imagine a man of his years and failing health subsisting in such an isolated environment. Nonetheless, he seemed to thrive there, and my father was never compelled to suggest that he relocate.

After Grandfather's death, I took it to heart to visit the old house, knowing that if my parents sold it, my chance would probably be gone forever. I was due for a week's vacation from my business, so after minimal consideration, I decided that Copper Peak was where I would spend it.

I drove alone from my Washington, D.C. residence, with a set of maps and written directions provided by my father. The mountainous countryside along Interstate 81 filled my view for the better part of the trip; southwest of Roanoke, the road rose and the green mountains turned to steeper, rock-walled towers. When I turned off the interstate onto the single-lane highway into Barren Creek, I found myself entering a picturesque, quaint world of pastures and woods, occasional farmhouses, and rare drivers passing in the opposite direction. Barren Creek lay a few miles west of a small community called Aiken Mill, which I judged to be relatively wealthy by the size and style of most of the houses I passed. Beyond the town, the road narrowed, and I found myself alone in a thickly wooded, rapidly rising countryside through which the road snaked and curled.

Between Aiken Mill and Barren Creek, I did not encounter another motorist going in either direction.

Barren Creek has a population of about 200 people. The town consists of several small buildings on either side of the road, including a bank, a post office (a mobile home painted red, white, and blue), a tiny grocery store, and a greasy-spoon diner. A few of the townsfolk were about, most of them old timers with missing teeth, wearing T-shirts and faded overalls.

Several of them waved as I passed, to which I responded in kind. Then, a mile or so beyond this strip of urbanization, a gravel road turned to the right and disappeared into the woods high above me. Checking my directions to be sure, I slowed and turned in, realizing I had arrived at my destination.

The road was little more than an eroded rut down the mountainside that had been poured over with gravel. In places, the hill grew so steep that my tires spun and spat rock, and I began to think that I might not be able to take the car all the way to the top. But my Japanese coupe proved itself a sturdy little animal and successfully negotiated the treacherous path.

Ahead of me, a patch of daylight marked a break in the foliage. I passed over a rickety wooden bridge, beneath which ran a spidery, shallow stream, identified by my father's directions as "the" Barren Creek, the source of which lay on this very mountain. And then, just beyond, I caught my first sight of the Asberry House, the birthplace and home of my father's father's fathers.

At first I was surprised by how small it was. The few photographs I'd seen made it appear larger, or perhaps seeing it amid the rearing trees created a different sense of scale than the tiny proportions of a picture. But the atmosphere of the place was much as I had imagined.

Shadows from the thick, sheltering branches fell darkly upon the house, and an undefined but unmistakable smell of age saturated the cool, early spring breeze. The weedy, unkempt grass that passed for a lawn disappeared into creeping, predatory brambles a few feet from the structure in every direction. Gray and green lichen stained the house's warped wooden siding.

Still, the building appeared sound and seemed like a natural part of the tranquil environment. I could imagine my dad as a boy, playing in what would have been a well-trimmed yard, while smoke curled from the chimney and the aroma of some splendid meal being cooked drifted across the clearing.

Again, I felt a pang of dismay that such a fundamental relic of my family's past would soon be either in the hands of strangers, or, more likely, demolished and replaced by some sterile piece of architecture that passed as someone's idea of a summer home. For a vain moment, I entertained the idea that I might buy the place; my profession as a graphic designer supported me comfortably, but I could barely afford my single apartment in D.C., much less an additional piece of property I could visit only infrequently. I would never be able to live here, for nowhere nearby could I secure employment suitable to my talents.

Dad had given me the keys, as he and Mom had been here shortly after Grandfather's death to remove a few valuables and generally tidy up. But after placing my few belongings just inside the front door, I immediately turned around and set out walking, hoping to familiarize myself with the surrounding land before the waning sunlight passed into impenetrable shadow.

I soon discovered several overgrown trails that must have been struck by my forefathers over the past two centuries. Following one of them, a short distance from the house I came to find the small spring whence came Barren Creek.

The stream wound down the mountainside, mostly parallel to the gravel road; I followed it for a time until I reached a sheer drop-off of at least a hundred feet, where the water leaped into space and plummeted to the valley below. In the summer, this stream all but dried up, hence its name—which had been coined by some family member in the late 1700s.

The scene was so quietly impressive, so stimulating to my city-numbed nerves, that I knew I *somehow* had to persuade my parents to retain the rights to this wonderful tract of land.

Upon returning to the house, I decided to begin a brief exploration of the interior before thinking about dinner. I had no idea what Mom and Dad might have already removed but, happily, I discovered a wealth of fascinating paraphernalia remaining: beautifully preserved antique furniture; photo albums of countless, as-yet-unidentified family members; and—most interestingly—a number of stringed musical instruments that appeared handmade.

In the little back room, I discovered a mandolin, a classical guitar, two violins, and a dulcimer, all exquisitely finished and in fine condition. I took this room to be a workshop, where my grandfather would have made these instruments himself.

In the tiny den, I found some exceptionally old books, an antique radio, and a reel-to-reel audiotape machine that looked to be of early 1960s vintage—apparently the most modern piece of electronic equipment in the house.

Fortunately, there was electricity (at least until the end of the current billing cycle), running water (both hot and cold); and an indoor toilet (which spared me having to use the ancient outhouse out back). Given these amenities, I anticipated a spartan but reasonably comfortable existence over the coming week.

Darkness fell early, and soon the woods came alive with the sounds of insects and nightbirds—something to which I was entirely unaccustomed. I sat down about seven o'clock to a dinner of chicken sandwiches and iced tea, which I had packed before leaving. The kitchen had been more or less cleaned out, so I figured that tomorrow I would visit the little store in Barren Creek to pick up a few necessities.

While I ate, I paged through some of the books I'd found, which included a couple of volumes on local history (courtesy of the Aiken Mill Public Library; someone in my family had not been above stealing), an original 19th-century copy of *Uncle Tom's Cabin* by Harriet Beecher Stowe, and a book of music by one Maurice Zann titled *The Spheres Beyond Sound*. I was not well-versed in musical theory, but this volume contained some odd and fabulous illustrations that immediately caught my interest.

I ate and read to a chorus of chirping and yowling from outside that was distracting at first but which, after a time, faded to the background of my awareness. The pictures in the Zann book captivated me, for they consisted of prints and drawings of imaginative, stylized subjects: lizards, birds, fish, skeletons (animal and human), and strange, monstrous-looking things straight out of science fiction.

Once I began skimming the text, I discovered that this book was truly no "normal" guide to music theory. Upon finding lines that read "...vibrations of this exact frequency and volume are required to complete the summoning process..." and "by combining the perfect tones and pitches, the very essence of primal power may be acquired...," I decided to start reading the book from the beginning.

I soon found that the strange illustrations perfectly complemented the text. The author's basic premise was that music could open gateways to other realms of existence—not just in the mind, but in the physical world.

Now, for me, music is indeed a spiritual experience. It may be hypnotic or stimulating. I listen to and appreciate all kinds of music, from folk to jazz, classical to rock, opera to technopop. When I was younger, nothing delighted me more than to sit for hours wearing my headphones, carried away by the power of music.

Zann contended that certain combinations of tones could actually alter space; that the precise modulation of frequencies could even reach beyond the barrier of death. Needless to say, my initial reaction was that *Spheres* was a work of pure fantasy; but, as I read further, the details became increasingly technical and beyond my grasp, leading me to assume that the author intended the work as factual.

This book occupied me well into the late hours. Even though the advanced concepts it detailed far exceeded my comprehension, the writer's sober, clinical prose captivated my imagination. I found myself almost shaking with excitement as I read this passage:

...I have seen the power the following strains will summon. Precise cadence is difficult but vital. The switch from the 3/4 to the 7/8 time signature followed by the 5/3 line illustrated below must be

instantaneous, without hesitation or pause. The standard tuning E, A,
D, G, B, E in perfect A must be altered to D-flat, A-sharp, E, B-sharp,
C, E-flat to facilitate the playing of the proper notes. The volume
produced by each instrument on each beat must range between 75 and
79 decibels for the summons to be effected. Depending upon
atmospheric conditions, results may be seen, if the process is completed
flawlessly, from within three minutes to one hour.

Farther into the text, I found passages relating to other types of musical power, from hypnotizing human subjects to communicating with the dead. But, to me, the most astounding aspect of all was the theory that certain musical arrangements could transcend the limits of time and space to be heard by *things* existing in other universes.

The concepts of parallel or alternate dimensions have been explored by both scientists and fantasists for years, I suppose, but never had I seen such a lucid and calculated treatise on the subject as this. After a time, I began to wonder why my grandfather would have owned such a book—and whether he had given its contents any credence.

I supposed the subject might have merely intrigued him, as it did me. Upon checking the front of the book, I learned it had been published by an independent firm in Providence, Rhode Island, in 1929, as a limited edition. Putting the book aside, I found that my imagination had surged into high gear, and spending the night alone in this old house suddenly seemed a chilling prospect.

When I at last began to prepare myself for bed, I found my hearing to be unnaturally sensitive, my state of mind strangely apprehensive. My chair legs scraped the bare wooden floor at shocking volume, sending a harsh shiver up my spine. I stopped and held my breath for a moment, half-expecting to hear ...something... other than the night creatures' cacophony in the woods.

When I heard nothing further, I went to the bedroom, made the huge, oak-framed bed with fresh linens from the closet, slipped out of my clothes, and buried myself deep within the covers, leaving the living room light burning and the door cracked so the darkness of the mountain night wouldn't totally engulf me.

I awoke early, to an absolutely brilliant morning. I had slept heavily and peacefully, and I now felt refreshed, free of the odd anxiety that had gripped me during the evening. Morning birds chirped outside my window in happy contrast to the eerie wails of the night creatures. In daylight, the house took on a fresh, new quality, and some of my previous enthusiasm for the locale returned.

I was hungry and, realizing I had next to nothing in the house to eat, I immediately left for the general store in Barren Creek. The town was practically deserted at this hour, but the store was open. The proprietor, a Mr. Avery, greeted me cheerfully enough, asking me from whereabouts I came.

When I told him I was the grandson of the late Timothy Asberry, he shrugged and offered his condolences. Apparently, Grandfather wasn't part of any close-knit group of locals. My family, like many of the back-country dwellers, had valued its privacy and seldom gathered with neighbors.

When I returned to the house, I prepared a breakfast of bacon, eggs, and toast; after eating, I let my attention return to the weird volume of Maurice Zann. In the golden daylight, it no longer seemed as much a warped, dreadful recording of factual data as a fanciful product of some long-dead writer's bizarre imagination.

I decided that, for the morning, I would forget it, explore more of the mountain, and conduct a thorough search of the house itself. A host of relics from my grandfather's day—and prior—awaited my perusal, which I hoped would help me assemble a more complete picture of my heritage.

About ten o'clock, I set out walking, heading north, in the direction opposite the previous day's expedition. I discovered another worn trail that led along the crest of Copper Peak, and I followed it to discover an exhilarating view of the surrounding valleys and slopes. Off to the east, far below me, I saw a few tiny buildings, which I took to be Barren Creek.

Farther on lay Aiken Mill, a haphazard cluster of buildings barely visible behind a thin veil of mist. Many miles to the west, I could see another little hamlet, which, if I recalled rightly, would be a little college town called Beckham.

About half a mile from the house, I came upon a flattened area beneath a canopy of limbs. To my surprise, I found it to be a small graveyard. There were maybe two dozen markers of varying shapes and sizes, all weathered with age, most nearly obscured by creeping flora.

I strolled into their midst, noting the engraved names that were still legible: Nicholas Asberry, 1761–1834; Stuart Asberry (my namesake), 1820–1914; Suzette Asberry Washington, 1823–1902; James Druid Asberry, 1895–1938; Sarah Asberry Collins, 1811–1899.

I found myself excited, for here lay my direct ancestors, those whose names I might have heard only in passing over the years. Here, the past surrounded me; the very earth contained the blood of my progenitors.

My parents had not told me specifically where my grandfather was buried. "In our family plot, in the mountains," Dad had said. My eyes roved among the stones, seeking. Then, in a far corner, standing alone...yes, a fresh marker above a patch of newly turned earth. I approached it, positive of what I would find.

I was correct. Timothy Cadden Asberry, my father's father, born in 1910. The remains of some flowers drooped next to the obelisk-like stone, probably those my parents had placed here upon Grandfather's burial. Thin shoots of grass were just beginning to burst from the mound of earth, and brown spots of mold had broken out on the granite. I stood there for a time, uncertain whether I should grieve, offer a prayer, or merely reflect. Finally, I murmured a low "Rest in peace," finding nothing within myself worth conveying to the dead. Then I turned and left the graveyard, feeling vaguely disconcerted. I didn't know why.

For a time, I wandered aimlessly. At last, I found myself back at the waterfall I'd discovered the previous day. The air was quiet and still and, gazing at the tiny houses and green slopes in the distance, I came to realize that some odd strain of music seemed to be running through my head.

It was low, harmonious, and pleasant, yet altogether unfamiliar. I am not a competent songwriter, and it seemed strange that something I'd never heard before could somehow wend its way up from my subconscious.

For a while longer, I stood musing; then I started back for the house. I decided I would make a light snack and then delve into a couple of the closets I had seen. I had to admit that the past—my family's past—had come to fascinate me.

Occasionally, whenever Dad spoke about his early life, my curiosity momentarily rose, but it always retreated as soon as I returned to my ordinary affairs. Here, I supposed, with little else to occupy my mind, the past simply loomed larger and more tantalizing.

By the time I reached the house, my enthusiasm for exploring had peaked. I built a substantial ham and cheese sandwich for lunch, chased it with an ice-cold beer, and then went to the bedroom to begin my foraging.

My parents had packed away most of the clothes and incidental personal items. But I soon came upon many neat little articles, such as an ancient shaving kit complete with boar's-bristle brush and straight razor, a slightly battered pocket watch, and a few bottles of age-old cologne, mostly still full.

I found some more books stacked in a corner, including a Bible, a dictionary (vintage 1939), and an exceptionally brittle-looking, moldy volume called *The Encyclopedia For Boys*. And then I spied some cartons that immediately caught my interest: a set of four 6-inch reel tapes for the machine I had seen in the other room.

Each was labeled with faded black ink in crabbed script that I assumed to be Grandfather's. Two of them were sermons recorded at a local church, which Grandfather must have attended; one was a radio show from 1964; and the last was labeled "Zann," recorded in 1966.

I immediately took the latter tape to the living room, found the machine in the corner, and proceeded to set it up for listening. I prayed the machine would work after so many years of probable disuse. Upon plugging it in, I found that everything seemed to function well enough.

The reel began turning, and I stood anxiously waiting as the small speaker began hissing and crackling. Then a voice, which I knew immediately was Grandfather's, began to speak: a slow, deep drawl with a pronounced southern Virginia accent, not unlike my dad's. The voice sounded tentative and somewhat nervous, perhaps due to his inexperience talking to a machine. What he said was this:

I am making this recording to test a few of the passages from the Zann text, on pages 121 through 128 of The Spheres Beyond Sound. I am Tim Asberry, I live on Copper Peak outside of Barren Creek, Virginia. I am making this recording with the help of my neighbors, John Eubanks, Fred Wharton, Ray Martin, and Bill Miller. I am in the backyard of my house now, facing the crest of the mountain.

Uh, we have practiced select verses, or, uh, lines out of the book, but this will be the first complete performance of what Zann calls, uh, the summons. My neighbors and I have all read the text, and we believe that if we follow the directions, as set down by the writer, we will actually experience the, uh, revelations he has described.

I have decided to record this activity on my new tape machine. We don't honestly know what to expect, but if we should be successful, then it is possible there may be some danger. Zann's text indicates that the, uh, existences on the other side are not necessarily malevolent, but they are destructive in nature, like a shark in the ocean. The musical composition that will send the, uh, results of the summoning back where it came from is printed on pages 135 through 137 of the text. We played that piece in full at several practice sessions.

As I have said, I believe the writer of this book is sincere, for the simple reason that I have had proof. Two months ago, I took my fiddle up to the graveyard and played the piece on pages 39 and 40—the prelude to opening the barrier of death. As I played, as surely as I am standing here now, I saw the corrupted bodies of my relatives appear to stand before me, as solid as the earth under my feet. I was so frightened, I quit playing and they vanished, but on two occasions, I have gone back to the graveyard and heard weird music, though there was no one there to be playing it. I believe it was an answer of some kind to the invitation I played. But I haven't responded. And I don't go back to the graveyard anymore.

Now I felt a tremendous surge of excitement, of complete disbelief in what I was hearing. But I continued to listen, hypnotized by the fear in the low voice on the tape, not sure now if my grandfather were wholly of sound mind. I could sense that he was terrified of proceeding with this plan of his...yet his longing to test the mysteries of Maurice Zann's book so outweighed his fear he was willing to risk unknowable consequences.

There came a series of tonal pluckings and whinings as the group tuned their instruments—probably the very same ones that hung in the small workshop next to the living room. A couple of unfamiliar voices said something incomprehensible; then my grandfather spoke again:

It's getting dark now, and we're about to start. I will admit that all of us are pretty afraid, but we believe the things we might learn are so incredible and so important that they warrant whatever risk. I think from what we have learned so far, we will be safe.

There was a pause, and a few more background voices. Then my grandfather's voice said, "So, you ready?" and, after a moment, a sudden discordant jangle rattled from the speaker. Harsh plucking and flat strumming echoed through what must have been a still mountain night more than thirty years ago.

The noise seemed to have no rhythm or melody. Insect-like chirps arpeggioed up and down unknown scales, bass thumps jumped from one time signature to another without any pattern or structure...so it seemed. What I was hearing sounded more like a random banging of instruments by inexperienced hands than a complex latticework of music holding some deep-hidden power.

But as I listened, I caught strains of some unearthly harmony occasionally breaking through the aural chaos. I began to hear tones that were not of stringed instruments, but of deep woodwinds or brassy pipes. The harmonic undertones of the mandolin, guitar, violin, and dulcimer were producing sounds unlike any I had ever heard, even in the most radical of electronic fusion.

Beyond this cacophony, a definite melody seemed to coalesce, but from somewhere distant, mostly drowned by the brash orchestration. I turned the volume up on the machine, straining to catch the sequence of the evasive notes. I began to get distortion over the speaker, but I shut my ears to the discomfort and concentrated only on what lurked beneath. Yes...a melody was forming, arias of thin, reed-like whistles and lower, rich tones that could only be blown from a French horn.

And then, beyond that, another distinctive tune, but so faint as to be lost in the crashing of insane strings. I sat there for a time, separated from my surroundings by a spell of mesmerizing power. My thoughts seemed to dissolve, and I allowed myself to be absorbed by this raw energy that explored every realm of ecstasy, tranquility, horror, and agony.

Suddenly, it was over. I sat facing the rear window of my grandfather's house, peering toward the depths of the forest. A clatter came from the speaker as the musicians lowered their instruments and simultaneously breathed exhausted sighs. For a full two minutes, no sound came except for a soft sigh of breeze and a few crickets beginning their chorus for the evening. At last, one of the background voices said, "What's that? Anything?"

My grandfather mumbled something low. Then: "No. It's nothing." I waited again as silence returned, picturing the group of men looking around expectantly, probably with fear-widened eyes and sweaty, trembling hands. Then, Grandfather said, "Wind's picking up."

Sure enough, the drone of the breeze was growing stronger. It rose and fell several times, whistled by the microphone that probably sat unprotected somewhere near the players. But still, nothing more than the increasing chatter from the forest crept from the speaker. Almost five minutes went by without a word from any of the men.

Then, Grandfather said:

Well, nothing is happening...so far. Guess we'll have to wait and see. The book said it could take a little while. I guess the weather has to be right, too, for the message to get through. But these are good conditions. Sky's clear, it's pretty cold. Sound really carries. Wind's holding, I'd say between five and ten miles an hour. I suppose we could've done something incorrectly...that damned piece of music ain't meant to be played by human hands...but it sure seemed like we did it right.

Outside, here in my own time, the afternoon sun was well on its way into the west. It would be dark within the hour. A gust of chilly wind swirled through the house.

To save tape, I'll shut off for the moment and come back at the first sign of anything happening. Still damned peculiar...absolutely nothing. Nothing at all.

There was a click as the tape was shut off all those years ago. Another click followed as it was turned back on some indeterminate time later.

It's been thirty minutes now. No sign of anything unusual. The crickets are going nuts, as you can hear, but apart from that, everything seems normal. Pretty disappointing, but also kind of a relief. Maybe it's better if nothing happens. I guess it ain't right for Christian men to fool around with powers that only the Lord should know about. 'Course, I suppose there's a lot this family has done that ain't considered right and true. It's common knowledge that the Asberrys make the best whiskey outside Franklin County...but I reckon in the eyes of God that's a small sin compared to messing around with the powers that be.

I frowned. I wondered if the Asberrys'"shady" side—moonshining—had been the source of my dad's discomfort in sharing his family's past with me. My father was a decent and proud man and, having broken from his rural mold and established himself in a well-to-do urban environment, it would be like him to feel some guilt about his family's less-than-upright background.

Now, though, I wondered if there might be other secrets my family had kept hidden...darker things...occult things. Perhaps the music of Maurice Zann was only one such example. Might this old family have been delving into unknown, forbidden lore since before they settled here from the Old World?

I have always considered myself rational, well educated, and reasonably wise in the ways of the world. Still, the purely intuitive side of my nature felt the stirrings of some primal dread; instinct had overridden reason, leaving me confused and uncomfortable. The woods and wilderness I had found so charming now seemed fraught with perilous mystery.

Another couple of clicks came from the player. Then my grandfather's voice said:

Forty-five minutes now. Still nothing. The boys and me are starting to breathe a little easier. John's gone inside to make coffee. I guess it's better this way. Maybe we messed up, or maybe the Lord just said it ain't to be. Anyway, if nothing happens in the next few minutes, I think we'll all sleep much better tonight. After this, I reckon I'll be forgetting all about what happened before, up at the graveyard. I'll put that book away and never bother with it again. I should never have taken it from Daddy in the first place.

So, the book had been in the family even before my grandfather. Interesting.

Well, unless something happens tonight, I might as well give up on this recording. I'm pretty tired...all of us are right worn out, matter of fact. It's been hard work. So, for now, I'll be ending all this up...unless the need arises later. This is Tim Asberry, signing off.

Grandfather ended on that uncertain note. There was nothing else on the tape, which disappointed me, as I had hoped for at least some explanation or commentary on the night's activities. Their attempt had surely failed, and I found nothing in the house to suggest they had repeated the experiment at any other time. And nothing mysterious seemed to have befallen my grandfather in the intervening years.

And what of this whole premise, I wondered to myself. Could I place any stock in the concepts my grandfather had sought—and failed—to prove? Surely not, I thought. There had indeed been some unusual, elusive depth to the music on the tape, but, surely, nothing that could convince me of any mystical power.

My grandfather sounded like an intelligent man, with a modicum of formal education. I wondered just what his experience in the graveyard had been that encouraged him to seek the greater power hinted at in Zann's text. Had he merely suffered some frightening manifestation of his own imagination? Frustration began to eat at me, for it seemed this mystery was destined to die with no resolution. Deciphering the technical data in *The Spheres Beyond Sound* was beyond my ability.

There had to be some other way of gathering information. Perhaps the neighbors that had aided my grandfather's performance could be of assistance, if any were still alive and of sound memory.

Then I remembered the strange tune that had entered my head while I was walking in the graveyard. Had not Grandfather spoken of hearing supernatural music when he had gone there? Could I have shared such an experience, here, more than thirty years later? Suddenly, I realized that I had to return to the woods to see if the same thing might happen again.

Late afternoon was creeping over the mountains, but I calculated I could easily get to the graveyard and back before dark. Maybe tomorrow, I could search for the men who had accompanied my grandfather on the tape. There might yet be hope for this venture.

I disconnected the tape machine and returned the reel to its carton. Then I set out walking, flashlight in hand in case darkness fell upon me sooner than I expected. The worst hazard would be the steep drop-off near the trail. Since I was a child, I have seldom felt the thrill of fear, the sense of foreboding cast by the unknown. That feeling was upon me now, and although I was skeptical of it, I also paid it a certain amount of respect.

It didn't take me long to reach my destination. The sun had already dropped beyond the wall of trees and cast long shadows over the graveyard. Now, I sensed something different here, an atmosphere I had not felt before. Tiny cyclones of dead foliage flitted and danced among the gravestones.

Strange dark patches grew here and there that were not shadows. A low rumble issued from the ground, as if something huge and distant were stirring from sleep. And, in the air, the faintest of high-toned wails blended with the whistle of the breeze in a wistful, eerie dirge.

None of these elements was spectacular or even blatant. But they combined to create an atmosphere of subtle *wrongness*. And something inside assured me these phenomena could not be ordinary acts of nature. Could it truly be that, somehow, the music of Maurice Zann lay behind all this?

But my grandfather's attempt to utilize that music had failed. Had my thoughtless playing of the tape conjured something unknown—something unnatural? Something *supernatural*? I had been so curious about the music itself that I had never considered the possibility of it actually working the effect that my grandfather had hoped—or feared—to witness.

I left the graveyard and ran down the path that led to the waterfall. All I could think of now was getting away from this place.

Behind me, a weird, wild shriek suddenly tore through the forest—something animalistic, subhuman. It was joined by another, and then another, like a choir of ghastly, agonized voices. Something beneath my feet boomed deeply; then the ground shook so violently I feared the earth's surface must have been rent, opening the way for denizens of the underworld to crawl from their blazing pits.

More chilling cries from the graveyard sent me running even faster, down toward the house that I considered my only retreat.

Suddenly, before I realized it, I reached the precipice where the stream pitched into space. I caught the trunk of a small tree just in time to save me hurtling over the edge, nearly dislocating my shoulder in the process. The stab of pain halted me in my tracks.

Then my eyes caught something moving in the valley below. The sun had just reached the horizon, and on this side of the mountain, facing east, only shadow filled the depths below. But in that darkness, something even darker—something gigantic—appeared to be crawling across the valley floor.

My eyes fixed on this mass of blackness, mesmerized by its immensity. My lungs stopped working and, for a moment, I felt I was falling. Somehow, I managed to keep holding on to that tree. It was the only thing that saved me.

From the woods behind me, there now came a multitude of shufflings and scrapings, as of many bodies moving through the foliage. Guttural groans and hoarse cries drifted through the dark woods toward me. A surge of panic sent me flying back from the edge and down the trail again.

But the woods had turned nearly pitch black, and I could no longer see where I was going. I slammed into a hidden tree, somehow avoiding being impaled on broken branches. Reeling from the force of the impact, I reached out to find support...and gripped a moist, muddy limb that hung too limply from something unseen.

To my horror, that limb moved of its own accord, and something hard and firm took hold of my wrist. I jerked back purely from reflex, and as I did, a shrill wail exploded from the shadowy figure before me. I launched myself past it and began my flight anew down the treacherous path, blindly hoping to reach the house without killing myself.

Many times in nightmares I have found myself fleeing from some terrible threat. As often as not, my car is my refuge, for in mobility there is hope of safety. I was now living one of my nightmares, and my one goal was to reach my car and escape from this terrible mountain. And, as in so many dreams, the darkness engulfed me, slowed me down, obscured my path.

I cannot count how many times my feet slipped out from under me or grasping branches clutched my clothing. At last, a short distance ahead, I saw inviting lights from the house's windows. With profound but temporary relief, I pushed my way through the back door, slammed it behind me, and fell heavily against it.

I didn't care about the few belongings I had brought with me. My only concern now was to find my keys and get away from here. From outside, the restless chatter of the night creatures, more urgent than usual, spurred me on. I ran into the bedroom, desperate to find my keys, which I located on the bedside table. Grabbing them up, I turned and headed for the front door, not bothering to turn off the lights or lock the door.

The moment I shakily inserted the key into the car door, I heard a grating rumble from the woods just above the house. Looking up, I saw the tops of the dark trees shaking and pitching back and forth violently. All around me, mournful wailing drifted out of the darkness.

I knew there was no way to get down the mountain in time to escape whatever was coming.

Still, I jerked the car door open with a burst of frenzied strength, slid into the seat, and willed my hand to carefully insert the key into the ignition. I somehow accomplished this on the first attempt, fired up the engine, and flipped on the headlights.

The car faced the side of the house, and caught in the beams of the headlights stood a figure whose appearance nearly stopped my heart. It was a parody of a man, or had once been a man. It stood facing me on two spindly legs, its body a mass of dark, moss-covered earth. Two black sockets gaped from its mud-encrusted skull, empty, but seemingly possessed of sight. For a long moment, it did not move, only stood there, apparently regarding me. Then, at either corner of the house, two similar figures appeared, both facing me but making no move in my direction.

Then, out of the empty air, I heard the mad strains of that mystical music, and to my shock, those corrupted bodies began to whirl and leap, spinning and pirouetting in a grotesque, fiery dance.

Above the roof of the house, a great mass of blackness rose into the night sky, blocking the glittering stars that had begun to appear. The night went utterly still; no wind cut across the mountaintop, no insect chirped. Only the notes of the supernatural music continued to rise into the sky.

The whirling figures ceased their dancing and dropped to their bony knees, prostrating themselves before the black shape that hovered above the house. At the farthest reaches of my senses, I discerned the wistful notes of my grandfather's stringed cacophony.

As I sat there, the features of the huge thing before me gradually came into focus. I could see what appeared to be thick, segmented legs, dozens of yards long and, in the midst of the solid central mass, myriad clusters of tiny, flickering lights. It was a gigantic spider-thing with a thousand eyes that glared down at me as if ready to pounce. The worshipping corpses began a new wailing chorus.

As the glare of those thousand eyes bore down upon me, I realized why my playing the tape recording had succeeded in summoning this monstrous entity where my grandfather's original performance had failed: I had turned the volume on the machine up to catch the subtle undertones of the music.

The lower, most subtle elements of the "live" performance on acoustic instruments had failed to reach the volume prescribed in the Zann text. Yet the very same music, played at a higher decibel level, had been in the exact range to complete the summoning process.

Then another cold fear seized me: due to the failure of his attempt, Grandfather had never recorded the passage that returned the extradimensional horror to its rightful place. There was no way to send the thing back!

Now, strange whispers, voices from somewhere beyond this plane of time and space, began to swirl around me like buzzing bees. Panic motivated my hand, and I slammed the gear lever into reverse and spun the steering wheel, turning my car down the road away from the house.

In mad fury, the car screamed and bucked over the potholed road, several times nearly skidding into the woods on either side. I did not slow down, though. Any fear of smashing myself into a tree or plunging into deep crevices paled beside the otherworldly threat I was fleeing.

At last, I reached the bottom of the mountain and sent my car hurtling down the winding highway toward Barren

Creek, never looking into the rearview mirror to see what might be following.

Even when the music and whispering faded from my hearing, my terror refused to subside. Once, while speeding down a long, curving decline that allowed me a brief view of Copper Peak, I swore I saw a portion of the sky blocked out by a gigantic, spiderlike shape resting on top of the mountain. But the road curved again, and Copper Peak once and for all slipped out of my line of sight.

In Aiken Mill, I stopped to fill my gas tank, which had fallen dangerously close to empty. As I nervously pumped the gasoline into my car, my eyes darted repeatedly down the road whence I had come, half-expecting to see some crawling, pitch-black silhouette advancing from the distance.

But nothing appeared, and I paid the nervous-looking attendant who must have thought I had escaped from the nearby Catawba Sanitarium. By the time I reached Interstate 81, I had seen nothing more, and the terror that consumed me at last began to abate.

And yet for me, the real fear lies ahead. Whatever the music of Maurice Zann summoned, it still lurks on the fringes of this world, somewhere in the mountains around Barren Creek.

The only way to send it back is by playing the proper musical arrangements from *The Spheres Beyond Sound*, and the only copy of that book in existence seems to be at my old family house. Even if I could find the right passage, someone who could read music would have to play the piece.

As it is, I have been unable to find another copy of that book, or any record indicating such a book ever existed. And I will never, *never* return to that place in the mountains, at any time, for any reason. I have urged my parents to sell the house, but to avoid going there at all costs.

Of course, I revealed nothing to my father of the events that had transpired there; yet as irrational as I must have sounded, he seemed to accept my words without question—and with a curious attitude of understanding.

As I said, however, the real terror for me has yet to come. For surely, those animated corpses were those of my own relatives, their eternal souls somehow drawn back to their wasted bodies. Even now, they dance and worship the black overlord of death that Zann's music called from beyond.

Thus, my fate has been sealed, for my own bloodline calls to me. At times, I can hear those demonic notes pounding in my ears, as if the long-dead Asberrys are beckoning me to join them. Whatever paradise may await others in the life after this one, I know it is never meant for me.

As long as that black spider remains free in this world, the gate to the other side is blocked and guarded.

Eventually, my time will come, and when it does, I will become one of those damned, dancing parodies that bewail their fate and bow to the demon master from some dimension beyond death.

Night Crier

2018

NOW:

His mother's dull gray eyes were focused inward, her smile wistful. After some long reflection, she looked up at him from her bed. "I remember when you were little, you were always scared on Halloween. Do you remember that?"

"Yes, I remember."

"It didn't seem to be the trick-or-treaters or the decorations. It was something else. I never really understood it. Did you?"

"I can't say I did. It was just a kid thing, I guess."

"You always were a good son. You're still a good son, and I thank you for all your care. I know so many people whose children don't visit them, even at holidays. It must break their hearts."

"I try my best."

"Tell me your name again."

"It's Bill, Mom."

"I know I've asked you before. I'm sorry I repeat myself."

"It's all right."

"It's frustrating not to remember. But I do remember long-ago things. Like your dad. I miss him so much. He was a good husband and father. And he was proud of you."

"I've always wanted to make him proud."

"He'd be proud of you now." She looked into the mirror atop the dresser at the far end of the bed, her face beaming, as if memories of every wonderful thing in her life had come rushing back.

That would be too much to hope for. Mom was just a shell, a poorly drawn caricature of the loving, intelligent woman she had always been.

Her disease was killing *him*.

"I'm so glad you're here. It's lonely when you're not. Sometimes I'm afraid."

"You don't need to be afraid, Mom. When I'm not here, you have good nurses staying with you."

"I don't remember them." She stared into the distance before looking back at him. "What was your name again?"

"Bill."

"Oh, yes. I remember when you were little, you were always scared on Halloween. It didn't seem to be the trick-or-treaters or the decorations. It was something else. Do you remember that?"

"Yes, Mom. I remember."

THEN:

Even with the nightlight on, the darkness felt smothering, like a cold, clinging blanket. He could hear his heartbeat—*buh-bump, buh-bump, buh-bump*—and the more he concentrated on the sound, the louder and faster it got.

Above him, the colorful birds that hung on wires from the ceiling looked mean and menacing. Tiny black eyes and ragged wings and sharp beaks, not nice and cute as they appeared in sunshine. With his thumb and forefinger, he kneaded a corner of the bedsheet, for the repetitive motion with the soft fabric soothed him. It helped slow his heartbeat.

Before he went to bed, the doorbell had rung and rung, and Mommy held him while Daddy kept opening the door to lots of faces hovering in the little island of light outside. They all looked different, but all were *wrong*, some with big staring eyes and gaping mouths; others with wild, stringy hair and huge ears; and some with glittering speckles on their faces and antennae sprouting from their heads.

There was lots of hollering and Daddy putting candy in the bags they thrust forward, and each time another group appeared, Mommy laughed and said, "Cute. So cute!"

They seemed kind of scary, but he didn't think they would hurt him. All they wanted was to make noise and get candy.

But that other noise—the one he could barely hear, for it came from far away—*it* was scary.

The sound drifted from the dark space beyond his half-open curtains: a weird, musical wailing that rose and fell, almost in rhythm with his heartbeat. At first, he thought it was a bird because he sometimes heard birds calling even at night. Then he thought it was a person singing, maybe even Mommy, but it couldn't be. She was with Daddy in their bedroom. Maybe the people with strange faces. Maybe candy wasn't all they wanted. But what else could they want?

The wailing went on for a long time, though it never seemed to get louder or closer. Finally, it rose long and shrill, and then went silent, but his heart kept going *buh-bump, buh-bump, buh-bump*, and he was breathing so fast he began to hiccup. After some time, and the hiccupping wouldn't go away, he heard footsteps in the hall. The door opened, and there was Mommy, a tall silhouette standing in the hallway light.

"Oh, honey," she whispered to him. She placed one hand on his chest and brushed his tousled hair back from his forehead with the other. "What's wrong? Were you scared? Did the trick-or-treaters frighten you?"

His heart slowed, and the hiccups subsided at her touch. He shook his head, and his eyes turned to the window. She left his bedside, pulled back the curtains, and peered into the darkness for what seemed a very long time. But when she came back to him, she smiled and said, "Everything is all right now. You go back to sleep, and it will be morning before you know it."

He nodded and smiled back at her. He didn't want her to leave the room yet, but he knew everything would be fine now.

She bent down and kissed him on the forehead. "I love you, honey. Good night."

"G'night, Mommy."

NOW:

The money was running out, and after a full year's time, there had not been a single call about the house. The local economy was too slow, the place too old and too big to sell.

A few more months, and there would be nothing left to pay the nurses. Medicaid would probably be his last option, but all he had heard about Alzheimer's patients on Medicaid were horror stories.

To save paying the nurses the time and a half weekend rate, he had been making the three-hour drive to Aiken Mill from Richmond almost every weekend for the past year, but overtime at the office had kept him away for a full month now.

"Her condition is getting worse," Vonda said. Of the trio of nurses that looked after Mom, Vonda was the best. From keeping the house spotless, to taking Mom to her doctor appointments, to handling all the shopping, she went beyond the call of duty when he wasn't there. "Mrs. Caswell has been getting ornery lately, and you know that's not like her. She's always been the sweetest lady I've ever known. She so reminds me of my grandmother."

He frowned. "She's never been impatient or short-tempered before. That's a big change."

"She's taken to wandering around the house at night too. Says she can't sleep, so she just goes back and forth from room to room. I don't think she's ever gone outside, but she could fall down the basement stairs or knock over a lamp and get cut. I try not to let her out of my sight, but she's getting where she doesn't want me to interfere with her, even if she doesn't have any idea what she's doing."

"That's all new."

"Dr. Barrow increased her dosage of Memantine and Donepezil, but there's not much else he can do." Vonda went quiet and stared past him for a moment. "Mr. Caswell, I do have to give you some news. I'm going to be leaving the nursing staff in two weeks. There's a great opportunity in Atlanta to start up a private nursing team with a couple of partners. I can't say no to that."

Despair lanced his heart and sent his head reeling. There was no one in Aiken Mill who could replace Vonda. He could not even try to smile at her. "I know that's your calling," he finally said. "I'm sure you'll do well, but I'll miss having you here. You've done more for Mom than anyone else, even her old friends." He gave a wry chuckle. "Of, course, most of her friends are no better off than she is."

"I'm going to miss her more than anyone," Vonda said. Her wide, amber-brown eyes were wet. "Since before her memory was so far gone, she's treated me like a member of the family. I'll never forget that."

"That's just how she is." He had to brush back a tear of his own. "Was."

THEN:

He was getting too old for trick-or-treating, but it was still the best thing about Halloween. He didn't relish the idea of sitting home alone watching movies or commiserating with his friends about the passing of their childhoods. He did enjoy dressing up in costumes, the scarier the better, and one of the few advantages of being short was that adults wouldn't peg him for twelve years old if they couldn't recognize him.

Tonight, he had worn a rubber scarecrow mask that fully covered his face, with an old sweatshirt and jeans stuffed with straw. Damn if it didn't itch, but he sure enjoyed the spooky look. He actually drew a few shocked stares from the neighbors when they opened their doors. Happily, he and Charles and Frank had made a good haul this evening.

It was getting on that time. Every year on Halloween night, the sound came out of the woods: the keening, mournful cry he had first heard when he was in the crib. Until a couple of years ago, it had always terrified him, but now it fascinated him. No, that wasn't right. It still scared the hell out of him. But since he had turned ten, on Halloween night, the sound drew him to the back porch, where he would stand peering and listening until it went silent.

Whatever it was, it remained far away, never approaching or receding. It wasn't going to hurt him, he told himself. It was just a noise. It wasn't a bird or an animal or a recording or someone playing an annual prank. He knew what it was *not*.

Beyond the porch railing, the backyard extended for a couple of hundred feet before ending at a steep, rocky ravine, through which a little creek ran. Then there was only a vast expanse of unbroken woodland—or so it had always been. Unseen amid the distant hills, bulldozers had begun clearing lots for new houses, and in the daytime, he could hear the heavy machinery and sharp cracking of falling trees.

If they kept cutting, would *they* find the source of that noise?

"Well, here you are," came Mom's voice. He didn't realize she had come out to the porch. "Did you enjoy your Halloween?"

"It was pretty good," he said. He had never spoken to Mom about his Halloween night terrors. Well, not since he was very little.

"Your friends have gone home, haven't they?"

"Yes."

"Since it's Friday night, if you'd like to stay up a little later, it'll be all right."

"Cool, thanks."

She stood beside him and peered into the woods. "You always used to close yourself indoors after trick-or-treating, like something upset you. I guess not anymore, huh? *Did* something upset you, Bill?" He felt her eyes studying him. "Does it still?"

He shrugged. "I dunno. I've always liked Halloween and all, but there's just something about it. Can't really explain."

It was just past ten o'clock.

The first strains of the wailing cry came wafting out of the woods.

"When you were little, you used to cry every Halloween night. It always seemed like something scared you."

An almost melodic, warbling noise, muted by distance, but still clear and resonant. A dirge, it seemed, as if something not quite human were crying out in soul-deep misery.

Mom's eyes turned to the woods. Her mouth was open as if to speak, but no words came. Together, she and Bill gazed into the depths of a world very different from its daylight counterpart. In sunshine, the woods appeared beautiful and wondrous. Now, in unleashing that sound from their dark, hidden heart, they had become grim and forbidding.

For another minute or so, the sound rose and fell, and some of his old, familiar dread came creeping back. He remembered lying in his crib, that very same sound drifting into his bedroom through the darkened window, his fingers kneading the bed sheet, his heart beating so hard it nearly drowned out the frightening noise.

And then, as it did every year, the wailing rose to a sharp screech and went silent.

Bill glanced at his mom. She was still staring into the darkness, her face thoughtful but not fearful. When she looked at him, she smiled.

His nerves nearly stopped him, but he asked, "What did you hear?"

Her eyes returned to the woods for a moment. "I heard wind in the trees. But it seemed different than usual. Somehow different."

"Yeah," he said. "That's what it was. Different."

"Don't eat too much candy, all right? You don't need all that sugar keeping you awake."

"I won't."

"I'm going to bed soon. Be sure and lock up, please. And turn out the lights."

"I will."

"I'll say good night then."

"G'night, Mom."

NOW:

He had dozed off on the living room couch after his mind wandered away from his book and settled on memories of his ex-wife. He'd had no contact with her for almost three years. On occasion, like tonight, he found himself *almost* missing her.

Kelly might have been the only soul on Earth who didn't care for his mother. Had they remained together, she would never have tolerated him devoting so much of his life to caring for Mom in her waning days.

He wasn't sure what had roused him, for the house was quiet. Mom usually kept the television on while she lay in bed, but he couldn't hear anything from the back bedroom. He groaned and dragged himself off the couch. His 55-year-old bones argued with him more than they used to. He shuffled down the hall to her room. When he poked his head through the open door, he found her bed empty, the television dark. He stepped inside and checked her bathroom. Also vacant.

Perhaps he'd heard her in the kitchen. *That* was what had roused him.

He went down the hall and found the kitchen dark but for the small light over the sink. She wasn't there either. With mounting alarm, he checked the door that led to the basement and, to his relief, found it closed and deadbolted. But then he noticed a draft from the mudroom that adjoined the kitchen. When he stepped into the small, dark space, a gust of frigid air swept over him.

The door to the back porch was hanging open.

"She's taken to wandering around the house at night. Says she can't sleep...."

"Jesus."

He would not have dreamed she might go outside on her own. She had never wandered off when he was there, but Vonda had said things were getting worse.

He hurried out to the porch and peered into the void beyond the railing. After several moments, the stars and silhouettes of the distant trees became clear. There, some indeterminate distance away, he saw a pale shape ambling away from him, toward the woods at the edge of the property.

"Mom!" he called. If she heard him, she gave no sign.

He leaped down the stairs and rushed after her, too late realizing he had left his shoes in front of the living room couch. Cold, razor-like grass and prickly sweetgum pods tortured his bare soles, and something sharp ripped into his heel, forcing him to slow his pace.

He had closed some of the distance between them, but she kept going, apparently unaware of his presence.

"Mom! For God's sake, *stop!*"

Disregarding the pain, he picked up the pace again. At last, he could make out her figure clearly. She was wearing her light blue robe—and almost certainly her bedroom slippers, since she appeared to have less trouble traversing the yard than he did.

At last, she stopped, her figure all but engulfed by the vast black night.

Panting, he caught up to her. He realized she was standing at the edge of the rocky drop-off to the creek. "Mom, what are you doing? Why did you come out here?"

"I heard something," she said. "I had to see."

"You can't see anything out here. You need to come back to the house."

She turned to him, her face a pale oval marred by vague shadows. "Who are you?"

"Mom, it's me. Bill. Your son."

She shook her head. "I—I don't know you."

She is not my mom anymore.

"Just trust me. Come on back to the house."

"But I heard something."

"Please, Mom."

Her gaze never left the dark gulf. "I can't go with you. I don't know you."

No, no, no, she cannot have forgotten me!

"Mom!"

She didn't answer him.

He didn't will it. He didn't want it. But he could not stop his hand.

It rose.

It touched her shoulder.

And shoved her.

Down she went. Down the rocky drop-off to the creek. He heard the *thud-thumping* of her body tumbling away in the darkness.

When the sounds of her fall died away, he peered into the chasm after her. At first, he could see nothing down there. Then he spotted her pale figure some thirty feet away, sprawled at the edge of the little stream. She wasn't moving.

"Oh, God. Mom."

That vacant shell is not my mom.

A soft moan rose from the gulf, and a frigid, iron fist seized him. She was still alive.

Jesus. Oh, Jesus.

He had to get back to the house and call 911.

She wandered off while I was asleep. No one will ever know any different.

The sound rose to a mournful, mindless wail, a plaintive cry of terror and confusion.

Rhythmic, almost musical.

He backed away from the edge, horrified by every mad thought that now swirled through his brain.

It was the last day of October.

He turned and bolted toward the house; swept away by all the terror he had known as a baby in his crib. The wretched wailing went on and on, kept pace with him until he reached the back porch.

His heart hammered like a piston in his chest. *Buh-bump, buh-bump, buh-bump.*

His mother's last cries ended.

And then, all those many years ago, began again.

Hell's Hollow

2017

Excerpt from a letter from Daniel Boone to Rebecca Boone, dated 12 June 1778

Dearest Rebecca,

I write this knowing you will not likely receve it, but I will try to see it into the hands of a mesenger in hopes that it may yet get through to you. I am safe and making my way eastward from Chalagawtha after a long ordeal amid the Shawnee. For my part in seeing to the surender of Boonesborough, the Shawnee chief Blackfish came to put trust in me. Thus, I eventualy managed to make my escape.

During these long months, I have witnesed many strange things, not the least of which is a nearby glen which grows lusher and thicker than any I have ever seen. There is a small stone in its center which gives off light of peculiar violet color. The Shawnee call it Star-stone and say it has laid in the glen longer than anyone remembers. They claim the stone makes the trees and plants in the glen grow tall, yet they are twisted and all tinged with that same peculiar color.

The Indians hunt inside the glen and bring back food and pelts of animals I do not recognize. Though the place provides the Shawnee with such abundance, it has a fearsome quality I do not like.

The sun is setting, and down in the valley miles away, even now I can see traces of that strange, violet light.

Mt. Zion, Tennessee — On the Nolichucky River, 20 miles southwest of Johnson City

April 11

"Sheriff, we got a call from Fred Traylor, over on Cemetery Hill. Said his neighbors' place has been demolished." The slow female voice on the radio might as well have announced rain in the forecast.

Janet Ashford. Little ever fazed her.

"Demolished?"

"Yes'm."

"Whose place?"

"Tom and Linda Imbuses'."

"Is Fred there now?"

"Yes'm."

"On the way." Sheriff Debra Sabourin steered the Ford Interceptor to the edge of the road and swung it back in the direction they'd come—up Clarke Road in the direction of Hell's Hollow. "Hold on, Robert."

Deputy Moses *harumphed*, one hand grasping the oh-shit handle above the window as the Interceptor accelerated up the winding road. "You know Tom and Linda?" he asked.

"Not really. I met her back when she worked the ER. Never met Tom."

"Good people. Known them for thirty years, thereabout."

"There's only four houses on Cemetery Hill. How does a place get demolished out there?"

"Gas explosion, maybe."

"You don't suppose Fred's already in his cups, do you?"

"Even if he is, he's rarely prone to misperception."

Sabourin flipped on the blue lights and siren and gave the accelerator an extra nudge. She took a couple of the snaking curves faster than necessary just to irk Deputy Moses.

"This is why you had me ride out with you today," he said. "You want me toss my lunch."

"I merely enjoy your company, Robert."

"As you should."

She chuckled. The older man had only a few months left till retirement, and for herself, she hated the prospect. She loved him like a second father.

Cemetery Hill Road ran along a steep ridge above the Nolichucky River. Sabourin switched off the siren as she turned the Interceptor onto the long gravel driveway that led to the house. She scanned the trees to either side for any sign of Tom and Linda—or anything that might appear amiss—but beyond the towering oaks, sycamores, and poplars, she saw only indiscernible shapes and shadows.

Until the car rounded a curve. Before her lay all that remained of the Imbuses' modest but well-appointed house.

"Oh, my lord," Moses muttered.

The northernmost end of the two-story wooden structure had collapsed into a pile of rubble. Only one wall and a portion of the roof remained intact. Inside, a jagged section of roof hung precariously over the remains of a flight of stairs. A couple of tall poplars had fallen across the driveway beside the house, but they clearly had not caused the damage. Nothing appeared burned.

Sabourin pushed her way out of the car. "This was no explosion."

"You see Fred Traylor anywhere?"

"No."

"I'm here, Sheriff." A hefty, bearded man with close-cropped gray hair stepped out from behind a large oak at the edge of the driveway.

"Do you know what happened here, Mr. Traylor?"

He shook his head. "I was at home asleep—been working third shift—and I woke up to a bunch of booming, like somebody was blasting with dynamite. Sounded like it was coming from here, so I ran right over, and this is what I found."

Deputy Moses made his way to the still-standing wall and peered in one of the shattered windows. "Tom Imbus! Linda!" Receiving no response, he moved on around the house, out of sight.

"Fred, do you know whether the Imbuses were at home?"

"Both their cars are in the garage—whatever's left of it. Since they both retired, they don't go out much, so I'd bet they were at home. I called Tom's phone, but it went straight to voicemail."

"When's the last time you saw them?"

"Couple of days ago."

Moses returned from his survey of the wreckage. "No sign of life anywhere."

"Fred, you don't know of anyone doing any blasting in the area, do you?"

"Well, that house wasn't blown up, not by dynamite. But you know those men out here, the ones on that government project?"

She felt a little jolt of surprise. "News to me, Fred."

"They came through a few days ago, heading into Hell's Hollow with a mess of electronic equipment and who knows what all."

"What about them?"

"Well, last night, I saw these flashes of light. At first, I thought it was lightning, but it was coming from *down* in the Hollow, not in the sky. Strange color, too—kind of purple. Now, there wasn't any noise last night, but when I heard that booming this morning, those men was the first ones I thought about."

"They aren't government people," Moses said. "They're from Beckham University, in Virginia. They're studying the effects of climate change and such."

"How do *you* know?"

"I know everything."

She scowled and looked back at Traylor. "You think *they* had something to do with this?"

"Well, I don't know. But I'm sure I don't like them."

"Why's that?"

"Seen them down at the Citgo on 81. Figured they was liberals, talking about climate change and all."

Sabourin gave the ruins a long, thoughtful stare. "Robert, let's get everybody up here. County rescue squad. Gas company. I have a bad feeling we'll be needing the coroner."

"I'm on it," Moses said, heading for the Interceptor.

To Traylor, she said, "You know, I might like to talk to those gentlemen from Beckham. Maybe they heard something."

He shot her a sour look. "Hell. I think they *done* something."

Sabourin finessed the SUV around the tight curves as they descended at high speed into Hell's Hollow. "What are you not telling me, Robert?"

"I'm not not telling you anything. I'm just trying to process something."

"Specifically?"

"Back in the woods behind the house. A long swath of downed trees. Like something very *big* passed through."

"What kind of something?"

"Maybe like a whale."

"Robert. Whales live in the ocean."

"Yes."

"So something like a whale came through the woods and demolished the Imbuses' house."

"Weird, ain't it?"

They reached the base of the ridge, and entered Hell's Hollow, a low-lying area so named after a fire had swept through in the early 1900s, burning hundreds of acres and taking a dozen lives.

"You sure the Beckham men went up Old Camp Road?" she asked.

"Fits with what Fred said. And Mayor Preston mentioned they were heading out here the other day."

"So *that's* how you know everything."

"Partly."

Sabourin turned the Interceptor onto Old Camp Road, a long-disused logging road that snaked through the gorge between Cemetery Hill and Bobcat Mountain. Fresh tire tracks in the dirt indicated someone had driven this way recently. Once upon a time, moonshiners operated a number of stills back here, but those were long gone. Nowadays, only the occasional camper ventured into the hollow.

Spring rains had turned the blossoming woods vivid green, and brilliant streamers of gold dribbled through the leafy canopy. But in an hour, it would be as dark as night beneath the trees, and she hoped to get back to the office in Mt. Zion well before then.

As the road wound up the ridge, stray tendrils of close-pressing mountain laurel slapped at the windows. Something caught Moses's attention, and he leaned forward to peer into the distance.

"Look at that, will you?"

She eased off the gas and followed his gaze. At first, she could not grasp what she was seeing.

A few hundred feet ahead, walls of dense, tangled foliage grew on either side of the road. Clinging, snakelike vines climbed high into the surrounding trees.

Pale, luminous, *violet* foliage.

As far as she could see, the inexplicable plants grew in profusion. Even the trees—many of them uncommonly tall with twisted, corkscrew-like trunks—glowed with the unnatural hue.

"Radiation?" Moses asked, his eyes widening.

"I don't see how. I don't see how *anything* could do this."

She drove at little more than walking speed, captivated by the frightening yet alluring flora. On all sides, the violet limbs, vines, and creepers grew denser until she could see only a few yards into them.

"When's the last time you came back here, Robert?"

"Four or five years, I reckon."

"How long do you suppose this has been growing?"

"I'd guess about as long as those men from Beckham have been here."

Around a curve, Sabourin caught sight of a vehicle parked in a clearing to the side of the road. It was a high-end, glorified RV, she thought, built on a Ford F750 chassis. An Earthroamer.

"Now *there* is an expedition vehicle," Moses said. "That cost a mint."

She parked the Interceptor next to the Earthroamer, got out, and took a moment to scan their surroundings. The thick, violet-colored vegetation appeared to have grown *atop* the existing foliage, like a weirdly woven blanket draped over it.

Moses took a walk around the Earthroamer, studying it with admiration. It was a big vehicle, painted iron gray with black trim, with a four-door cab, the windows all tinted dark.

"Bet this thing cost a million," he said.

"Try a million and a half," came a gruff voice from somewhere amid the trees. A second later, a tall man stepped from behind a cluster of purple-tinted creepers, just beyond the Earthroamer. He was wearing a khaki vest over a gray sweatshirt, cargo pants, and a papyrus brim sunhat. His eyes hid behind a pair of opaque shades. "Can I help you?"

"I'm Sheriff Sabourin. This is Deputy Moses. May I assume you're one of the researchers from Beckham University?"

"Dr. Derek Westerman." He gave her a sardonic smile. "You have clearly taken notice of our little anomaly in the woods."

"Clearly. Dr. Westerman, just what *are* we seeing?"

"Sheriff, you're looking at the results of a brand new, very ancient agricultural experiment."

"Thank you. That tells me everything I need to know."

He chuckled. "Forgive me, Sheriff. We are using material many centuries old to cultivate new organic strains, designed to counteract the detrimental effects of climate change on global food supplies. Basically, you're looking at a supersized agricultural laboratory."

"Is there any danger of radiation here?"

"There is no radiation danger, or danger at all. I can assure you our procedures are safe, and we have every necessary permit to work here. But I can appreciate that it appears disconcerting."

"I understand you're not working alone."

"My partner, Dr. McGufficke, is engaged in some tests a short distance from here."

"If it isn't radiation, what produces this luminous effect?" Moses asked.

"Biology. In simple terms, it's not unlike the glow produced by certain undersea creatures, such as jellyfish. I'm afraid I can't be more specific than that."

"Would any of your experiments produce bright flashes of light?" Sabourin asked. "Light that could be seen several miles from here—at least after dark?"

"Not likely. You might detect some faint glow from this area at night, but not from far away."

"How about blasting? I don't suppose anything you're doing would produce an explosion. Or a concussion?"

"Not at all. Sheriff, I assume you have a specific reason for asking these questions."

"This morning, a few miles from here, a house was destroyed, and two people are missing. Earlier, a witness reported hearing noises that might indicate explosions. That same witness also claims he saw flashes of violet light last night in Hell's Hollow—which, in case you're not aware, is where you are now." She gestured to the luminous vegetation. "*Violet* light."

"As I said, nothing we're doing could account for such things."

Moses pointed to the Earthroamer. "This is an impressive vehicle, Doc. A million and half dollars? Beckham U. must have serious petty cash on hand."

Westerman gave a dry chuckle. "The university matched a small percentage, but Dr. McGufficke and I paid for most of this out of our own pockets."

"I'm something of an RV geek myself," Moses said in a genial tone. "Think I could take a look inside?"

"Nice try, Deputy. As much as I would love to show off our hardware, our work is highly proprietary. For you to inspect the interior, I'd have to insist you get a warrant."

Moses held up a placating hand. "I understand."

Robert isn't buying all this.

She glanced up through the branches. The sunbeams infiltrating the canopy had all but petered out. In the near-silence, she detected a low rustling in the woods. She realized that some of the tangled vines nearby were moving, rising from the ground with a slow, undulating motion. *Like snakes wriggling up to stand on their tails.*

"Good God!"

"Did I hear—?" A figure stepped from behind the Earthroamer, bespectacled eyes widening when they registered the newcomers. "Oh. Officers."

"Dr. McGufficke, I presume?"

The man nodded. He appeared to be about fifty, heavyset, dressed in garb almost identical to Westerman's.

His eyes, magnified to immense proportion by the thick lenses, flicked toward the woods.

"Is everything all right, Doctor?"

"I suppose so. I didn't expect to find anyone else here, much less police officers."

"Deputy Moses, I wonder if you'd mind asking Dr. McGufficke a few questions," Sabourin said. "One on one."

"Not a bit." He motioned to the Interceptor. "Doctor, if you would accompany me to our vehicle, I'll only take a few minutes of your time."

"I'm sorry," he said, glancing toward Westerman. "But I'm going to have to ask you both to leave. For your safety. I've become aware of a small problem here."

"A 'small' problem?" Sabourin asked. "Dr. Westerman has assured us your experiment is safe. Gentlemen, I think we may need to have a more serious conversation. Not out here."

Westerman held up a hand. "A moment, please. Ian, can you elaborate?"

McGufficke appeared an inch shy of panic. "Wildfire."

For a second, something like satisfaction brightened Westerman's features. But then his somber expression returned.

"Sheriff, Dr. McGufficke is correct. It would be prudent for you to leave. First thing in the morning, I will come to your office, and we can talk then."

"'Wildfire.' So, something has gone beyond your control. Perhaps your experiment is not as safe as you've made it out to be?"

McGufficke said, "Sheriff, we have a situation that requires our immediate attention. Failing to address it will set us back in ways you wouldn't understand. The scientific—and financial—loss could be devastating."

Moses pointed to the nearby vines, now entwined so they resembled a lattice, taut enough to prevent anyone passing through. "Anything to do with this?"

Behind the shades, Westerman's eyes seemed to linger on the vines. "This *is* an unusual side effect."

A deep, resonating *boom* rolled out of the distance.

Now, even Westerman appeared concerned. "Sheriff Sabourin. Deputy Moses. I urge you to leave right now. I fear some danger does exist."

Her hand went to her holstered Glock 21. "What kind of danger?"

In the distance, another *boom*, followed by a sharp *crack* and *crash*.

Trees falling.

"Hey, Debra."

Moses pointed down the dirt road in the direction they had come. Another lattice of luminous vines was forming across the road, blocking their exit. Beyond them, a huge, trunk-like root that resembled a massive serpent came creeping out of the woods.

"Jesus," she whispered. "Westerman, are you in control of all this?"

"Control? No."

Sabourin drew her pistol, guessing it would be useless against the animated flora but tempted to turn it on Westerman. She resisted the impulse.

"Sheriff, that is no use to you. Remember, we did ask you to leave. It appears that option is no longer viable." He pointed to the Interceptor. "Not in that, anyway."

A shuffling, scuttling sound rose from the underbrush. A nearby branch broke with a sharp *crack*.

"We should get inside," McGufficke said. "Please."

Westerman appeared to ponder the situation. Then he gave Moses a wry smile. "Well, Deputy, you did want to see the inside of the Earthroamer."

McGufficke tugged open the cabin door, just behind the rear wheel. "Please."

Moses took the cue, and Sabourin followed him up the metal stairs and through the narrow door.

The interior was spacious but loaded with electronic and laboratory equipment she did not recognize. At the rear of the cabin, there was a compact kitchenette, a door that presumably opened to a closet-sized bathroom, and a narrow dining table with four seats that folded down to provide a sleeping area. Toward the front, a pair of computer stations and multiple banks of electronic consoles lined each wall.

Next to the computer station on the right, a tall, vertical cylinder about ten inches in diameter went up through the roof. Running down its length, a series of narrow slots glowed with violet light.

The two scientists scrambled inside. With trembling hands McGufficke locked the door behind them. He then went to one of the computer stations, entered a series of commands, and flipped a few switches on the console above his head. The light in the cylinder went dark. He hurried to the cab to peer out the windows, his face ashen.

"Gentlemen," Sabourin said, "you may be looking at any number of serious charges, including manslaughter. So let's have it. First of all, tell me what the hell is out there."

"As I told you. We have produced varieties of flora and fauna, unlike any modern man has seen."

"That doesn't explain why we've locked ourselves inside your vehicle."

"In case you didn't notice," Moses said, "those plants out there were moving. Like they knew what they were doing."

"You're ascribing intelligence where none exists, Deputy. Simply an involuntary response to various stimuli—such as the sun going down. Many of these organisms thrive nocturnally."

"Sheriff," McGufficke said, eyeing his partner with distaste. "What Dr. Westerman says is true, but there are——"

"Ian!" Westerman barked like pit bull. He faced McGufficke, the eyes behind the shades evidently glaring. But when he turned back to Sabourin, he nearly choked on the muzzle of her Glock 21.

"Let him speak."

Westerman raised a conciliatory hand, and she lowered her weapon.

McGufficke said, "For years, we have been experimenting with a crystal of unknown origin. Back in the frontier days, Daniel Boone, of all people, brought a fragment of it to Washington, D.C. Under the right conditions, it stimulates a unique type of organic growth. Or that's what we've always thought."

"A crystal?"

"Some believe it came from a meteor. No one actually knows. Whatever it is, it differs from conventional matter on a quantum level. It had fallen through the cracks of government bureaucracy until a decade or so ago, when Beckham University acquired it."

"When I acquired it," Westerman said. "It has been my project from the start."

"The federal government misplaced something of this magnitude?" Moses said. "Seriously?"

Westerman chuckled. "The last administration that was even aware of it was probably JFK's. No one knew whose jurisdiction it fell under. The Department of Defense? The Department of Agriculture? Eventually, the government decided it was best turned over to university specialists contracting with the Department of the Interior. That would be us."

"On its own, this object produces an insignificant effect. But we found a way to construct an amplifier to enhance it, to generate these organisms you have witnessed." McGufficke indicated the cylindrical pipe.

"You said this was a 'fragment,'" Moses said. "What about the rest of it?"

Westerman shrugged. "No one knows. It may no longer exist."

"The Indians believed the stone spawned unusual plants and animals," McGufficke said. "But in reality, it's different. It emits rays that create a kind of rift, so that the native flora and fauna from an entirely different dimension phase into ours. You understand the term multiverse? Alternate universe, perhaps? Yes?"

"What we learn here will shape the direction of scientific research in more fields than you can imagine," Westerman said. "But at this point, we don't know what's out there."

"'Wildfire.'"

"Yes."

"Yet you've continued working with it, even as things have gone beyond your control."

"I am a scientist. Once I begin an experiment, I am committed to seeing it through."

"At the expense of your safety? Of public safety?"

"If those responsible for the Manhattan Project had not been willing to assume such risk, imagine how different our history would be."

Another *boom* reverberated through the woods. McGufficke hunkered down in the backseat of the cab and peered out the window. "It's getting dark."

"These things out there," Sabourin said. "Do they have eyesight like ours? Can they see us?"

"The higher specimens we've studied do have sight organs. The most advanced of them have sixteen cones, compared to our three. They see colors in ways we do not. Their night vision is basically perfect."

"You turned your amplifier off. Will that stop what's happening?"

"More or less. It will halt the expansion of the rift field."

"You gentlemen appear to know more about less than you do about more."

"Which is why we came to Hell's Hollow," McGufficke said. He gave his partner a distasteful look. "This test area should have been more than adequate. But Dr. Westerman exceeded our mandate. We have disagreed."

"Listen," Moses said, peering out the window. "Something's just outside."

Sabourin peered out at the swaying creepers. Fifty feet away, beneath an umbrella of spindly, luminous fronds, something upright appeared to be making its way through the undergrowth—something that, from this distance, resembled a gnarly tree that had acquired mobility. Twelve, maybe fifteen feet tall, advancing in stiff, halting motions.

At its apex, a pair of bright, violet eyes materialized. They rolled back and forth within dark, oddly angled sockets.

Sabourin pulled away from the window, her heart pounding. McGufficke ducked down and covered his head with his arms.

Something struck the Earthroamer with such force she nearly went sprawling. Another blow, and glittering fragments exploded in the cab. With a panicked cry, McGufficke scrambled from his seat and rushed back into the cabin.

Up front, a dark appendage, like a jointed, articulated tree limb, slid in through the shattered window. Something that resembled a hand—a hand with a dozen, gnarled fingers—groped around the dashboard and seats.

Searching for McGufficke.

She heard a low creak and felt a subtle change in air pressure. *Westerman!* He had slipped out the back and left the narrow door hanging open. With Glock drawn, Moses rushed to the door and peered outside.

A second later, he pulled the door shut, eyes blazing with shock. "There's more than one of those things," he said. "Coming through the woods."

"Westerman is finished, then."

"I don't think so," McGufficke said. "He has changed. I've been trying to figure out what he's doing. This is not an experiment gone out of hand. Westerman *made* this happen."

Something slammed into the wall, and a kitchen cabinet flew open. Several boxes of packaged food tumbled to the floor. In the cab, with a metallic crash, the right rear passenger door whirled into the darkness.

"We can't stay in here," Moses said. "We've gotta go out the back. And run like hell."

McGufficke groaned. "We'll never make it."

Moses motioned them toward the door. "Debra, you go first. McGufficke, you next. I'll be right behind you. Somehow, we've got to get past that mess that's blocked us in."

From the cab, the monstrous limb came scraping and scratching toward them like a questing arm. Moses raised his gun and aimed, not at the limb, but at the cylindrical amplifier. He pulled the trigger, and the device exploded.

Sabourin's eardrums felt as if they had burst. She gave Moses a pained, questioning look.

He shrugged. "Can't hurt."

"All right, we're getting out of here." She gave the deputy's shoulder an affectionate squeeze and then, without hesitating, leaped out the door. She landed running and raced into the ghost-lit night as if living fire licked at her heels.

Ahead, she could see the web-like mass of glowing fronds that blocked their escape. She glanced back and saw Moses and McGufficke sprinting after her.

Something was chasing them: a towering, misshapen figure, darker than the night but suffused with glowing, purplish veins. It strode after the men with a stiff loping motion.

She screeched to a halt, spun around, and raised her Glock.

"Keep running!" Moses called. "Go around those things!"

McGufficke reached her, but she shoved him past her into the darkness. The huge silhouette loomed over Moses, only a few feet behind. Realizing he was leading it straight toward her, he veered toward the woods to her right.

She took aim at the approaching monstrosity and fired—again and again—the reports ripping apart the night. For a few seconds, smoke obscured her view. When it cleared, Moses—and the creature—were gone. As the echoes of the shots faded, she made out a heavy, arrhythmic thumping that receded into the woods.

"Robert!"

Oh, no.

"ROBERT!"

All fell silent. Not a rustle in the darkness. Not even a whisper of breeze.

Robert was gone. He had given his life for her.

"Sheriff," came McGufficke's voice. "Over here."

She wiped tears from her eyes and pushed her way through tangled brush toward the sound of his voice. He was standing next to a vine-covered cedar, pointing up the steep side of the gorge. "There is a small cave up there. I think that's where Westerman has been working."

BOOM.

Through her soles, she felt the earth vibrate. "Take me there."

His face fell. "It's only a few hundred feet. You can find it if—"

She shoved the gun toward his open mouth. "Take me there. Now."

Palpable dread oozed from his body. But he started up the hillside on quivering legs. Sabourin followed, gun at the ready, eyes searching every shadow. As they climbed higher, the luminous vegetation grew sparser. But pale violet limned the top of the ridge, as if some vast source of radiance lay beyond it. Soon, she could make out, just short of the summit, an outcropping of rock. Below it, violet light emanated from a craggy opening in the earth.

A sharp voice rang down from the cleft. "Ian! You'll want to see this."

As if mesmerized, McGufficke plodded toward the outcropping. Sabourin followed, prepared to shoot any threat, human or otherwise.

Westerman waited for them at the glowing fissure, his dark glasses ablaze with reflected violet. "Ian. We don't need the electronics. Not anymore. All we needed was another piece of the crystal, and now I have it. It's here. Right here!"

"Another piece? How could you—?"

He pointed into the opening. "By bringing it from the other side. Our amplifier opened the way temporarily. But now we can *keep* the door open."

"Dr. Westerman," Sabourin said, "your amplifier has been destroyed."

"That no longer matters. I brought the fragment here two days ago." He gave McGufficke a remorseful frown. "I'm sorry, Ian. I knew you wouldn't approve."

"Whatever you've done, Doctor, it's time to undo it."

Westerman made a sweeping gesture. "Undo this? I cannot, and I wouldn't if I could. Sheriff, this may be the most important discovery in the history of science— achieved with such a small thing, and for so little investment."

"People have been killed. That's no 'little' investment."

"Progress can be painful. But you can't turn away from the light just because it hurts."

BOOM!

To McGufficke, he said, "I now have a portion of crystal five times the size of our original. Placing them together in a precise fashion potentiates the power of both. Ian, we are on the verge of something magnificent."

"Derek, this has affected you. I've watched you change. You're like an addict."

"If acquiring extraordinary knowledge is an addiction, then I admit to it."

"This is not about knowledge. It's about a dangerous unknown that has spiraled out of control."

Sabourin felt a deep rumbling beneath her feet. Along the length of the ridge, the violet corona intensified. Peering through the trees, she made out a tall, narrow silhouette—a dark spire—rising through the haze above the summit.

"All is precisely under control," Westerman said.

Another huge, black pillar appeared above the crest of the ridge and began a slow, steady ascent.

Another. And then another. Rising higher. *Faster.*

Gigantic, black, violet-veined trees, she thought, all taller than the tallest redwood, soaring into the sky one after the other, groping for the stars in the midnight blue sky.

Rising by the dozens.

She took a few steps forward and peered into the fissure beneath the outcropping. The space within was small, only a few feet deep, but lit by two brilliant, translucent crystals that pulsed with unearthly light. They hung suspended in an intricate metal frame—some device of Westerman's making, no doubt.

On the ridge, the lofty towers began to fold in on themselves, their upper portions arcing downward until they smashed into the earth with explosive force.

Beyond the violet-limned crest, a monstrous bulk, spanning hundreds of feet, rose up like a massive, swelling tumor.

It pulled itself free of the earth.

Legs. Those pillars were the *legs* of some unimaginable behemoth, now lifting itself higher and higher above the forest. The earth itself rumbled and shook.

McGufficke appeared beside her, his eyes locked on the unfolding spectacle. Then, from close behind him, she heard a rustling, clumping sound. She spun around in time to see a gangly, glowing limb materialize from the darkness. In an instant, McGufficke was gone—vanished as if he had never existed.

Her eyes made out something that looked like a huge banyan tree—a banyan tree that was *trying* to become human. At least fifteen feet tall, it stood on "legs" that ended in clusters of tangled, tendril-like roots. An array of crooked, twisted arms, each ten feet long, extended from its cylindrical core. And from two asymmetrical, crevice-like sockets in a knobby dome atop the trunk, a pair of brilliant violet irises peered down at her.

Westerman had not moved. He stood, statue-like, before the opening in the rocks, oblivious to the chaos erupting all around them.

Something inside her broke, and she began to run. She had no idea where she was going, just *away* from the approaching horrors. It was only when the night had turned almost as bright as day that she realized she had bolted *up* the ridge. Now she stood on its crest, gazing into the valley, toward Mt. Zion.

Out there, several miles distant, amid an endless field of black, the clustered speckles of white, gold, yellow, and red resembled the embers of a dying campfire.

Hundreds—no, *thousands*— of pale violet tendrils were creeping through the darkness toward the town. The ground vibrated as the massive beast from beyond lumbered down the ridge toward the unsuspecting hub of human life.

"Impressive, isn't it?" came a voice from behind her. "They *needed* to come here. The other side has its own environmental issues, you see. But I believe those have been permanently solved."

She turned and saw Westerman standing ten feet away, his body seeming to *drip* with glowing, liquid violet.

"Shall we watch what happens together?"

One of Westerman's hands rose to his face and removed his sunglasses.

Sabourin shot him. Shot him dead.

Then she collapsed on the trembling ground, to watch and wait as the doors between two worlds shattered and fell into oblivion with her.

Masque of the Queen

2014

She should have made her way to Hollywood five years ago, back when she had enough money to travel farther than Upper to Midtown Manhattan. She would wager that, by now, she could have at least snagged a part in some sitcom or second-rate motion picture—something to make her name known beyond one block off Broadway.

Finances were tighter than ever, and though she had no problem lining up auditions, landing a role that paid for something more than a few drinks was tougher now than the day she had spoken her first line on the stage at Fugazi Playhouse, now closed.

She sure as hell couldn't afford to move to a new place. By any standard, her cozy apartment in Manhattan Valley was a bargain, though uncomfortably far from the law office where she temped as receptionist, and even farther from the theater district.

Tonight, as usual, the bus was jammed with bodies, but she had managed to grab a seat near the back. To get it, she'd had to physically remove a large shopping bag owned by an older Hispanic woman who had strategically placed it to discourage potential seatmates. On a crowded bus, Kathryn Stefano refused to tolerate such discourtesy, and now the woman, her bag tucked under her seat, sat peering out the window radiating hot, silent hatred.

Kathryn had felt so good about the last audition. They seemed to love her, but her phone had been silent for two weeks, and they had promised her an answer within a few days. Bryon Florey, her ersatz agent, had pestered the director enough, perhaps beyond his tolerance level, clearly to no avail. The damned thing would have paid well, too.

She was 28, and her time for grabbing choice roles was rapidly slip-sliding away.

She had never heard of the play before. *The King in Yellow*, a two-act exercise in surrealism, produced by an unfamiliar company—Mythosphere, it was called. Still, she knew of the director, one Vernard Broach, who had gained notoriety two decades earlier by helming a production of *Jesus Christ, Superstar* that took a page from the Gospel of Phillip.

In it, Jesus and Mary Magdalene were engaged in an amorous relationship, portrayed quite graphically on the stage. For *The King in Yellow*, Kathryn had read for the part of Cassilda, the queen of a mythical city called Hastur, somewhere on or off the earth. She had not read the entire play, but it supposedly ended on a tragic note, and she'd always had an affinity for tragedies.

At 109th, she disembarked, ignoring the whispered "*Reina puta*" from her seatmate. She had walked most of the block to her building when she felt her jacket pocket vibrate.

Bryon!

"You got Cassilda," came his excited voice. "She's all yours."

"Well, thank *you!*"

"Rehearsals start Friday night."

"Seriously?"

"The schedule's going to be intense. Hope you're up for it. Can you get to their office tomorrow afternoon and get the paperwork done?"

"I guess I can take a long lunch."

"Do it. I have a good feeling about this one."

"So do I. I think."

"You impress Broach, things are going to start falling into place. See if they don't."

"I'll hold you to that."

"You'd better."

She signed off just as she reached the front door of her building, an ancient, nine-story monstrosity that took up half the block between Amsterdam and Broadway. Her apartment was on the top floor, a single-bedroom cubbyhole she shared with her roommate, Yumiko, whom she actually saw about twice a month. She found herself hoping Yumiko would be there now.

At first, she thought it was simple excitement that set off an unexpected series of little tremors; but as the elevator took her up to the dim, deathly silent hallway, she realized it was not excitement but apprehension. Not the little butterflies that came before stepping on stage, but the cold anxiety that came when a stranger fell in behind her and rapidly closed the distance.

Unfortunately, when she opened the door and entered darkness, she found the place deserted, except for Koki, Yumiko's cat, who occupied his traditional spot on the windowsill. The gray and white tabby gave her a brief, unconcerned glance and returned to peering out at his vast, unreachable kingdom.

For a second, she glimpsed an odd reflection in the glass: a kind of swirly pattern in bright yellow-gold, as if cast by a neon sign. But no such sign existed out there. The weird image lasted only a few seconds and then vanished.

That was strange, she thought, but hardly worth dwelling on. Koki displayed no unusual interest in anything, indoors or out. If the Feline Early Warning System hadn't gone off, all must be right with the world. Such as it was.

Damned peculiar: the script the office manager had given her was incomplete. A number of random pages had been excised, including the final scene. Still, from it, she pieced together as much of the story as possible:

The play opened with Queen Cassilda—many thousands, perhaps millions of years old—gazing on the vast Lake of Hali from her palace in the far-off city of Hastur. For eons, Hastur had been at war with its sister city, Alar, and the endless siege had turned Cassilda into an embittered, impotent monarch.

She occasionally entertained the idea of passing her rule to one of her two sons, Uoht or Thale, she cared not which. Both princes desired to marry their sister, Camilla, and Cassilda finally decided that whichever son won her daughter's hand would ascend to the throne and take the name "Aldones"—the name of every king that had ever ruled in Hastur.

Then Cassilda would give Camilla the royal diadem, which had been worn by Hastur's queen since the beginning of time. Camilla, however, dreaded such a transfer, for legend told that the recipient of the diadem might also receive the Yellow Sign—a harbinger of death, or worse—from the mysterious King in Yellow: a nightmarish entity that resided in the fabled, spectral city of Carcosa, which existed somewhere beyond the Lake of Hali.

One day, a stranger wearing a pallid mask appeared in Hastur. To Cassilda's horror, he also bore on his garment the Yellow Sign: an intricate sigil rendered "in no human script." The queen's high priest, Naotalba, declared that the stranger must be none other than the Phantom of Truth, the King in Yellow's most dreaded agent.

However, the stranger explained that he was in fact Hastur's truest ally. His pallid mask concealed his identity even from the all-powerful Yellow King, so he could wear the Yellow Sign with impunity. And any kingdom that could bear the Yellow Sign as its standard would be invincible.

To make this possible, he suggested Cassilda put on a "masque," wherein the attendees would wear their own pallid masks in the presence of the Yellow Sign. At an hour of the stranger's choosing, the attendees would unmask and find that the Yellow Sign no longer held power over them. Despite suspecting treachery, Cassilda accepted the stranger's offer, for no matter the outcome of such a gamble, the conflict with Alar would at long last end.

Act 2 opened with the masked ball in progress. Cassilda and all members of her court wore pallid masks. At the sound of a gong, all removed their masks—all except the stranger, who then revealed that he wore no mask at all. He had deceived them so that Alar, not Hastur, might emerge victorious from the endless war.

Suddenly, with a cry of "Yhtill!"—a word meaning "stranger"—the King in Yellow appeared. Taller than two men, garbed in flowing, tattered, golden robes, the King struck down the faceless stranger, proclaiming himself a living god who could not abide such mockery. He told Cassilda that Hastur *would* prevail over Alar, but with a heavy price: from that moment on, every inhabitant of Hastur, including Cassilda, would wear a pallid mask.

Cassilda, regaining her regal manner for the first time in eons, approached the King and boldly refused to accept his terms.

And there the script ended.

There was clearly more to the final scene. Whoever had collated this copy, Kathryn decided, was anything but thorough at his or her job.

Something in the script had seized Kathryn's attention and, for reasons she couldn't fathom, sent her mind reeling, as if gripped by vertigo. She flipped back through the pages until she found the passage.

"The city of Carcosa had four singularities. The first was that it appeared overnight. The second was that it was impossible to distinguish whether the city sat upon the waters of the Lake of Hali or on the invisible shore beyond. The third was that when the moon rose, it rose in *front* of the city's spires rather than behind them. And the fourth was that as soon as one looked upon the city, one knew its name was Carcosa."

Something about that name, *Carcosa*. She felt a strange, tingling excitement, as if she had discovered something indecent or forbidden—the way she had felt when she bought her first vibrator all those years ago. She had taken it home feeling dirty, giddy, almost breathless with anticipation. *How could she possibly feel this way now?*

That night, she dreamed of a soft, reed-thin voice saying, "The truth *is* but a phantom—a ghost that can be used or murdered at whim. Have you found the Yellow Sign?"

The first read-through with the full cast in the rehearsal room of the Frontiere Theatre:

Upon her request for a complete copy of the script, the production manager, Earl Blohm—a bearded, long-haired young man who dressed as if he had fallen out of the early 1970s—told her it was all she would get. "You'll find out the ending when everyone else does," he said. "It never ends the same way twice."

"I didn't think this play had been produced before."

"Oh, it's very old. It's just that no one alive has ever seen it."

Strange, *strange* man, Kathryn thought. In fact, the whole ensemble struck her as peculiar. Usually, when cast members gathered for the first time, a certain excitement ran through them like a humming electric current, but here, a somber, almost funereal atmosphere pervaded the chamber. Director Vernard Broach, a portly, swarthy man with dyed black, slicked-back hair and a pencil-thin mustache, spoke so softly she could barely make out his instructions.

"The audience is *there*," he said, pointing to the farthest wall of the long, deeply shadowed rehearsal room. "We do not concern ourselves with them. You are in the city of Hastur on the Lake of Hali." He gave the group his most theatrical scowl, pointed to the opposite corner of the room, and said, "The King in Yellow lives *there*. We do not look there, we do not speak of there, we do not go there. Now, look at your scripts, look at them. We have Queen Cassilda and her daughter, Camilla. Who is Camilla, where are you?"

"Here." An attractive young black woman raised her hand and then pointed to herself. "Jayda Rivera."

"Your name doesn't matter," Broach said. "Read, will you?"

Jayda Rivera gave him a questioning look, and Broach replied by stamping one foot.

Jayda glanced at Kathryn and drew a steadying breath. "'Forgive my bluntness, my queen, but you have been looking for Carcosa. Again.'"

"'The Hyades have not yet risen, thus Carcosa may not appear. I am simply watching the Lake of Hali swallowing the suns. Again.'" Kathryn's gaze at Jayda was haughty, but her voice carried a wistful note. She felt Broach's eyes warm with approval.

"'If only the lake would swallow our enemy,'" Jayda said, her voice gaining assurance as she began to immerse herself in her part. "'But, Mother, does it not lie within your power to destroy Alar?'"

"'It does not, and you know this.'" She drew herself up and in a commanding voice said, "'Listen well, daughter. Do not mock me, for I still have power in Hastur, and I would as soon you never live to succeed me.'"

Jayda's eyes widened in pure, authentic fear. "'I do not mock, my queen. You withhold powerful secrets. I desire only to learn.'"

"'I should first share them with agents of Alar.'"

The ensuing silence felt so deep that Kathryn swallowed hard to make sure she could still hear. From the direction that Broach had indicated lay the purview of the King in Yellow, a movement caught her eye. *Do not look there.*

She looked. Just for a second.

A tiny figure, standing in the shadows, barely visible. *A child.*

A sudden rhythmic clattering drew her attention back to director Broach. The stout man was doing a weird little two-step dance to himself, a blissful grin broadening his already broad face. The sounds of his feet tapping on the floor were soon joined in syncopated rhythm by another set of echoing, *tap-tapping* footsteps.

In the room's far shadows, the child was dancing as well.

Three weeks later: lunch at Brodjian's Café with Jayda, who, it turned out, worked by day in a nearby office.

"I don't like those damned masks," Jayda said, giving her chicken salad wrap a suspicious glance. "They're creepy and uncomfortable."

"Creepier on some than others."

Jayda smiled and nodded, then looked back at her lunch. "I asked for no walnuts. Screw it, they won't kill me. You think this play has a chance of taking off?"

Kathryn's turkey and brie croissant must have sat on the counter overnight. It was not thrilling. She shrugged. "It's the weirdest thing. I tell you, if I were in the audience, I don't know I'd sit through it—at least as much of it as we can perform."

"Please! What *are* we going to do at the end? Stand there like dummies as the curtain falls? And who's that little girl? One of the cast members' who can't find a babysitter?"

"Little girl?" For a second, she drew a blank. "Oh, wait. I thought it was a little boy."

"Pretty sure it's a girl."

"Okay." Boy or girl, the kid was a mystery. Always lurking in the shadows, never quite revealing his or her face. Six or seven years old at most. She had never heard the child speak, yet he—she was *sure* it was a boy—sometimes mimicked the actions of the players during rehearsal. She didn't think the kid was Broach's; he was reputedly as gay as they came and had been an old bachelor since before Moses' day.

"We still don't even know who that is playing the King."

"Nope. Could be anyone, since we never see his face."

"The orchestra's on tonight. You ready?"

Kathryn nodded. The play featured a single musical number, "The Song of Cassilda," in the second scene of Act 1. Till now, she had simply sung it *a cappella* from the sheet music, which, most curiously, Broach had transcribed by hand. This evening, the prior production having finally cleared out, the theater proper would be open for rehearsal, and she would sing with orchestral accompaniment. She had a fair mezzo-soprano voice, best suited to singing in a chorus, but in college she had held her own as Lady Macbeth in their production of Verdi's *Macbeth*, and more recently as Luisa in a revival of *The Fantasticks*. She had no doubt she could nail the song, yet for some reason she was on edge about it.

Like about so many things in this play.

"What are you doing?"

Jayda was looking at her, one eyebrow raised. Kathryn realized one finger was tracing a pattern on the table and had twisted a portion of the tablecloth into a knotted mass. She'd had no idea she was doing it.

A chilly worm slid down the back of her neck. "I'm done," she said, pushing away her half-eaten croissant. "Not hungry. And I gotta get back to work."

"You really are nervous."

"Something about being poor as dirt, I guess. I need this play to fly, and I'm not sure it's going to."

"If it doesn't, it won't be on your account."

"Well, thanks for that."

They settled their bills and headed out of the café into the afternoon sunshine. Lunchtime pedestrians and traffic choked West 47th Street, the usual barely controlled chaos. For the moment, the aroma of cooking meat from a dozen nearby eateries overwhelmed the exhaust fumes, just barely.

"Till tonight, then," Kathryn said. She gave the younger woman a little wink. "If you see crowds of people running away, it's because I'm practicing my song in the streets."

"Now, that I believe."

"Oh, and Jayda?"

"Hmm?"

"It's a little boy."

Jayda returned an exaggerated sneer. "Yes, Mother."

Dark, *dark* theater.

himself was played by some anonymous actor, whose identity only Broach knew.

Kathryn's roommate, Yumiko, after one read-through, refused to practice with her any further. "This play is not happy for me," she had said. "It feels bad."

Two weeks remained before the opening. Broach had promised the sets would be "phenomenal," and the stage crew had their work cut out for them. Until then, there would be rehearsals every night, but they still had no inkling of how the play would actually end.

However, as Kathryn had hoped, the first stage rehearsal felt different. *Good* different. Even without the sets in place, the theater aura bolstered her confidence, and as Cassilda slipped inside her, the two of them breathing together as one, the orchestra sent up swirling, mystical strains from woodwinds and strings, weaving an otherworldly atmosphere that was at once dark and lovely.

As Scene 2 of Act 1—Cassilda's song—loomed nearer, the music became more intense, the brooding bass deeper and more ominous, the ethereal flutes more melodic.

The introduction to the song began. Weird and wistful, the instruments assumed the quality of human voices, humming and warbling in an eerie melody that gave Kathryn a chill.

She needed no cue to begin.

"'Along the shore the cloud waves break,
The twin suns sink beneath the lake,
The shadows lengthen
*   In Carcosa.'"*

Her voice was not hers. *Alien*, it seemed, more assured and more beautiful than any her vocal cords could produce. She felt herself diminishing. All she could perceive—all that remained of *her*—was her voice.

"'Strange is the night where black stars rise,
And strange moons circle through the skies
But stranger still is
*   Lost Carcosa.'"*

"'Songs that the Hyades shall sing,
Where flap the tatters of the King,
Must die unheard in
*   Dim Carcosa.'"*

Her heart swelled, and her feet seemed to leave the floor, her body as light as a dust mote, her emotions overflowing, spilling into all those within her presence.

"'Song of my soul, my voice is dead;
Die thou, unsung, as tears unshed
Shall dry and die in
Lost Carcosa.'"

The last syllable echoed away into pure, empty silence. She had no breath left in her lungs.

Camilla—no, *Jayda*—stood nearby, her eyes bright jewels, tears glistening on her cheeks. Kenton Peach lifted an arm and propped himself on Les Perrin's shoulder, as if to keep from toppling. Somewhere beyond the island of light, a soft female voice breathed, "Oh, my."

At the edge of darkness, stage left, Vernard Broach stood with his hands folded together as if in prayer, knees slightly bent, face to the heavens, eyes closed. After a moment, he began to shiver as if clutched by bone-numbing cold. Then he was not shivering but *vibrating*, his entire body quivering in a way no human body could or should move.

Behind Broach, a shadow stirred, and the reed-thin voice Kathryn had heard in her dream sang out: "Aldebaran."

Sometime in the night, she woke to an odd flapping noise, unlike anything she had ever heard in her apartment. She rose and peeked into the darkened living room. Yumiko was not on the pullout sofa bed, and she didn't see Koki anywhere. The heavy flapping came again, and she now determined it originated outside her window, which overlooked the narrow alley. She drew up the venetian blinds and then staggered backward with the realization that she was not awake but dreaming.

Where the opposite brick wall should have been she saw vast, dizzying space: a midnight blue sky lit by alien stars over an endless body of inky water. High above and to the right, a huge, blood-red star lit the night sky, and she knew *this* was Aldebaran, the sun that blazed above the city of Alar. Around it, a cluster of stars—the Hyades— glittered like the jewels adorning Cassilda's diadem. And now, slowly, the rim of the silver moon breached the farthest edge of the Lake of Hali and rose until it resembled a cyclopean eye, its gaze burning through her body straight to her hammering heart.

Then, on the horizon: an impossible array of gleaming, dizzying spires that wavered like ghostly tendrils before taking solid form *behind* the bright, full moon.

Carcosa.

Moments later, it came: the thin, childlike dream voice she had heard before; distant, barely comprehensible.

"Doggy!"

No. The word only sounded like "doggy." That wasn't what it had really said.

"Joggy!"

It was still too far away, too difficult to understand. The flapping sound came again, and now, in front of those distant, luminous spires, a silhouette appeared in the sky, its contours vague, imprecise. It was coming toward her, trailing black smoke, as if it were on fire.

"Blocky!"

A little clearer now, the reedy voice sounded excited. The shape in the sky was no clearer to her eye than the voice was to her ear. It seemed ghostly in its way, surrounded by an aura of indeterminate color. Was this what it was like to be color blind? It was neither gray, nor silver, nor white, nor violet. But it *was* color.

"Byakhee!"

Now the thing was rushing toward her, and she could see its eyes, burning with that indefinable, radiant gleam. She backed away from the window, knowing the thing had become aware of *her*.

Then a hand touched the small of her back. She spun around and looked down. Standing before her was the child she had seen at rehearsals. Even now, she couldn't tell whether it was a boy or a girl. Curly dark hair hung low over big blue eyes, its short, slightly pudgy frame garbed in a pale blue robe, a tiny replica of Cassilda's jeweled diadem adorning its oversize head. Those eyes were too mature to belong to a child.

The tiny, cherubic mouth spread into an overly huge grin, revealing two rows of polished, very large, very adult teeth.

"Grandmother!" it said.

"I want out of this," she said, and from the long silence, she didn't know whether Bryon had even been listening to her. "I can't do this play."

The low voice that finally replied was disbelieving. "You signed a contract."

"Screw the contract."

"You do *not* back out on Vernard Broach. Are you fucking serious?"

"There's something wrong with him. He's not *right*."

"What's he done? Tried to rape you or something?"

"No, of course not. But I can't eat anymore. I can't sleep—not without these nightmares. I see things that can't be real. Bryon, no play is worth my health." Then she whispered, "Or my mind."

"You break this contract, you'll be temping and waiting tables till that drama mask tattoo on your ass is sagging to your knees. Are you that damned stupid?"

"This is not negotiable. Call. Him."

"You're not my client anymore. I'm done with you. You tell Broach yourself."

Bryon Florey hung up on her.

Her eyes were swollen from crying, and her throat felt as if she had swallowed razor blades. She'd had to call in sick at the temp agency, and they were hardly happier with her than Bryon was. For that brief moment, when she had sung Cassilda's song on stage, there seemed a chance that everything might yet turn out as she had hoped. But then came the aftermath, so repulsive, so full of unendurable *dread*.

She had barely put her phone down on the nightstand when it began to vibrate. It was not a number she recognized. "Hello?"

Director Vernard Broach's voice. "I know you wish to leave the play."

"How did you—?"

"If you stay, I promise something wonderful will happen. Kathryn, you are our shining star."

"Mr. Broach, this is taking too much out of me. I feel awful, physically and mentally. I just can't do this."

"I will double your pay. No. Triple it. Kathryn, you *are* Cassilda. Trust me when I say that, after the first performance, things will be very different."

"I don't know what that means."

"I've treated you well, have I not?"

She had to concede that, personally, Broach had shown her only respect. What if she *were* to face her fears and finish out this play? All kinds of new doors would open to her. And this bullshit would be behind her.

"When you wake up in the morning, the money will be in your account. And you will have a new agent. A real agent."

"Mr. Broach, I—"

"Kathryn. Please?"

"All right. All right. I'll sleep on it and call you in the morning. I promise."

There was a long silence. "I trust you, my good friend Kathryn. Now I ask you to trust me. Tomorrow morning, call me and say you will stay. I will honor my word to you."

"I'll call."

"Until then, Kathryn."

Opening night:

Upon her arrival, her first reaction had been to the brilliant sets. Everything looked as it had during the final dress rehearsal, but nothing *felt* like it. The balconies of the palace rose almost to the ceiling, and—more disturbing to her—the backdrop of the Lake of Hali uncannily resembled her vision from that night.

The lavish interior sets were modular and could be moved by stagehands to their designated marks almost instantaneously. She had seen all these during their construction, but now she felt as if she were viewing for the first time a realm that actually existed.

Vernard Broach had been true to his word. By any standard she could measure, she was now a wealthy woman, about to sign a contract with a brand new, very reputable agent.

The King in Yellow opened with an overture: a haunting, wistful composition built on the melody of "Song of Cassilda," but that ended on a series of harsh, dissonant notes that set her teeth on edge. As she took her place on the palace balcony, she felt a moment of vertigo, and just for an instant, an image of that black, smoking silhouette with burning eyes flashed in her mind.

There was a rumble as the curtains separated and spread wide, and then the spotlights were on her. Beyond those lights, only a gaping abyss, blacker than the sky over the city of Alar. Behind her, Jayda spoke her lines, and the play commenced. Uoht and Thale argued over which of them would take their sister's hand in marriage. Cassilda turned thoughtful as she decided that one of the brothers would succeed her and that Camilla would inherit the royal diadem.

Something seemed wrong. The space beyond the stage was too silent, too still. She felt as if she were trapped within a sealed sphere of light, barely able to breathe. But it was when she was supposed to describe to Camilla the four singularities of Carcosa that she received her first shock.

It wasn't Jayda who knelt before her to listen. It was the child.

"Grandmother!" it said. "Tell me of Carcosa."

Deaf and blind, existing somewhere apart from herself, her body continued to play her part, speaking the lines she was meant to speak. When awareness returned to her, the music told her it was almost time to begin her song. For a moment, the spotlights were turned away from her, and she chanced a look out at the darkened chamber.

It was empty. No living soul occupied a single seat.

She stepped in front of Brad Silva, who played the priest, Naotalba. Her disbelieving eyes swept the empty space. "There's no one there. There's no one out there!"

She felt something tugging at her long, crimson skirt, and she looked down to see the child's huge blue eyes peering up at her.

"There is an audience, Grandmother. But sensible souls in Hastur hide their faces."

Inside, she began to scream. She tried to leave the stage. She pleaded, cajoled, threatened Cassilda, but the character refused her, and Kathryn played on.

The masked figure—the Phantom of Truth, played by a young man named Zack Cheauvront—appeared before her, and for the first time, she saw it. Not a crude, painted "X" but a blazing, yellow-gold sigil, simultaneously adorning the character's robe while floating in some dimension in front of it. She could not have found words to describe the Yellow Sign, for it was rendered by no human hand.

The masked stranger was full head taller than Zack Cheauvront.

Kathryn sang "The Song of Cassilda." And the empty, soulless auditorium erupted with thunderous applause.

This was all in her mind.

She agreed to the stranger's proposal, and the curtain came down on Act 1. She fell to her knees, sobbing, barely aware of tiny hands pulling the pallid mask down over her head.

The child took the stage and spoke to the emptiness.

"'Your chance to escape has passed. Bound to us, at last.
No harm can come to you in fantasy, and this is not reality.
No sensibilities offended; no immorality decried.
But 'tis now too late, for your sin is complete.
You have crossed the threshold and the door is barred.
Lament what you will, but here you abide;
Sit and listen, for you are ours forever,
And until the end of time, we are also yours.'"

The gong sounded.

Zack Cheauvront—it *had* to be Zack—as the Phantom of Truth stood before her, pointing to her face. She was supposed to remove her mask, but as long as she wore it, she couldn't be seen. She did *not* want to be seen.

But she tore the mask from her face and regarded the horrid Yellow Sign on the stranger's robe. She heard Camilla say, "You, sir, should unmask."

"Indeed?"

That was not Zack's voice.

"It is time. We have laid aside our disguises. All but you."

"But I wear no mask."

"No mask!" Camilla's eyes turned to Cassilda's, bright and bulging with horror.

"*Yhtill! Yhtill! Yhtill!*"

The King in Yellow appeared before her and, with a glance, struck down the masked stranger. The monstrous figure floated above the stage: a giant garbed in tattered, brilliant yellow robes; its face covered by a golden mask that revealed only its eyes—eyes so black they glowed. One hand rose to point at her, and the King's voice boomed across space: "Have you found the Yellow Sign?"

It was not the costume from their rehearsals.

It was not the same man.

It was not a man at all.

The King pronounced Hastur's fate. Declared its victory over Alar. Condemned every man, woman, and child in the city to wear a pallid mask for the rest of eternity.

Cassilda felt another soul inside her, one struggling to escape, protesting these events that never began and never ended. At last, it was time for her to rule in Hastur, to no longer revel in the ennui of perpetual siege. She stepped forward and gazed into those blazing sockets in the golden mask. "No," she said, her voice firm and strong. "This will not do."

That was where the script ended.

Kathryn stood under the hot stage lights, glaring at the thing floating before her. It seemed diminished somehow, as if wilted by her refusal. She heard rustling and other little sounds in the darkness, and her attention shifted to the great, empty hall beyond the orchestra pit.

The theater was filled to capacity. Not a seat remained empty. As she stared, the applause began, at first sparse, then rising to a consuming thunder. People rose to their feet and began to shout. When she looked back toward the King, he was gone. Only the unmasked people of Hastur—these actors—surrounded her, radiating approval.

Her children—Jayda Rivera, Les Perrin, and Kenton Peach—came to her, smiling, and the two men took her arms, evidently to escort her offstage. But no; at the far end, on a dais, there was a throne. The original throne of Hastur, first occupied by King Aldones, before the beginning of time. *Not one of Broach's sets.* They led her to the throne and knelt as she ascended the dais and took her rightful place.

The child appeared and stood before her, its big blue eyes gazing at her, inquisitive, appraising. The eyes turned cold and black, mimicking those of the King in Yellow. Kathryn heard a series of metallic *snaps*, and a second later realized that manacles had closed around her wrists and ankles, binding her in the throne.

"What is this?"

She heard a clatter behind her and smelled something thick and pungent. From the shadows offstage, actors were carrying bundles of wood and piling them on the dais beneath and around the throne.

My god, they were going to burn her.

"No," she whispered to the child. "What are you doing? Why?"

The small creature laid one finger beside its nose and said, "Grandmother. Did you think to be human still?"

Jayda appeared, carrying a lit torch, her eyes reflecting the flames until they burned pure gold. From the painted stage backdrop, Kathryn detected movement, and—as in her dream—saw a smoking silhouette with glowing eyes drifting through an endless, star-filled sky.

"When all is done, Byakhee will feed," Jayda said.

The child pointed to a blood red star above the Lake of Hali. "Aldebaran."

She could see Carcosa behind the rising moon, and as Jayda dropped the torch and flames began to rise around her, catching her skirt and enveloping her sleeves, she saw the distant spires glowing gold.

Before her screams became the only existing sound, she heard the child addressing the audience.

"This ends the story of *The King in Yellow*, a tragedy told in fire and verse."

The child danced its way off stage, while Kathryn and Carcosa burned together.

She woke to a pair of blurry figures leaning over her and discovered she could not move. Something covered her face, something with slits for her eyes that barely permitted her to see out.

"Stay still. We just want to help you," a young male voice said.

Paramedics.

"We need to try to get that off her face."

"What is it?"

"Looks like some kind of mask."

"No!" she cried; her voice muffled. "Don't take it off."

"What did she do?" another voice asked.

"She burned herself."

"Oh, my god."

"It's bonded to her skin," the second voice said. "We can't remove it here."

"Look at that pattern on her chest. Why is it *yellow*?"

"Who knows? Let's get her in the ambulance."

Kathryn closed her eyes. She felt no pain, felt *nothing*. As long as she wore the mask, she would never have to face the King again.

"How bad is it?" the first voice said.

"Bad. No one will ever recognize her."

Ever.

And so, at last, Kathryn and Cassilda were free.

Somewhere, My Love

1994

She lived in our town's one and only haunted house: a century-old, two-story Victorian with a pepperbox turret, windows of leaded glass, a sagging roof with missing shingles, and a wild array of blackened brick chimneys.

The little paint remaining on its aging wooden skin was no longer white but crusty gray, so the structure lurked almost unseen behind a thick shield of cedar trees that ringed the property.

Rather than a neat, paved driveway like all the others in the neighborhood, only a short, gravel apron, tucked tight against the house, existed for the owner's car. The man of the manor had died before I was born, so the woman had lived alone in that place for over ten years.

At night, no light ever shone in any of the windows. But sometimes, after dark, I would hear her voice echoing out of that old house, singing songs that seemed to me unearthly.

Her name was Jeanne Weiler, and she was my music teacher when I was in elementary school.

Of course, she was a witch.

Looking back now, I would have to say she was quite an attractive woman, though at the time, she presented such an imposing figure that just being in the same room with her intimidated me to the edge of fright.

She stood nearly six feet (which, when I measured barely four feet, seemed so very tall indeed); had long, wavy black hair, which she often piled high atop her head, adding to her commanding height; and possessed the most piercing green eyes I have ever seen, even to this day.

She virtually always wore smart, tight-fitting black outfits that showed off a figure my youthful eyes could not yet appreciate, but her clothes insinuated no impropriety—only dignity.

Despite my fear of Mrs. Weiler, I did adore her. In those pre-pubescent days, the concept of sexual attraction was still a mystifying, nebulous thing, which only the future would elucidate, but my typical physical response to her presence consisted of stammering, chills, and uncontrollable trembling. Had she but asked it, I would have fallen to my knees, kissed her feet, and been excited enough by the prospect to wet my drawers.

All the more proof that she was a witch, at least to me, for I recognized this effect as pure *power*—miles and leagues beyond any held by my parents, or any other teachers, or the minister at church, or any of my fellow fourth-graders. She terrified me because she could have made me do things. Anything.

Mrs. Weiler always spoke kindly to me, and showed me the same respect she showed my classmates. All the parents liked her. I know she was aware of the effect she had on me because I would often glance up and catch her looking at me appraisingly, one hand curled beneath her chin as if she were contemplating things in store for me that I could hardly imagine.

And, oh, her voice! She would sing so many songs to us as she attempted to teach us music, and that sweet alto would weave its way down to my deepest core, tugging at my soul with sorrow or joy, or whatever emotion to which the song was tuned. I remember she would sing "A Time for Us," the theme to *Romeo and Juliet*, with such passion that the whole class would be in tears.

No one else could have ever done that to me, or to any of my friends.

She was a witch.

Some of the songs we had to learn were stupid, and she took great pleasure in watching us humiliate ourselves by singing them—badly, at that—and I loved her all the more for it. Songs like "Morning Comes Bringing" and "Dreidle," and "Cherry Ripe" made my teeth grind, but because she desired it, I would sing my little heart out, and she would smile with joy.

She was our mistress, and we could not refuse her. Sometimes, she would reward us with chocolate milk and cookies, or even let us out five minutes before the bell rang in the afternoon, for hers was the last class of the day.

It was late in the school year when I learned what she had held in store for me from the beginning. Not only for me, I might add, but for Johnny McCrickard and Tina Truman as well. The horror of it nearly destroyed me, and I think the day she announced it was the first and only time I ever hyperventilated.

Johnny and Tina's reactions were not so violent, but the dread showed just as plainly in their eyes and chalky faces. The rest of the class, of course, cheered and sang their praises to Mrs. Weiler, no doubt relieved that she had not singled out any of them.

Johnny, Tina and I were to sing solos. Not only in front of the class, but in front of the school. We had shown such superior achievement that Mrs. Weiler was certain we would shine, and make her, our parents—everyone—very, very proud.

Johnny would sing "The Impossible Dream." Tina would sing "Love is Blue." And I—I would sing "Somewhere, My Love (Lara's Theme)" from *Dr. Zhivago*, the big blockbuster of the day.

Mrs. Weiler looked pained and fearful when I began breathing and sobbing so hard—and came immediately to me and stroked my hand, and gazed at me with such sadness in her green eyes. Almost immediately the paroxysm passed. Kneeling before me, she looked truly beautiful, and I wanted to kiss her. But she said, "Warren, you can do it, I know. Won't you sing for us? Won't you please?"

And taking a deep breath, I said, "Yes, Mrs. Weiler," because I could not refuse her.

The big event would happen two weeks later, at a special assembly held in the evening so the parents could come. There was plenty of other programming: scholastic awards, athletic awards, a farewell presentation for Mrs. Clairmont, who would be retiring at the end of the term. The music event would not occur until almost the end of the assembly, which gave the three unlucky participants all the more time to sweat and fidget.

And through it all, Mrs. Weiler stood by me, whispered little encouragements in my ear, ran her fingers affectionately through my hair—making me melt as her power coursed through my body like an electrical current. She was kind enough to Johnny and Tina, but her attention was focused on me; an attempt, I suppose, to cast a spell upon me like none she had ever conjured before.

It must have worked, for by the time I was to sing my song, my heart was thumping and my knees were weak, but I went out on stage after Tina and Johnny, consumed with desire to please Mrs. Weiler. The multitudes of eyes on me, and all those expectant faces—including my mom and dad's—meant nothing. Only the green eyes gazing at me with such tenderness had any influence, any meaning, whatsoever.

The record began playing over the loudspeakers. It was an instrumental version, which left the vocals entirely up to *me*. I glanced at my teacher, who nodded at just the right moment, giving me the cue to begin. I stepped up to the microphone, and the voice that came out was no longer mine. It was a rich, hearty stranger's voice, entirely on key, and absent any trace of quaver.

"Somewhere, my love," I sang, and nearly fell over right there on stage, surprised and shocked by the entity that must have entered me for the sole purpose of releasing its voice. I saw my teacher leave her place behind the curtain and make her way down the stage steps, coming slowly to stand at the edge of the platform before me.

Her eyes gleamed at me, and this thing of Mrs. Weiler's making, having seized my lungs and my vocal cords, had its way with me until the music ended, and I stood there alone in a vacuum, without so much as a whisper of breath to break the silence.

Until I looked down at the green eyes, and saw them smiling. And then a single pair of hands came together, cracking in the air like a gunshot, and a moment later a thunder erupted in the auditorium: a monstrous peal of applause joined by hundreds of voices crying out.

I nearly swooned, for it seemed that a cold wind swept past my body, threatening to topple me as my adrenaline high faded, leaving me unsteady and on the verge of hyperventilating again.

Mrs. Weiler's strong hands supported me, though, for in an instant she was beside me, and I looked into my parents' eyes and saw them beaming with pride. I smiled, probably for the first time since the news of my "performance" had been broken to me.

Without looking at her, I knew that Mrs. Weiler's eyes were focused on me, perhaps in attempt to take back the thing she had released to take possession of my body. Was it a kind thing? I wondered. A dangerous thing? All I knew was that for time it had been mine, and Mrs. Weiler had made it so.

Because she was a witch.

That night became something special in my memory. Afterward, I sang and I enjoyed the sound of my voice, but it was always *my* voice. The sounds falling from my lips at that assembly had come from something apart from me, and try as I might, I could not regain it. Only Mrs. Weiler knew the secret.

Shortly after school ended for that summer, Mrs. Weiler died. I do not know how or why, only that I never saw her again. I cried, harder than when my grandparents died, more bitterly than when my father passed away a couple of years later. My mother is still alive, and I love her dearly, yet I cannot imagine shedding tears more meaningful when her time comes than those I shed for Mrs. Weiler.

One day when I was eighteen, I went to the house where she had lived, for it still stood then, and indeed, remains today as something of a monument in this old town. On that day, though, remembering so well the effect she'd had on my life, I wandered around the place, taken by a feeling of melancholy. I stepped up to the rickety front porch and tried the front door, not expecting it to be unlocked.

But it was. As if I were expected.

So I went inside and, as soon as I stepped over the darkened threshold, the scent of her rushed into my nostrils, still potent after so many years. Dust-shrouded furniture remained in place, as if nothing had been touched since her death.

A grand piano occupied one corner of the large living room and, stepping up to it, I touched a key. A clear note rang out, and so I played a few chords, to my surprise finding each key in perfect tune. I had become proficient playing the piano, though never so well had Mrs. Weiler been there to guide my hand and attune my senses to the music.

But what came out in that dusty old chamber was a clear melody—"Somewhere, My Love"—a song I had never played myself, now played as perfectly as I had sung it on that night in fourth grade. I felt the same current in my soul as on the night she had released her power into me, and I would have sworn then I heard her voice singing in accompaniment.

When I stopped playing, the notes echoed into the darkened halls of that house, stirring *something*. Something that whispered my name and touched my cheek and brushed my lips with a sweet caress.

I left there knowing I would return. Soon.

And I did.

When I graduated from college, I disavowed the ritual practiced by my friends and virtually all the rest of the town's youth—leaving home for greener pastures, never to return, or if so, only for brief family visits. Instead, I managed to place myself as music teacher in the local school system.

I moved into the old Weiler place, which is where I still reside. I often wish I had been able to know her as an adult, for I had come to understand her power and her love of music. I came to feel what she must have felt when a beautiful melody played and touched her heart. I still feel her and hear her and smell her in the halls of this house, and within these walls, I feel the magic she once gave to me on the stage of our little elementary school.

I take that magic with me every day, and when I encounter a little one who shares, however vaguely, the power that Mrs. Weiler bestowed upon me, I give to that child all I can spare, conjuring up that *thing* that once took me and that still lives within the walls of my old house. It doesn't like light, but favors the dark, so in the evenings, I walk with it and sing, or play the piano or the guitar, or whichever instrument brings it pleasure.

It prefers the old things, so I don't change the furniture, or otherwise renovate the place any more than necessary to keep it habitable. And I remember those times when I was a child and heard Mrs. Weiler's voice in the night, and didn't understand.

But I am older now, and I understand so much more. And though most children don't understand, there are those few who one day *will*. Those are the ones upon whom I focus—to perpetuate the spirit that Mrs. Weiler passed on to me. I can do this; I have that power.

Because I am a witch.

Of course.

When Jarly Calls

2013

Of the dozen or so vineyards Sarah and I had visited during the past few months, Lavinder Hill was the most isolated, hidden in a shadowed, remote corner of North Carolina's Yadkin Valley, surprisingly far from any main traffic arteries.

Most of the region's wineries lay off the beaten path, but as we drove down a winding, potholed road along some unnamed stream, I began to wonder if we had taken a wrong turn.

But the polite, feminine voice of our virtual navigator assured me we were on the right track, and as we rounded a sharp curve, I glimpsed a row of grapevines creeping up and over a long, rolling hillside. Moments later, I saw it: an arrow-shaped wooden sign bearing the name "Lavinder Hill" in faded blue script, pointing to a barely visible gap in the long row of cedar trees that lined the road.

As I turned the Mini Cooper into this nebulous opening, I was surprised to see, standing next to the gravel driveway, a lone figure with a large cylindrical object tucked under one arm. A wooden drum, I realized, its ends covered by dark skins pulled taut with leather thongs. The man himself was black—not dark brown but onyx *black*—and strikingly tall. Despite the chilly day, he wore only a frayed black T-shirt; ragged, ill-fitting jeans; and no shoes.

His face was long and thin—equine, I thought—and the afternoon sun turned his eyes amber-gold, the same hue as the brightest autumn foliage. His elongated head was hairless and uncovered. As we approached, he hefted the drum, focused his brilliant eyes on mine, and began to pound the taut skin with the heel of one hand, beating out a repetitive cadence that thundered above the running engine.

Boom, boom, boom, BOOM-BOOM, boom, boom, boom, BOOM-BOOM....

Sarah gave a wry chuckle. "Bet he never worked as a Walmart greeter."

"God forbid he owns the place."

The driveway led through thinning woods, which gave way to reveal an ancient, two-story Southern Colonial that might have boasted affluence a century or so ago. The place appeared dilapidated to the point of near-collapse, and at first I thought the winery must lie some distance ahead. Then I noticed the little sign that read "Tasting Room" affixed to one of the porch columns. Sarah saw it at the same time and huffed in dismay.

"Do we really want to go in there?"

In the little parking area in front of the house, I saw one other car: a white Buick Century that was shedding its paint, half-hidden in the corner nearest the woods. I shrugged. "We've come this far."

"What sound logic."

I parked the Cooper, and as we stepped into the brisk air, I paused to listen for any hint of that distant, pounding drum, but a whistling breeze vanquished all other sounds. Rickety wooden stairs led us to the front porch, whose floorboards groaned in agonized protest. Next to the front door, a couple of distressed wooden rocking chairs faced the woods that surrounded the house.

I pushed open the warped door, whose hinges issued a long, feline yowl. As soon as we stepped inside, I became aware of a heady mélange of aromas: vanilla, cinnamon, cloves, cedar. It was a cozy room with a bare hardwood floor. A couple of small, ornamental lamps and several wine bottles filled with glowing Christmas lights dispelled the shadows.

An elderly gentleman, rather hefty—what Sarah would call "puffy"—sat behind a long wooden counter, peering over narrow wire-frame glasses at a newspaper, taking scant note of our presence. After a few seconds, he laid his paper aside, drew himself up, and focused his attention on us.

"Y'all want a tasting?" he asked in a thin, tenor voice.

"I believe we do," I said.

"I'm Jack Lavinder," he said, his gaze lingering on Sarah with clear appreciation. The lady did possess a tolerable physique, and today she appeared particularly distinguished in her black cashmere sweater, variegated gray scarf, form-fitting blue jeans, and black leather boots. The wind had tousled her shoulder-length auburn hair, adding a sassy touch I knew would please her.

"It's seven dollars for seven," Lavinder said, handing us each a sheet of paper displaying the wine list.

I briefly examined the page. The varieties appeared typical for the region: in the white column, a Viognier and two Chardonnays; in the red, Sangiovese, Cabernet Franc, the ubiquitous Chambourcin, and a blend called 1841 Reserve.

"We're the only vineyard in the area that grows our grapes in slate earth. Everyone else grows them in North Carolina clay. You'll notice the difference."

"I'm sure," I said. "Listen, let me ask you something. When we drove in, there was a man at the entrance, banging on a drum. Does he work here?"

Lavinder froze, and his dull aqua eyes rolled up to peer at me over his glasses. "Tall black man? Drum like a tom-tom?"

"Yes."

He turned toward a door at the back of the room and called out in his thin voice, "Vera! *Vera!*"

We heard a creaking and a shuffling, and after a few seconds, a stooped, gray-haired woman, also puffy, appeared in the doorway. "Yeah?"

"Jarly's out there."

The woman's eyes flicked toward us. "Again? But it's too soon!"

I was struck by the look of alarm on the woman's face. "I take it he doesn't work here."

"Not exactly." The old man nodded toward the woman. "This is my wife, Vera. I'm gonna let her take over the tasting." Without another word, he stalked out from behind the counter, gave his wife a look of something between fear and disgust, and disappeared through the door.

Vera Lavinder stepped behind the counter, and sparkling green eyes gave Sarah and me a thorough once-over. "First time here?" she asked.

"Yes," I said. "Is everything all right?"

"He'll sort things out," she said, her voice edged with ice. But then she smiled an apology, reached beneath the counter, and brought forth a pair of wine glasses, which—to my surprise—were full-size rather than the miniatures customarily used for tastings. "We're going to start with the Viognier," she said with a cheerful lilt, falling into well-practiced routine. "I think you'll find it crisp and refreshing. You'll taste some peach." She poured a healthy amount into both glasses.

I tipped mine back and swallowed the entire quantity at once. Unobjectionable was the best I could say for it. Sarah was a little more reserved, taking several small, thoughtful sips before draining the glass and offering a non-committal nod.

"Where y'all from?" Vera asked.

"Aiken Mill, in Virginia."

"Oh! That's a fair distance."

"An easy enough drive," I said, reluctant to mention the last few miles of potholed road.

Next, Vera served us the two Chardonnays, each portion far larger than typical for a tasting. I hoped she would be as generous with the reds. Indeed, when she poured the first of them, the Sangiovese, she filled both glasses more than half full.

I took a few slow sips and let the flavors wash over my tongue. This one was delicious, with hints of cherry and vanilla, with no trace of the typical North Carolina clay flavor, and my hopes for Lavinder Hill soared.

Vera poured us each a substantial quantity of Cabernet Franc, followed by a similar measure of Chambourcin. Both were excellent. When she brought out the bottle of 1841 Reserve, she gave me a huge smile. "I think you'll really enjoy our reserve blend."

"Why 1841?" Sarah asked.

"That's the year this farmhouse was built—by my husband's great-great-grandfather. How did you hear about us, if I might ask?"

"The NC Winery website," I said. "There wasn't much information about this place, though."

"Jack and me don't know anything about computers," Vera said. "We got a friend to put up a barebones website just so we'd have something to show."

"Now, that's something I could help you with," I said

"Do you have a card?"

I reached for my wallet, extracted one of my business cards, and handed it to her. She gave it a cursory look and scowled.

"Bill Kidd. Is that a joke?"

"Not at all."

"And I reckon she's Calamity Jane. Well, Mr. Kidd, let's see how you like our red blend." She filled both our glasses more than half full. I swirled the glass and took a small sip. A veritable burst of fruit and spice filled my mouth, followed by traces of vanilla and tobacco. It was one of the most delicious wines I had ever tasted.

This little vineyard was a hidden gem, I thought. Still, as I glanced around the tasting room, something about it seemed less than congenial. Despite the warm lamplight and agreeable aromas, behind it all lay the taint of mustiness, of *squalor*, more in keeping with my first impression of the house.

However, I thrust away my misgiving, as I felt the first traces of warmth seeping into my bloodstream. By now, Sarah and I both must have consumed the equivalent of three full glasses of wine, but as one who could claim considerable experience with spirits, I remained some distance from intoxication.

"Bottles of the reserve are thirty dollars," Vera said. "Tell you what. I'll give you two bottles—and your tastings—for fifty. You can't get a better deal than that."

I chuckled. "You may have just talked us into it." I gave Sarah an inquiring glance. "Drink one here and take one with us?"

She was looking out the window that faced the front of the house. "Sure," she said with a distracted air.

"The view is best from our back porch." Vera then gave me an apologetic look. "Now, if you don't mind going ahead and paying? And you wouldn't happen to have cash, would you? Our card reader isn't working."

This request irked me more than it should have, but I took out my wallet and laid fifty dollars on the counter. She whisked it away, verified I had given her the correct amount, and proceeded to uncork a new bottle. "Y'all are welcome to wander around. In fact, I recommend you walk back among the grapes." She handed me the bottle and smiled a sweet smile. "When you're ready, just stop back inside to collect your other one."

Sarah grabbed our two glasses, and we headed out the door, which again screeched like a scalded cat. We followed the wraparound porch to the back and saw a pair of rocking chairs, siblings to those in front. They looked inviting enough, so we settled into them, and I filled our glasses.

Beyond the house, the broad expanse of green sloped toward a distant sea of red, brown, and gold foliage. In the distance, a black cloud appeared to be oozing from the earth to hover above the trees. I hoped a storm wasn't brewing, not with us so far out on a rutted, winding back road.

"You know," Sarah said. "Vera's trying awfully hard to get us drunk."

"Yeah. And I wonder why." I found myself again listening for any hint of faraway drumming, but I detected only the moan of the constant breeze. "You looked a bit disturbed in there."

She frowned. "Something about that man Jarly."

"Vera said he was here 'too soon.' I wonder what she meant."

Sarah had an amusing habit of swirling her wine until it sloshed over the rim, and sure enough, a moment later, some quantity of red liquid splashed onto the table. She raised a hand to her mouth and squeaked an abashed, "Oops!"

"Klutz."

She giggled one of her endearing little giggles. But then we both heard a faint *thump-thump*, and Sarah's face paled. "I'm guessing Mr. Lavinder didn't quite sort things out."

"Would you rather go back inside?"

She shook her head. "I shouldn't be so jumpy." But then she wrinkled her nose. "What's that smell?"

I took a deep breath and at first detected only the pervasive, loamy scent of autumn. But a second later, I smelled something burning. Not the familiar, pleasant aroma of wood smoke or even the taint of some smoldering synthetic; more a nauseating blend of sulfur, gasoline, and scorched flesh. The kind of smell my imagination might associate with bodies being incinerated.

Boom, boom, boom, BOOM-BOOM, boom, boom, boom, BOOM-BOOM....

Jarly must have made his way to the front of the house, possibly even the porch.

"I don't care how good their wine is, this is ridiculous," I said. "Shall we go back inside?"

"Let's."

We rose from our chairs and started toward the back door, but then Sarah stopped. "Jesus," she said and pointed toward the vineyard. "Look at that!"

At first, I didn't notice anything unusual—until I realized, at the farthest edge of the vineyard, where I had first seen the dark clouds, a black, inky splotch appeared to be spreading into the sky like a gigantic, ebony spider.

"Is that a tornado?" she asked.

"I don't think so." I twisted the rusted handle of the back door, only to find it locked. "Shit. Let's just go around front, get our wine, and go. What say you?"

"Yes, please."

I grabbed the half-empty bottle and led the way to front door.

It, too, was locked.

"What the hell?" I peered in through the window, but drawn curtains prevented even a glimpse inside. I pounded hard on the door but was met with a long silence.

"Let's just leave," Sarah said.

I beat on the door again, with the same result. By now, I was tempted to give it a good kick, but an ounce of remaining good judgment prevented me. Then Sarah grabbed my arm, her eyes so wide I could see white all around her emerald irises. "Bill, look."

My focus shifted to the Mini Cooper, and I saw that both tires on the right side were flat. I rushed around to check the left side.

There were deep cuts in all of them.

"Son of a bitch," I growled, setting the wine bottle on top of the car. For the first time in a long time, I wished I still carried my Glock 38 in the glove compartment. Whatever was happening here, it went far beyond mere mischief.

Sarah drew her phone from her pocket, glanced at the screen, and shook her head. "Nope."

"We had service when we got here."

"Not now."

My phone was also a paperweight.

Now curious, I went to inspect the old Buick parked nearby. The tires were intact, but grit and grime covered the peeling white paint, and I suddenly doubted it belonged to the Lavinders. For the first time, I noticed its license plate was missing. And the hood was not latched. I tugged it open.

I hardly qualified as an automobile expert, but I knew enough to realize the spark plug wires were all missing.

"Sarah, you have your pepper spray?" I called.

"In my purse, under the seat."

"Grab it."

She didn't question me but went to retrieve the canister. Then, with little other recourse, we started back toward the house. We had just reached the stairs when a figure appeared at the corner of the porch.

It was Jarly, drum at his chest. One hand began to feverishly pound its skin. His gold-tinted eyes peered at us, betraying no emotion whatsoever.

"You'd better explain yourself," I said.

In response, he drew himself up and, in a rich, mellifluous baritone, began to sing. Not in English or any other language that I recognized. Smooth, rolling syllables that descended into harsh, guttural clicks and grunts, then again ascended to melodious, lyrical non-words.

"O lai, eeno-weetch ya so lah! O lai, shee ma keeyo na lah!

Yogo, ah-vee moh gahn!"

The voice poured over us like warm liquid, so mellow, so soothing, I was barely aware of my knees beginning to sag. Only when one struck the ground, sending a jolt of pain up my leg, did my mind grasp that I was mesmerized—*under a spell*—and that realization snapped my senses back to stark clarity. I righted myself and saw Sarah succumbing to the same influence. I tugged hard on her arm, and awareness returned to her eyes.

"What the hell?" she whispered.

"Come on." We rushed to the porch where, with a single, forceful kick, I sent the door flying open. Jarly's drum continued without pause, though he was no longer singing.

What the hell had happened to us? Did those incomprehensible words have meaning, or were they simply some weird, hypnotic mechanism to render us helpless?

Helpless against what?

Sarah shoved the door closed, but my kick had broken the lock. The tasting room was now dark and empty, and the pleasant aromas from earlier had given way to the scorched odor from outside. I noticed our bottle of 1841

Reserve on the counter and the tasting bottles still open, as if the proprietors had evacuated in haste.

If we were lucky, the Lavinders owned a house phone. Perhaps we could yet call 911.

"Look in here. I'll check the other rooms," Sarah said and disappeared through the door that led to the rest of the house. The old couple *must* have a land line, I thought, but I quickly determined that if they did, it wasn't in the tasting room. Then Sarah called, "Bill! Come here! My God, hurry!"

I rushed through the door and found myself in a short hallway. At the far end, Sarah was standing at the locked door to the back porch, peering out at a shockingly dark sky. She lifted one quivering hand to point out the window.

It was a cloud—almost. More like a black gash in the sky from which inky, weblike threads sprouted and spread from horizon to horizon. At first, the massive apparition appeared motionless, but after a few moments, I realized it was growing larger, as if the threads, like ghostly fingers, were tearing the gash wider and wider, causing the sky itself to unravel. The sight of the thing confused my senses so that I couldn't tell whether it was convex or concave, solid or the ultimate emptiness.

Boom, boom, boom, BOOM-BOOM, boom, boom, boom, BOOM-BOOM....

It was not the drum I was hearing. The sound was deep, *gigantic*, like a series of rhythmic thunderclaps, steady and hypnotic. *Echoing Jarly's song.* From afar, I heard Sarah's voice. "Vera wanted us to go out among the grapes. She wanted us out *there.*"

"That's why she was trying to get us drunk."

I backed away from the door, the cold fear in my stomach intensifying with every reverberating *boom.* The spectacle unfolding in the sky was no freak storm, no meteorological anomaly.

"Where are the Lavinders?" she asked.

I glanced behind me and saw a smaller door, which was adorned with some kind of printing, indecipherable in the dim light. "What is that?"

Sarah crept forward and knelt before it. "Jesus. Look at these."

The door was covered in strange figures and symbols, etched or burned into the wood. Some resembled Arabic characters; others were pictographs, a black, spidery starburst prominent among them—clearly, a representation of the shocking phenomenon now unfolding in the sky.

Sarah put her ear to the door and listened. "I hear them. The Lavinders." She tried the doorknob, which gave a mocking rattle. "Locked."

I motioned for her to stand back and gave the door a solid kick. With a crash, it flew open. Below, I saw dim, amber light and heard the yammer of panicked voices. I rushed down the flight of wooden stairs and came face to face with Jack and Vera Lavinder. They were huddled inside a small chamber with exposed brick walls, unfurnished but for a few stacked crates. A flickering oil lamp rested atop one of them.

"What the hell is out there? Tell me."

Jack Lavinder shook his head. "You get out of here."

"You wanted us outside," Sarah said. "Why?"

"It comes when Jarly calls it," Vera said, her voice shrill and warbling. "We just do what he wants. We *have* to."

"Who is Jarly?"

Vera made an expansive gesture. "He is the air, the land. *This place*. We do what he says, and he lets us stay."

"If we didn't, he would take us," Lavinder said.

"It's usually every couple of years, that's all," Vera said, as if to placate us. "But Jarly was just here, a few weeks ago. I don't know why he came back so soon."

"Those symbols on the door. What are they?"

"Jarly made those. To protect us," Lavinder said.

"When Jarly calls, everything changes," Vera said, her voice hushed. "It's like outside of this valley, nothing exists. There is only *here*."

"This is a safe room," Sarah said. She glanced at the broken door. "Or was."

Thunder shook the brick walls.

"You need to go," Lavinder said. "You have to be outside."

"Well, someone does, don't they?" My gaze burned into Lavinder's eyes.

"No," Lavinder said, his thin voice rising. "No, don't you put us out there."

"How many people have *you* put out there?" Sarah said. "You wanted us to go out among the grapes!"

"We didn't! It's what *he* wants. Jarly!"

Knowing time must be short, I grabbed Lavinder by his shirt collar. "Up the stairs."

"Please," he said, his voice cracking, his body becoming dead weight. "Don't!"

"What happens if we all stay here?" Sarah asked.

Vera's eyes bulged. "Then it's the end of everything. It takes us all."

Boom, boom, boom, BOOM-BOOM.

"Come on." I began dragging Jack Lavinder up the stairs with me.

He struggled but was too feeble to break my grip. Vera tried to grab one of his arms, but Sarah blocked her.

"No!" The old man flailed with renewed panic. He tore himself away, but then cried out in agony and began wiping his eyes with frantic hands.

Sarah had hit him with her pepper spray.

Vera lunged at her, only to receive a face full of spray herself. Her tortured screech nearly shattered my eardrums. Driven by adrenaline, I dragged Lavinder up the last few steps, tore open the back door, and shoved his puffy bulk through it.

I didn't think I had enough strength left to do anything about Vera, but she solved my problem by stumbling, half-blinded and wailing, up the stairs after her husband. For a second, the prospect of what we were about to do stopped me from hurling the wailing hellcat outside.

But this was no time to think, to consider morality; we had to act, to *survive*. This was me facing my moment of personal annihilation and defying it.

I grabbed one of Vera's arms and slung her through the gaping portal. Then, without another glance at the pathetic pair, I rushed back into the stairwell, and Sarah slammed the broken door shut behind me. We pressed our backs against it, sealing it with our weight. I felt Sarah's hands entwine with mine. Any second now, I expected the door to burst open and admit death.

Or whatever fate the alien sky had designed for us.

The door held, but outside, the screams began. Agonized, terrified screams, shrill and mortal, the shrieks of human beings being taken apart, as if by frenzied sharks. Then came the smell. A hellish, charred smell that saturated the air and seared our lungs.

I didn't know when the screaming and booming outside gave way to the pounding of my heart. At some point, the air seeping into my lungs turned clean, free of that awful stench.

I felt Sarah's arms encircle my shoulders. As her body pressed close to mine, the subtle, pleasant aromas of vanilla, cinnamon, cloves, and cedar came wafting to my nostrils, and I wondered if, for some brief time, we had both simply lost our minds.

When we staggered out of the cellar room, the house was empty. Jack and Vera Lavinder were gone without a trace. No blood, no clothing, no visible damage to the house except for the pair of broken doors, for which I was responsible.

From the back porch, I saw the late afternoon sun shining down on the vineyard, the grapes sparkling as if they had turned to gemstones.

"What have we done?" Sarah's eyes were glistening. "We killed those people."

"No. They made their choice a long time ago. We made sure they saw it through."

"That's how you rationalize it?"

"*We* had to live."

"How do we live now, knowing what exists out here?"

"We *don't* know. We don't know anything."

She sighed. "No. We don't." She slid an arm around my waist, half in reassurance, half to support herself. "It'll be dark soon."

"Jarly got what he wanted, I expect."

"For now." She stared into the distance, out where the black gash had first appeared in the sky. "I wonder. What would we have done in the Lavinders' position?"

"I'm afraid we know."

We went back into the house, and this time, I found the telephone—in the Lavinders' bedroom. A room that might belong to any older couple. A room that betrayed no hint its occupants had destroyed countless lives. It seemed ironic—absurd, even—that they had left that old Buick on the property, in plain view. At one time, they must have been experts at covering up all evidence of the events that occurred here.

Maybe they just hadn't cared anymore.

Maybe they had *wanted* a way out.

I doubt I will ever know who—or what—Jarly actually is. But I am certain that somewhere, sometime, he will reappear to enlist or entrap others to assume the Lavinders' place, so they might continue to *feed* the monstrous thing that lurks behind this innocent facade.

This place ought to be burned, I thought. Yet no fire in the world, I knew, could ever touch the horror we had experienced.

We did not dare call the police. Instead, I phoned my brother in Winston-Salem, explained that my car had been vandalized, and he agreed to pick us up. It would take him an hour to reach us. By then it would be dark.

We were still in shock, and I was glad of it. Once we recovered, I feared madness lay in store.

I retrieved my bottle of 1841 Reserve from the tasting room. I had paid for it, and I intended keep it. That bottle I would never drink, but I had left the partially finished one on my car. It was still there. So, as night fell over us, Sarah and I settled into the rocking chairs on the porch, drank wine, waited, and listened.

Messages From a Dark Deity

2006

NOW:

Blair finally realized that the things lining the roadside were severed heads.

He had spent time in Iraq during a particularly violent spell, and if he were driving through Baghdad or Fallujah, he would have been just as disturbed, if perhaps less stunned.

But this was Hinton, Ohio, a tiny smudge on the banks of the Ohio River. In every corner of the world, people made statements through violence, but in America's heartland, they rarely did it this way.

He slowed his Buick LaCrosse, keenly aware that the perpetrator might be watching him even now, intent on adding another cap to his collection. He counted nine of the awful things: three men, three women, three children, all placed neatly, about ten feet apart, on the road's solid shoulder.

Only a few trickles of still-wet blood leaked out from beneath the cleanly sawn necks, and all bore expressions of vivid shock, as if they were still alive and pitiably aware of their condition. The dead he had seen in the Middle East never actually looked like that.

He brought the Buick to a slow halt, grabbed his camera, and clambered out, scanning his surroundings before moving away from the safety of his car. To the right, there was only high grass, a stand of oak trees, and a crumbling barn emblazoned with an ancient Mail Pouch Tobacco advertisement; to the left, a grassy slope led down to the banks of the river.

He saw no other remains, for which he was grateful, and no one alive in his field of vision. When he thought about it, he could not remember the last car he had seen or which way it was traveling. This afternoon, he might as well be the only living soul in Hinton.

As he crept toward the nearest of the heads, which belonged to a young, possibly once-attractive woman, he drew his phone from his pocket, only to find no service. For the assignment he had just put to bed in Charleston—the busting of a deadly arson ring—he had opted to drive, rather than make the O'Hare–Yeager roundtrip, because he had wanted to stop in on his brother in Cincinnati. At the last minute, Jim had canceled because of a strep infection. Now this.

Unable to suppress his reporter's instincts for capturing a story, however ghastly, he braced himself and snapped several photos of the heads. If it came down to an assignment, though, he hoped Sibulsky, his editor, would put someone else on this one.

Fat chance.

Blair had witnessed many horrific sights in Iraq— particularly the bodies of children torn apart by shrapnel from homemade explosives and bullets from automatic rifles. But somehow *these* remnants of lives ended so brutally hit him like a vicious punch to the gut. It was the awful *awareness* in their eyes, he decided, both heart-wrenching and terrifying, as if the dead gazes portended for him an imminent, equally dreadful fate.

This place felt *sick.*

He had seen evil, especially overseas. People anywhere and everywhere were evil. But no location in his experience had ever felt like this—drenched in some tangible, noisome horror.

Photos done, he slipped his camera into his pocket and returned to the car. He had a duty to turn this matter over to the local law, and he would. At this moment, to his profession, he felt considerably less committed.

As he started the LaCrosse, for a second or two, he thought he glimpsed something beyond the old barn: a hovering patch of darkness in the sky, like a hole punched in the fabric of the world.

A dark cloud.

No.

A black hole with soulless, spying eyes.

"What did Sibulsky say?"

"I didn't tell him."

"You serious?"

"Very."

Debra's hands on her hips, her head cocked quizzically at him, indicated that she thought his brain stem must have snapped. "You called the State Patrol and vamoosed? You?"

"I couldn't stay and deal with that."

"After the things you've seen?"

"This was the worst."

"Is it on the news?"

"Not that I know of."

"But you're checking on it?"

"Diligently."

Blair stepped around the wet bar in the corner of the living room and poured a second martini, very dirty, from the shaker. Debra followed and held out her glass, which he filled before turning to the window, wondering if he might again glimpse the strange image that had drifted into his field of vision several times since his discovery of the Hinton Heads.

His 30th-floor apartment overlooked the Kennedy Expressway and the northern Chicago skyline, now ablaze with brilliant, kinetic light—a view that, as far as he was concerned, justified his spending more than a third of his income on his residence. He saw nothing unusual, other than a single, brilliant star in the sky, which must have been Mars or Jupiter, since no other celestial bodies besides the moon had the candlepower to cut through the city's canopy of smog and light pollution.

"Why do you keep looking out there?" Debra asked as she half-danced over to him and slipped an arm around his waist. "You're so preoccupied."

"I'm looking for a message from God," he said, with an ounce more solemnity than she would understand. "He doesn't seem to have left any lately."

"Something to ease the memory?"

That wasn't exactly what he was getting at, so he shrugged. "I think God's stopped watching because the movie's too nasty."

Debra's amber-brown eyes blinked away the remark. Every now and then, some remnant of her mostly forgotten Christianity asserted itself. "He doesn't stop watching."

There. At one o'clock. In the general direction of Lincoln Park.

A dark splotch. A black hole drilled in the midnight blue sky, from which *something* peered out at him, unseen except for a few barely discernible bubbles of color, a hue he couldn't quite describe, vaguely resembling a spider's bulbous eyes. As before, the thing existed for three seconds and then was gone, but his sporadic glimpses were just distinct enough to convince him it was not an optical illusion.

The fact it had first appeared in Hinton might be coincidence or it might not, but somehow, insidiously, it brought to mind the dark days of two summers ago, when he was firmly entrenched in the atrocity that was the Persian Gulf.

He would remember why in his own sweet time.

He opened the sliding glass door and stepped out to what he called the Afterdeck: the sole remnant of a long-disassembled fire escape, a four-by-eight rectangle of iron grillwork anchored to the building's superstructure by a few bolts that looked rusty enough to pop under little more than his weight.

Debra wouldn't set foot out here, but he had outfitted the platform with a table and lounge chair, and on pleasant evenings, he enjoyed reclining with nothing but 300 feet of turbulent air between him and Monroe Street. She knew when he went out there he had entered his own private world, and she let him be, if sometimes with more than a touch of anxiety.

Sipping his martini, he fixed his eyes on the northeastern horizon and the countless glittering towers that soared out of the sizzling ocean of light, hoping to take a bearing should the ghostly image appear yet again.

A steady breeze from Lake Michigan swept away the humidity before it could turn his skin to moist clay and, along with the alcohol, lulled him into a contemplative stupor. Every now and then, the grillwork platform would shift subtly, just enough to induce a touch of vertigo, and he wondered how long those old bolts in the wall would continue to hold. However, he enjoyed the thrill of the wind's tug and the perception that he was actually floating on a current of air, so the danger was more alluring than daunting.

He closed his eyes to enjoy the invigorating sensation, and when he opened them again, the moon had risen and the sound of traffic on the expressway below had changed from a slow, steady rumble to the occasional *swish-thrum* of vehicles passing by at high speed.

His martini glass, empty, lay on its side on the metal latticework beside his lounge chair, and his chest felt heavy, as if something were pressing insistently down on him. Glancing northeastward, he half-expected to see a gaping pit in the sky, barely visible globular eyes peering out, their inscrutable gaze weighing on him like frigid stone. But there was nothing.

Except stars.

Holy God, the sky was full of them. Brilliant, multicolored jewels cutting through the greenish haze like smoldering embers that stretched from horizon to horizon. He'd never seen anything like it—at least, not in the city. Maybe in a distant desert, some years ago.

He sat up and nearly choked, and he realized the pressure in his chest was from a horrible, gut-wrenching stench, which hovered like a layer of thick, sulfurous smoke just above his reclining body.

"Fucking awful," he muttered, wondering what kind of hellish atmospheric cocktail had wafted to this altitude. He picked up his glass and returned indoors, where it was now dark and silent. Apparently, Debra had already gone to bed. The kitchen clock read 1:09 am; five hours had flashed by since he had ventured out to the Afterdeck.

Age, alcohol, and fatigue, he thought. Traveling long distances wore him out more than it used to, and lately he'd been aware of a low, slow burn as the stress of endlessly delving into man's inhumanity to man took its toll on his mind and body. Lots of newsmen burned out quickly, especially now that the world had shrunk to the point that there was simply no such place as "over there." It was all one big mass of humanity on an aging, cancer-riddled sphere edging ever closer to its final days of existence.

He'd smelled something like that stench out there once before, he thought. But somewhere else, back in the past; never in Chicago.

He went to the bar, made himself a nightcap—a thing he had lately come to cherish like little else—and returned to the window to marvel at the inexplicable, star-stippled sky.

Two Summers Ago:

A few glimmers of light cut through the pulsating darkness that had become his entire field of vision, and, finally, he began to hear the sounds of mass confusion around him: haranguing voices, none in English; the grating rumble of HUMV engines; the distant, arrhythmic thuds of artillery fire—whether from the Americans, the Islamists, or both, he couldn't tell. It was heavy and constant, *so it must be ours*, he thought.

He was lying on his back on a rough, uncomfortable surface. As sight and hearing slowly returned, he took stock of every sensation, praying he hadn't been ripped half-apart by the nearby mortar blast. His back ached, but he didn't feel any other focused pain. He found he could move his hands and feet—thank God!—and apart from a dull pounding in his temples, he counted himself little the worse for wear.

Overhead, he saw a cracked plaster ceiling; to his right, an open window, through which a few wisps of smoke trickled in; and to the left, a cracked wooden door, slightly ajar. There were no furnishings, and the walls were bare. At the moment, he appeared to be alone.

Soon, the shelling stopped, the motors faded, and the voices grew fainter until all he could hear was the soft whisper of desert wind outside. No further hint of incoming ordnance.

Thus reassured, he relaxed somewhat, a bit nervous about his unknown whereabouts, but still too dazed to worry much about it, at least for the time being. He was alive and seemingly whole.

He had no idea what had happened to Edward Hollister, the British journalist with whom he'd been traveling, or the young Iraqi translator, whose name he couldn't remember. He'd last seen them just before the shelling started—before the road had been completely obliterated by smoke and every vehicle and person in the convoy had scattered in search of cover.

He didn't remain relaxed very long. A new chorus of voices rose somewhere just beyond the window, and he sat up, slowly, carefully, wondering whether he had been brought here by friendlies or by murderous fanatics. But no—the window and door were open. If the Islamists had abducted him, they would never have left him unattended.

Or would they? Out there lay only miles of desert. He wouldn't get far even if he were to walk out of here unhindered.

He rose to his knees, shuffled to the window, and stuck his head into the arid afternoon air. To his surprise, he found himself looking out over an expanse of blinding white sand from three stories up. Maybe he was in a mosque, or some vacant apartment building. From this vantage point, he couldn't see any other structures, but off to the right, he discerned a pale, thin ribbon that extended to the horizon, which he figured was the road his convoy had been traveling when the mortars hit.

Something on that horizon—which lay to the east, according to the sun—drew his attention and held it. A long, dark smudge, like a blotch of murky oil paint, had turned a portion of the powder-blue backdrop to yellow-brown soup. For a long minute, he couldn't figure out what he was seeing until he remembered seeing something like it rolling across the endless, flat plain as he drove through western Indiana late one spring.

Dust storm.

A huge one, by the look of it.

A tremor passed through his gut, but he wasn't sure why. It wasn't just the approaching sand storm. Something here seemed wrong. *Evil*, even. As if more than danger lurked somewhere around him, hidden, waiting.

Plotting.

Now:

The next day when he saw the thing in the sky, it lasted for several minutes, occupying that same space above the horizon, becoming more substantial with every passing second, like an onyx-hued moon materializing through a thinning haze.

Debra hadn't seen it when he'd pointed straight to it. He doubted anyone else would either.

So he went after it.

Like a black star of Bethlehem, it led him northeastward until he arrived in a Wrigleyville neighborhood he passed through only rarely: an attractive, tree-lined residential street, quiet and restful, between Belmont and Addison. He knew when he had reached his destination because of the sudden tremor of cold, pure dread that passed through his body.

The same as in Hinton, Ohio.

And some other, still unremembered time.

An ancient, hulking church stood silently on a street corner, watching over the neighborhood with somber dignity, its tall spire thrusting skyward—toward the gaping black mouth that had climbed to a zenith directly overhead, occasionally revealing a shifting array of oddly colored orbs on which his eyes refused to focus.

He parked at the curbside, got out of his car with his camera, and snapped a series of photographs. Hardly unexpectedly, when he looked into the preview pane to see what the lens had captured, he saw only azure blue sky and a few ruffled altostratus clouds.

The implication nearly sent him into a screaming rage. That some portion of his mind had become unhinged and was causing him to hallucinate seemed sickeningly certain.

"What you s'pose that is?" came a cracked, dry voice from behind him.

Blair whirled to regard the speaker: a stooped, gray-haired woman who wore a moth-eaten overcoat and a ratty woolen scarf, even though the morning was already quite warm. A gnarled finger pointed, not to the sky, but toward the distant street corner to the north. At first, he saw nothing remarkable, but after a few seconds, he detected a movement among the tree limbs, just above the sidewalk.

A dark shape was gliding slowly earthward: a black cat pawing its way out of the branches and creeping down the trunk, he thought, until he realized, by way of comparing it to the car parked beside the tree, that the thing was easily larger than a man. It had a long, lithe torso and four spindly limbs, but he could discern only a black, featureless silhouette. When it reached the ground, it vanished behind the cars and did not reappear.

"An animal?" he asked, glancing back at the old woman, realizing he had failed to lift his camera for a shot.

"No. It came from outa that, up yonder." The pointing finger turned upward.

Blair's blood froze. He tried not to stammer, nearly succeeded. "You see it?"

"You think I'm blind? 'Course I see it."

Blair squinted, a little suspicious. "What do you see?"

"Don't get wise with me!"

"You mean the hole in the sky."

"Yeah. The hole in the sky."

The old woman's eyes shifted and turned north. Blair followed her gaze and again saw the black silhouette, almost a man, but not quite, and this time it began to dance.

Jerky, erratic. A puppet on strings pulled by a madman's hands.

Blair broke into a sprint, something he hadn't done in too many ages, and his lungs and heart protested after a hundred yards. When he blinked, the silhouette had again disappeared.

"No way."

As he passed a parked car, something caught his eye, and he stopped. There, half jammed into the grille, half hanging on to the asphalt: a shapeless mass, all pink and red, surrounded by a pool of liquid crimson.

No, it was not a child. It couldn't be.

A fractured, dripping skull hung from a few peach-colored, fleshy strands, its eyes glistening blue and staring vacantly skyward. Two crooked rows of teeth between bleeding, blistered gums grinned endlessly, and he heard a wheezing gasp, which seemed to come from the ruined figure hanging from the front of the car, though he knew it couldn't have.

This time he took photographs. Several.

He looked left, across the street, down the alley between two of the houses. From a tree in the backyard, barely visible, something small was hanging from a rope, swinging slowly back and forth, and for a couple of seconds, it appeared to wriggle helplessly.

To his right, from beneath the wooden stairs that led to the side door of a house, a small, ivory-white arm protruded, doll-like, but too clearly not a doll.

The odor that suddenly wormed down his trachea and expanded in his lungs was like an injection of brimstone.

He turned, gagged, and emptied the contents of his stomach onto the sidewalk.

Sometime later, he struggled back upright and glimpsed the black silhouette pirouetting away to the north, where it vanished in the distance.

"You see?" came the voice of the old woman.

It was a little Clark Street tavern; he might have visited it a time or two before. At this hour of day, it was nearly empty. The bartender, a burly young man with a goatee and small but very bright emerald eyes, watched him curiously as he sucked down a bourbon on ice, its burn as beautiful as the caress of Debra's hand.

"Another," he said, passing back the empty glass.

"What did you see?" the bartender asked, his small eyes a little too intent.

"What makes you think I saw anything?"

"Intuition."

"I'll just bet."

"Lots of people lately. They see things, they come in here, they drink. Sometimes they talk."

Blair raised an eyebrow, but then his phone in his pocket burred softly.

"Yeah?"

"Why didn't you tell me about Hinton?" It was Sibulsky's voice.

"What about it?"

"You know what about. Did you get pictures?"

"Yeah. I got pictures."

"Somehow, I have not seen them."

"You will."

"I'm wondering why you didn't bring this to me straight away. And why—if you saw what you say you did—it hasn't been picked up by any of the majors. Or even social media."

"How do you know about Hinton?"

"I just talked to Debra. Wanted to know why you hadn't checked in."

He sighed. "Look, Ben. Don't even think of sending me back there. I can't go. Not now."

Sibulsky's voice turned sharp. "If this is something big, it belongs to you, Blair."

He hated where this train was heading, but there was no way to turn it. "Okay. Here's the deal. Something's happening here. In the city. I think it's part of the same thing."

"What the hell are you talking about?"

"Whatever happened in Hinton. It's here now."

"That calls for an explanation."

"Yeah. Later."

"This afternoon."

"Tomorrow morning."

Another long hesitation and a sigh. "Shoot me those pictures. Today. Now."

"I will."

He put his phone away and downed the last of his drink. He contemplated a third, but a lingering shred of reason dissuaded him. The bartender's little hyena eyes remained fixed on him.

"So what do people talk about here?" he asked.

"Black holes."

Blair barely kept his jaw from hitting the counter. "Black holes?"

"Yep."

"Have you seen a black hole?"

"Nope."

Blair leaned closer, the back of his skull buzzing. "So who has?"

"Nobody who claims to have seen one ever comes back."

He barked a laugh. "Well, I tell you what. When I find out what I aim to find out, I'm going to come back in here and have a drink. That, my young friend, is a solemn promise."

"I could use the business."

Two Summers Ago:

Footsteps echoed from somewhere beyond his room, and then the door burst open and four men entered, all dressed in sweat-soaked fatigues. Blair raised his hands, but they waved him down, speaking rapid gibberish that sounded reasonably friendly. At least they didn't seem intent on separating his head from his shoulders, he thought with some relief.

One man was much taller than the others and had very dark skin, but bright blue eyes. Another one carried a primitive-looking radio-transmitter set, and he sat down on the floor, slipped on the headset, and began speaking in Arabic into the mouthpiece.

The two youngest, barely past their teens, pointed excitedly out the window to the approaching storm; the tall man, however, was watching it with grim fascination. The one with the radio seemed to be having trouble reaching his intended contact and finally shut it down, giving it a disapproving frown. Then he glanced at Blair and said in halting English, "Stay there, my friend. We find help for you after the storm goes."

Blair nodded and mumbled "Thank you," trying but failing to suppress his escalating anxiety. Outside, the great brown smudge had grown to cover the entire horizon, and he could now hear a faint, rumbling *whooshing* sound that grew gradually nearer and louder.

The man who had spoken turned, picked up his radio set, and disappeared through the door, his footsteps clattering away into silence. The others continued to gaze out the window, transfixed, as the thunderous rumble grew deeper and more menacing.

Soon, Blair could see the huge wall of brown sand and dust bearing down on his window: an endless series of huge, roiling columns that ascended into the sky and then collapsed, kicking up more sand, which, in turn, grew into towers, swirling and crawling and melting into an increasingly chaotic mass. In the center of the great cloud, a huge, black opening appeared and slowly expanded, like a mouth gaping wide to swallow anything and everything in the raging storm's path.

The two youngest men turned to face Mecca, knelt, and began to pray aloud, as if aware of the reek of *evil* that surrounded their little room. Their frenzied voices only added to Blair's apprehension. The air now felt charged with some dreadful electricity, and he detected a hideous odor—a nauseating mélange of sulfuric acid, ammonia, and rancid meat.

The tall, blue-eyed man remained standing and, if anything, appeared more captivated than concerned. Ignoring Blair altogether, he stepped closer to the window and began to speak softly, so softly that, at first, Blair couldn't make out a thing he said. The words were guttural and ran together, but when they did become more or less clear to him, they sounded like "Ee-eye-ee-eye-oh, cuckoo who'll fool you, foe tag again, glue a gnarly toe tap."

Within two minutes, the winds died and the sandstorm collapsed upon itself, leaving only a few slowly rising columns of dark dust several hundred yards from their vulnerable window to mark its violent passing.

4Without a word, the tall man turned and left the room, while the two young Iraqis shakily rose to their feet, exchanged shocked glances, and stared out at the now-empty desert. Finally, with what he took to be pitying glances at him, they followed the tall man out the door. Once again, he was alone in some tiny chamber in the middle of a God-forsaken land, feeling as if, at any moment, the hand of some unknown—unknowable—dark deity might strike him down.

Now:

"Oh, God. It *is* a baby."

Debra's face was chalky as she handed the camera back to him.

"And nobody cared. It took the police forty-five minutes to get there, and then they wouldn't talk to me. No questions, no interviews, just a curt 'go away.'"

"That's awful. Horrible. But why do you think this is related to the other killings?"

He didn't want to tell her that God had said so in a message, or that God was looking more and more like a spindly black dancing thing that had dropped from a hole in the sky. "Well, I had an interesting interview with a bartender. Where this thing shows up, people die."

"This *thing*. This thing that I can't see. That nobody can see—except for some people a bartender told you about."

Coming from her lips, it did sound ridiculous. "Something like that."

"You don't think the bartender might have been having a good one on you?"

"No."

He went through the sliding glass door to the Afterdeck and gazed at the afternoon sky. The sun blazed behind a thin layer of clouds, but an ocean of twinkling stars glittered across the azure backdrop. Overhead, Ursa Major and Polaris looked down at him with disdain, and closer to the horizon, Cepheus and Cassiopeia danced lewdly together in the sun's vain glare.

He snapped a few shots, wondering if the lens might deign to capture more than it had when he'd photographed the hole in the sky. It didn't.

Debra joined him at his side, eyeing him thoughtfully. "So what's up?"

"Ever see a sky full of stars in broad daylight?" he asked.

"Is that what you see?"

He had never lied to her, but he could hardly stand to tell her the truth. "I wish I didn't. But I see stars, yes."

"So, what makes you—and those others—see things the rest of us don't? That the camera doesn't?"

"If I knew that, I'd know the rest of the story."

"Are you going to write this one?"

"I am now in what we officially call the investigation stage." He gave her shoulder a squeeze. "At least you haven't called me a liar."

Deep shadows surrounded his eyes. "I know you're not a liar. I wonder about your senses, though."

"I'd wonder too—if it weren't for those dead. Those were no hallucination."

She glanced distastefully at his camera. "No. Those weren't."

Such an absurdity. The camera's eye apprehended the bodies of the dead, but not the black hole or the stars in the daytime sky. Conversely, shockingly few human eyes—or brains—registered the very real dead in the streets.

Blair noticed that Debra still stood with her eyes locked on the sky, so intently that he wondered whether she might have finally observed the insane phenomenon above. But when she turned away, her eyes barely held his, and her sad, heavy sigh indicated that she was vitally worried about him.

He spent the rest of the day trying to interview detectives at the Belmont District Headquarters, but after three fruitless attempts to see Lieutenant Ingram Trotter— usually one of his most reliable contacts at the department—he threw up his hands, went back to Wrigleyville, and walked the streets for two hours. With no sign of the hole in the sky or its attendant black dancer, he returned home, only to find an empty apartment and a note from Debra that she had gone out with her friend Sharon for the evening.

A night out with Sharon meant some serious commiserating, which often lasted until the following day. He would likely be sleeping alone tonight.

He dutifully flipped through the news channels, checked websites, every social media outlet for even a hint of some vindicating report. A story about the higher-than-usual number of random murders in Chicago and elsewhere raised his hopes slightly, but in the end, it was little more than a footnote to the major international news of the day.

Then something drew his attention to the television screen during a report about corruption in the Justice Department, and his chest immediately constricted so that he could barely breathe.

A few blocks behind the cheerful-looking young woman narrating the story, a building was burning, but neither she nor the cameraman paid it one moment's attention. And not an emergency vehicle to be seen. As the segment ended, the fire appeared to be spreading, while the news crew and a dozen or so bystanders went blithely about their business.

That was in Washington, D.C.

Blair shut off the television, rose from the couch, and made himself a drink. Then he went to the window, and there they were: a billion stars in the sky, their jeweled faces flashing with sinister light behind a dense layer of haze. He automatically reached for his camera, before his brain had a chance to remind him of its futility. He paused, but then took the camera from the kitchen table, removed the flashcard, and plugged it into his computer, suddenly fixated on the fact that he had not bothered to examine his photographs except via the small preview pane.

Once he had brought the images up on his monitor, he selected the first shots he had taken of the sky—which by all rights *should* have pictured the black-hole thing—and began to study them at various zoom levels. In one, he now saw a faint, oblong shadow hovering above the distant buildings: the vaguest suggestion of some massive, airborne object.

There *was* something there.

Something that had cloaked itself—almost—from the camera's eye.

He brought up a more recent shot of the afternoon sky and zoomed in on the seemingly empty field of blue, only to find numerous scattered pixels of slightly different hue than the rest of the backdrop. Then, by meticulously tracing the patterns of some of the off-colored dots, he was able to discern the shape of Ursa Major.

It was all there. Indiscernible to anyone who wasn't specifically looking for the signs in the sky, but there nonetheless.

A low, foreboding voice in his head told him that the source of the phenomena simply wasn't ready to reveal itself to a global audience. But it would be. Soon.

What the hell would happen then?

A little later, he went out to the Afterdeck with a fresh martini. He saw several fires in the distance but didn't hear a single siren.

Blair had only been asleep a few minutes when the creaking of the bedroom door drew him back to consciousness. His eyes opened only reluctantly, but when they found their focus, he saw Debra's naked body in front of the window, limned with electric blue. She slid onto the bed next to him and leaned down so that her hair spilled over his face. She kissed him lightly on the mouth.

"Surprised to see you," he mumbled.

"Wanted to make sure you were okay."

"How about you? You all right?"

"I'm okay."

"Did you cry on Sharon's shoulder?"

"You know better than that." Her eyes sought the ceiling. "But she..."

"What?"

"She's saw them."

He bolted upright and gripped her bicep with a taut claw. "What? What did she see?"

"Stars. During daylight."

"I've got to talk to her."

"Calm down. It's late. She's coming over tomorrow, so you can compare notes then." Debra extricated her arm from his grasp. "She's afraid."

"Did you see any fires?"

She blinked. "Fires? No. What do you mean?"

"Buildings. Cars. Anything burning anywhere?"

She seemed to struggle for a moment. Then she shook her head. "Not that I can remember."

"I think we're going to."

"You've got me worried now. And Sharon...I've never seen her like that." She searched his eyes for a long time. "What do you think is happening, Owen?"

"Something unprecedented."

"What? From *where*?"

He inhaled deeply and caught a faint whiff of sulfur. "A very dark place."

She pressed close to him, and he lay back, pulling her with him, cradling her head in his arms. Her presence was calming, though blood and adrenaline raced recklessly through both of their bodies.

Finally, once her hand began to move down his chest, past his stomach, and then lower, the fires in his head went out for a time.

At some point, sunlight replaced the electric glow beyond the blinds. Blair opened his eyes and found himself alone in the bed, but he could smell coffee brewing in the kitchen, and he felt a warm rush of relief to know Debra was still here. Somehow, he feared she might have gone off again.

The coffee called to him, so he tugged on a pair of boxer shorts and set out on his quest. As he entered the dining room, he was surprised to see Debra standing in front of the sliding door to the Afterdeck, her head craned back slightly, her brown eyes reflecting the ten o'clock sun.

"Christ, Sibulsky's going to have my head," he muttered, moving toward her, wondering what caught her interest. But he stopped as she lifted a hand and pointed toward the door.

"I see them," she said softly. "God almighty, I see them."

His heart lurched, but he could only watch as Debra opened the sliding door and stepped out to the Afterdeck, her eyes never leaving the sky. He felt a faint twinge of unkind amusement, for she had only been out there once before, and that was with stark terror.

But the stars in the mid-morning sky had snared her completely, and now he saw them, ten times more numerous and far more brilliant than the day before.

They must be almost *right* by now, he thought, wondering where that peculiar idea had come from.

Right for what?

She slowly turned to look at him, her face drawn, defeated. "I see them," she said softly. "Are you happy now?"

For a moment, the world fell unnaturally quiet. The breeze whispering past the door went still. Then, with a sharp *bang,* one of the bolts in the wall snapped, and one end of the Afterdeck dipped abruptly, pitching Debra off-balance. She threw out a hand to steady herself, but a second later, there came another *bang* and then a scraping sound, and the iron platform, railing and all, simply disappeared. He had been looking right into Debra's eyes, but now he was facing only sky—a vivid, nightmarish canopy splattered with millions of twinkling stars, like speckles of fiery blood hurled from a sun laid open by a vast, sweeping scythe. At the edge of his vision, something huge and black hovered in the blue.

"Debra?" he said to the sky. "No. No!"

He lunged forward and gripped the door jamb to keep from following her down, only to see her fall terminate on the Oak Street sidewalk, his trusty old lounge chair following and shattering a half-second later.

Several pedestrians sauntered past on the street, though none of them stopped to look. One old woman did glance briefly upward, as if she might have felt a stray drop of rain, before continuing on her eastward shamble.

"No," Blair said again, as an odor like sulfur, ammonia, and rancid meat drifted to his nostrils. "She doesn't go out there. She just doesn't."

The odor intensified, and he stepped back into the room, pulled the door shut, and locked it, half-afraid he might forget and walk out there before it registered that his favorite retreat had collapsed into ruin.

The sun's light failed to reach into the living room, and here, shadows swirled like living, dancing thunderclouds. As the terrible smell burned sharper and more menacingly in his nostrils, he saw, standing before him, the black silhouette that had yesterday danced on the sidewalk in front of the old church.

That was all it was—a silhouette, vaguely man-shaped but with disproportionately long arms and legs, an elongated, misshapen bulb that might have been its head, and some kind of horn-like protrusion curling outward from its torso. It was tall. So tall it had to stoop to clear his ten-foot ceiling.

The voice sounded like mighty stands of timber splintering. "Until the stars come right, only a few shall spy us, and those only dimly."

As if it had merged with the swirling darkness around it, the silhouette lost its contours, became a shadow of a shadow, and Blair felt a frigid, oily wave rush past him, drenching him with cold brimstone. In that moment, he expected to be scattered to the four winds, swept into oblivion.

He struggled for air, though after a few moments, he realized the hideous odor had dissipated. His skin, however, felt coated with vile slime, and the unnatural darkness in the room only slowly gave way to light from outside.

Unsteadily, he made his way to the bar and poured himself a glass of straight gin. He threw it back, poured another, and then went to the sliding door to peer into the well of empty space that had swallowed the only things in the world that actually meant anything to him.

He tugged the door open again and stood on the precipice, wondering briefly if he should take one more step and add his body to the wreckage thirty stories below.

While he thought, he drank. And breathed in the acrid smoke that was rising from the countless fires that blazed in clusters around the city as far as his eyes could see.

Smoke that was beginning to take form—vaguely resembling the dark deity that had briefly acknowledged his existence.

It was almost a relief when his brain registered, at long last, the rising wailing of sirens.

And screams.

From all over the city.

From all over the world.

Countless Summers Ago:

Fifteen minutes after the strange man had left, Blair heard the sound of a helicopter approaching, and, looking out the window, he saw a UH-1 Blackhawk bearing down on the building, and damned if that wasn't Ed Hollister leaning out its door, his eyes anxiously scanning the terrain. Somehow, he caught sight of Blair in the building's window and began waving.

Blair waved back, only to freeze in surprise. For one brief second, beyond the approaching bird, the bright daylight sky appeared full of stars. Endless, brilliant, insane, *dizzying* stars.

He looked away and then back at the sky. The stars were gone. A migraine coming on, maybe. Not surprising after all he had been through.

The vertigo passed quickly, but he knew he never wanted to see anything like *that* ever again.

Short Wave

2014

It was a Heathkit GR81 short wave radio set, and it belonged to my friend Charles Fleming—or, more accurately, to his dad.

I didn't have the first idea how the thing worked, but it could supposedly pick up broadcasts from London, Paris, Rome, Tokyo, or just about anywhere in the world. I found this a big deal because, on any other radio, all you could hear were the few nearby stations—although, on my little MBC transistor radio, under the right weather conditions, I could sometimes get WSB from Atlanta, over 300 miles away.

This excited me no end, since my family and I visited my grandparents in Atlanta at least twice a year, and any Atlanta station beat the hell out of our local ones.

We lived in Aiken Mill, Virginia, and it was July 1969. I was twelve years old.

Compared to the radios at my house, Charles's short-wave set looked like some kind of space-age device you might expect to see in an Apollo space capsule. In fact, it was because Apollo 11 had landed on the moon the day before that Charles and I decided to mess with the short wave. We figured that if we could pick up transmissions from all over the world, we might also be able to hear broadcasts from outer space.

Charles's dad had hooked the set up to a super-powerful antenna—later I found out this was because, without it, you'd never hear *anything* other than static—and we hoped it might be just the ticket to pick up the astronauts talking from the moon. That day after school, I went over to his place and we headed straight to his dad's attic den to start up the radio.

The set, which sat on Mr. Fleming's huge wooden desk, was a bit bigger than any of the radios we owned, with a distinctive blue and silver case; the frequency dial and fine-tuning knob on its left side; the speaker and band selection, regeneration, and volume knobs on its right. Giving me a look that suggested we were about to commence something momentous, Charles switched on the set, and we waited what seemed a couple of ages before the speaker issued a low, wavering hum.

"Dad was listening to Czechoslovakia last night," he said with a proud smirk.

"He was not. It's behind the Iron Curtain." I was pretty sure radio signals couldn't come out from there.

"No, it isn't."

"Is too."

Charles was the kid for whom the word "dork" was invented. He was my age, but he still wore every ounce of his baby fat, and any casual observer would have reasonably thought him a tall seven-year-old. Still, I rated him pretty cool, mainly because he had a Lil Indian minibike, which he let me ride whenever I wanted to; my folks wouldn't get me have a minibike because they were dangerous.

On top of that, the baby-faced bastard had made out with Carrie Crowe, who was a year older than us—and that wasn't just horseshit because I had actually seen them kissing. Most importantly, he had sworn to get me together with Carrie's friend Gretchen Wylie, for whom I was more than a little hot. So yeah, for a dork, Charles was all right.

He twisted the radio dial, and the speaker let out a shrill, whistling tone that hurt my ears. He quickly changed frequency, and an unsettling series of chirps, buzzes, and burps replaced the whistling. As he rotated the dial back and forth, we did hear just about every alien noise that existed in the universe. What we didn't hear was the sound of a human voice, speaking in any language.

"Kinda eerie," I said, as the radio warbled and moaned. "That sounds like it's coming from outer space."

"Atmospheric conditions," he said, crossing his arms and putting on his best "I-know-more-than-you-do" face. Smuggest dork that ever breathed, that was my friend Charles. "Short waves bounce back and forth between Earth and the clouds for a long way, and you get a lot of interference."

I nodded as if I understood, though I had a hard time imagining terrestrial weather being responsible for the unearthly sounds we were hearing. I did hope those radio waves were bouncing a hell of a lot higher than the clouds so we might yet receive transmissions from the Apollo spacecraft. A few moments later, a male voice came over the speaker, but so fragmented we couldn't tell whether the language was English or something else.

"Get it back," I said, daring to admit a rush of excitement. "That might have been it!"

He turned the dial back with excruciating deliberation, and then, there it was—the voice we were hoping to hear. Or so we thought.

"E l'uomo nella luna riso e pianto."

"Where's that from?" I asked.

"Not outer space," Charles said, his face drooping with disappointment.

The voice continued speaking in some language we didn't know, periodically interrupted by harsh crackles and crashes. Eventually, Charles rotated the dial, but now the eerie electronic noise dominated every frequency.

"Damn," he muttered. "I can usually get *something* on this."

I thought I detected a voice amid the noise, so I leaned close to the speaker, trying to make out words. All I could discern was a strange cadence somewhere within the scrambled layers of sound, but it was engrossing, hypnotic. Whatever it was, I wanted to hear it in full clarity. After some time, I came to believe it was female voice, singing. Charles futzed with the regeneration knob, and—just for a couple of seconds—I swore I heard the voice plaintively moan, "Whoooo aaaare yooou?"

It was so buried in the noise I couldn't be sure what I had heard. But Charles smacked me on the shoulder, and I saw that his chubby face had gone a little pale.

"That was *weird*," he said.

"What did you hear?"

"Didn't you hear it?"

"I heard something."

"It said, 'Who are you?'"

I nodded. "That's what I heard too." Then, unable to explain or stop myself, I leaned close to the speaker and said in a soft voice, "I'm Todd Crane. Who are you?"

"That doesn't transmit," Charles said, regaining his usual composure. "Nobody can hear you. Anyway, it was just a song."

I brushed him off and continued to listen. At first, there was only that endless noise with the strange pulsing cadence in the background, but then the soprano voice sang out, this time with crystal clarity: "Todd Crane. Number two million, nine-hundred ninety-three thousand, six-hundred one."

I was so startled; I nearly fell out of my chair. "They *can* hear us!" I gave Charles a slug in the arm that brought a grimace of pain to his face.

"But it isn't a transmitter. How can this be?" But he leaned close to the radio set and, after a long hesitation, said, "Hello, there. Can anybody hear me?"

Just noise for a time. Then, barely audible, the soprano voice sang, "Whoooo aaaare yooou?"

We exchanged amazed looks, and then he said, "Charles Fleming."

"Charles Fleming. Number three million, five-hundred eleven-thousand, four-hundred ninety-eight."

"That's unreal," I said, understanding for the first time in my life what it meant to be stunned. "Just unreal."

For another hour, we tried, unsuccessfully, to detect the mysterious voice again, or the Apollo astronauts, or anyone broadcasting from anywhere, but all our efforts went for naught. We heard no more human voices that evening; only the mysterious, endless noise, which even know-it-all Charles had begun to think must be the result of something other than ordinary atmospheric interference.

At my house, a radio was almost always playing. In the morning, at breakfast, we had the kitchen radio tuned to our local AM station, which played pop music, fluffy chat, and stats from the Vietnam War, which were usually to the effect that 400 Vietcong had been killed, with two U.S. servicemen slightly injured.

Mom didn't work outside our home, so she always listened to the morning talk shows before putting on the TV for her afternoon soap operas. When Dad came home from the office—he was an executive at the local DuPont nylon plant—the first thing he did was fix a martini and turn the radio on for the evening news, weather, and sports. After dinner, he spent most nights in his den working on his stamp collection, accompanied by easy listening and samba music, which he clearly enjoyed, usually until the wee hours.

As for me, I had my nice little transistor radio, which I oftentimes tucked under my pillow to listen to until I went to sleep. I had to keep the volume low, knowing Mom and

Dad would not approve, and my dad in disapproval mode could be a fearsome thing.

But it was comforting at night to listen to our local rock show—"Night Train," it was called—which always played my favorite songs, such as "Born to Be Wild" by Steppenwolf, "Crimson and Clover" by Tommy James & the Shondells, and "Aquarius/Let the Sun Shine In" by the Fifth Dimension. The DJ was a local guy named Paul Bluhm, whose endless jokes were so bad they made my father's lame sense of humor seem sophisticated.

That night, rather than music, the show was almost all talk about Apollo 11, which was okay by me because I felt the moon mission represented a door opening to the world of *2001: A Space Odyssey*—my favorite movie, which I had seen at least five times since its release the previous year.

But before I drifted off to sleep, an advertisement narrated by Paul Bluhm came on that sent my young heart into a frenzy. In his deepest, most dramatic voice, he said, "This Friday and Saturday nights at the Skyview Drive-In Theater: *Godzilla vs. the Thing* and *Gorgo*. The giant monsters are coming to Aiken Mill, and Godzilla is sure to win this one!"

Well, I knew otherwise because I had seen *Godzilla vs. the Thing* on television, but holy gods, *this* was big—much bigger than the moon landing. Charles and I were both rabid monster movie fans, and there was no way we could miss such a fantastic double bill. I figured I could talk my dad into taking us, as he was generally pretty sporting about drive-in movie outings.

Consumed by mounting, feverish excitement, I could barely refrain from leaping out of bed and flying down the hall to press him into chauffeuring service, but I knew that doing so would only end up dashing my hopes for the weekend.

It took almost an hour to calm down enough to begin drifting off to sleep. I was about to turn off the radio when I heard strange, rhythmic moaning and thumping sounds behind the song that was playing—"In the Year 2525" by Zager & Evans—sounds that distinctly brought to mind those that Charles and I had earlier heard over the short wave's speaker.

As before, the electronic noise took on the cadence of speech, and though I couldn't identify any words, I sensed that someone or *something* was attempting to communicate with me. My youthful intuition told me that our voyage to the moon had alerted an extraterrestrial consciousness, some non-human entity, which was now attempting to make contact with some of us here on Earth.

This both excited and terrified me, for I could not conceive of an encounter with alien intelligence that did not end badly. Rationally, I knew this idea came from a lifetime—short though it might have been—of living and breathing science fiction movies and comic books. The more sensible part of my brain insisted there *had* to be some other logical explanation, but at the same time, I could not escape an overwhelming rush of intense, icy fear.

After a few minutes, those strange noises faded away. The clanging of my heart did not.

My bedroom was in the basement, down a short hall from our family room; my parents' room was upstairs on the main floor, at the other end of the house, and Mom and Dad suddenly seemed very far away. My window faced the backyard and the woods that occupied several as-yet undeveloped lots.

I thought I heard something moving out there: a series of soft, almost inaudible shuffling and whirring sounds. At first, I attributed these to either an animal or my over-stimulated imagination, and I turned up the volume on my radio, hoping the music—now Bobby Vinton's "Blue on Blue"—would present a bulwark, if only psychological, against the unknown stirrings.

But then, above the music, a deep, wavering hum vibrated from the speaker. And there *was* something outside. It was scratching at the windowpanes, faint, tentative, but the sounds were perfectly synchronized with the humming on the radio.

Out of the speaker came a voice—a male voice, yet not altogether human. Artificial, I thought; a *reconstruction* of a human voice.

"Todd Crane. You are Todd Crane."

And from outside the window, a low, whispering voice—as inhuman as the one over the radio speaker— replied, "Number two million, nine-hundred ninety-three thousand, six-hundred one."

I didn't even realize until I was barreling up the stairs at top speed that I had launched myself from the bed, intent on reaching the perceived safety of my parents' bedroom. I flew around the upstairs corner in blind panic, only to slam into a solid object, one that twisted and tottered before falling backward in the darkness.

"God *damn*, son!"

"Oh!"

"What the hell's wrong with you?"

"Oh. Dad. Oh, Dad, I'm sorry!"

I stood at the hallway entrance, gaping into the void in disbelief, the profound terror I had felt downstairs transforming into an altogether different though no less chilling fear.

I might die right here and now.

"Can't even get up to get a drink without being bowled over by a goddamn out-of-control pint-sized half-witted reprobate."

Fluorescent light exploded in the hall, illuminating a lanky, bathrobed figure struggling to his feet, dark hair mussed, pale gray eyes squinting as my dad tried to make heads or tails of what was happening to him.

"What is going on?" came my mom's voice from the far end of the hall.

"It's just the miscreant, Brenda."

"It was an accident!"

Dad raised an eyebrow. "Personal emergency?"

"You have a bathroom downstairs," my mom said. "It works, right?"

"No!" I said. "I mean, that's not it. I heard something outside. And on the radio. Voices."

"You heard voices on the radio," Dad said. "I'm amazed."

"Dad." I felt myself barely holding back tears. When he realized it, his face abruptly changed.

"What is it? What's wrong, son?"

I knew then I couldn't tell him what had happened. It wasn't just that he wouldn't believe me; it was that, suddenly, I didn't believe me. I could *not* have heard the things I thought I had heard. It had been a waking dream. It must have been.

I shook my head in honest confusion. "I don't know, I guess I was dreaming. I was scared. It was terrible."

"Must have been a bad one."

My mom came down the hall toward me, her stern features softening a little. "Maybe you ought to move back up to your old room if you're scared down in the basement."

"No!" I blurted, knowing I could never give up my private little sanctuary, which I'd had to fight the world's most stubborn parents to win. "No, I'll be all right," I said. "Just a nightmare. That's all."

My dad gave me an earnest look. "You're at that age, I guess. I remember when I was about twelve, I used to have terrible night horrors. I remember dreaming your granddad turned into a bear and came after me to kill me." His eyes took on a far-off gaze. "That *was* scary."

"All right, then," Mom said. "Let's all get back to bed, shall we?"

I nodded and was about to turn around and face the darkened stairwell again when I paused. "Hey, Dad?"

"Yes?"

"Could you take Charles and me to see Godzilla at the drive-in tomorrow night?"

He gave me a quizzical look. "And miss *Star Trek*?"

"I guess so. It's a rerun, anyway."

My mom frowned. "You'd be up way past your normal bedtime."

Dad's eyes brightened. "If it'll make him tired enough to sleep all night, then I'm all for it. Sure, we can go to the drive-in."

Oh, my wonderful dad! My heart soared, my fears now all but forgotten. When I turned to make my way back to the dark downstairs, I dared the night to so much as make an errant noise at me. I *dared* it.

I loved going to the drive-in theater. In the summertime, Charles and I always attempted to persuade our folks to take us to several shows, preferably a monster movie double-feature. Mr. Fleming usually demurred, but my dad rarely seemed to mind. Charles and I would camp outside in our lawn chairs while Dad sat in our red '67 Mustang convertible and drank beer or bourbon and ginger ales, at least until the second show started, and then he stopped.

Tonight was a beautiful July evening, and the excitement of monster movies at the drive-in completely wiped out any lingering effects from the previous evening's trauma. The spectacle of Godzilla tromping on Japanese cities, burning up entire tank brigades, and battling the spectacular winged Mothra was almost more than my young heart could stand. I had seen the movie once on television, but here, on the big outdoor screen, it was pure magic.

The second feature, *Gorgo*, was a British giant monster movie, which I had seen once as a little kid. It was good, though not as impressive as Godzilla. Between the shows,

Charles went to the concession stand to grab us a couple of barbecue sandwiches, while I made my way around the back of the building to use the restroom.

I had to wait for a few older guys to do their business, but once I got to the urinal, I found myself alone in the dimly lit chamber, which reeked of ammonia and pine-scented sanitizer. "Night Train" was playing at low volume on a radio speaker mounted in a shadowed corner of the room, and Paul Bluhm was carrying on about Mangum-Berry Shoe Shop on Walnut Street, where you could not only outfit yourself with new shoes and get your old shoes repaired, but some lucky kid was going to win an authentic shoe phone, just like Maxwell Smart's on *Get Smart*. I could not say I was enthused.

I was about done and ready to flush when a crash of electronic noise drowned out Paul Bluhm and then lowered to a warbling, droning moan.

Just like the short wave.

The inhuman male voice I had heard before began to intone: "Three billion, six-hundred thirty-one million, one hundred thousand eight, six hundred twenty-nine. Mark. Three billion, six-hundred thirty-one million, one hundred thousand eight, six hundred twenty-nine. Mark." There was a long pause, and the speaker was silent. But then the voice said, "Todd Crane, number two million, nine-hundred ninety-three thousand, six-hundred one."

What the hell?

So I had not been dreaming last night!

I hurtled out of the bathroom, dodging a few figures outside, and careened pell-mell back toward the car, where I saw my dad standing outside, stretching his legs. I slowed down, trying to regain my motor and mental control, realizing nothing was actually after me. It was only sound. It couldn't hurt me. I couldn't explain it any more than I could leap to the moon, but the sound *could not hurt me.*

Out here, there was music over the speakers, lights from cars and the concession stand, people milling about. I saw Charles making his way toward the car with a couple of paper bags in his hand, and when he saw me, he gave me a thoughtful frown. Could he tell something had happened just by looking at me?

I resolved to say nothing to my dad. Charles and I had shared the initial weird experience, and the two of us needed to talk it all out.

Charles sat down, and I lowered myself to my seat, only to lurch and knock it over. As I righted it and sat down, I realized I was still shaking. I saw Dad mouth the word "klutz," but Charles's face was white—just as I reckoned mine was.

We both spoke at the same time.

"I heard something."

"I saw something."

"Wait." I gazed into his wide, bulging eyes. "You *saw* something?"

He nodded. "By the woods at the back of the parking lot. Shadows. *Big* shadows. With eyes."

"But there's cars back there."

"I don't think anybody else could see them." He shuddered. "But they were looking at me."

"I heard that voice over the radio. Numbers again. In the billions."

"Space coordinates?"

I shrugged. "I don't know. It said my name again."

A moment later, the speakers crackled, Angelo Lavagnino's score swelled, the King Brothers logo appeared before us, and the main title for *Gorgo* splashed across the screen. Charles handed me my barbecue sandwich, but even though it was one of my favorite things in the world to eat, I could barely choke it down.

Charles spent more time looking behind us than at the screen, though each time he shook his head to indicate there was nothing back there. Regardless, I knew we had been identified, singled out by something not human. Something not of this earth. A dull inner sense assured me that if it intended to harm us, it could have easily done so by now. So what the hell *did* it want?

That was the only time in my life I ever sat through a drive-in monster movie without seeing a frame of it.

As the theater lot began to clear out, we stowed our lawn chairs in the trunk and settled ourselves in the car, I in the front passenger seat, Charles in the back.

Fortunately, Dad didn't offer much conversation; I think he took our uncomfortable silence for sleepiness.

The drive-in was on the outskirts of town, on an old, wooded country road, and as we rode through the night with the top down—ordinarily an exhilarating experience—a sense of profound vulnerability struck me with the force of a thirty-pound sledge. I chanced a look back, then up. And if it were possible for one's hair to turn white on the spot, I know mine would have.

High above and just behind us, a vague blackness was blocking out a portion of the clear, starry sky. Not motionless but moving. *Pacing us.*

I thought I was seeing a pair of bright, jewel-like stars in the midst of the solid black mass, until I realized they were the eyes that Charles had seen. They were gold, green, silver, red, blue—shifting, glittering gems, strangely beautiful yet horrible. Monstrous. Alive. Aware.

I almost cried out. I so wanted to alert my dad, for surely he would see this thing and believe me, and understand the terror that had gripped Charles and me. But *something* held my tongue, and when I glanced back around, the thing had vanished, leaving only the stars and a pale quarter moon leering down at us from the deep midnight sky.

There were three men up there, now on their way back home. Had they awakened something that should never have been disturbed?

Dad reached forward, switched on the radio, and then Paul Bluhm was introducing Three Dog Night's "Heaven Is in Your Mind." It was such a great song that, for a fraction of a second, it filled me with warmth and hope, tugged my mind away from the fear within.

But then I saw, in the back seat, Charles was sitting rigid, staring straight ahead, his eyes never meeting mine. He was in shock.

This was it, then, I thought. Our doom had been spelled.

We were both dead, and we knew it.

The next night, Saturday, I went over to Charles's house to sleep over. It felt less lonely for both of us, for no one else could understand what we had experienced, even if they might believe us—which seemed beyond doubtful. Whatever it took, whatever it cost us, we had to do something, *anything*, if not to escape dire fate then to somehow learn what all these weird occurrences really meant. Our only method, our only option, was the short wave.

It was just after sunset when Charles turned on the set. His dad's upstairs den was an oasis of warm light, a place we ordinarily felt as secure as secure could be, but as the weird warbling sounds issued from the speaker, a dark, ominous atmosphere crept through the room, as if the sounds themselves cast shadows.

He rotated the tuner to random frequencies, knowing he could never reproduce what he had done when we picked up those strange voices. I didn't think it mattered, though—they seemed to find *us*, no matter where we happened to be.

"Who are you? What do you want?" Charles begged the radio set to answer him, knowing it didn't matter that the set could not actually transmit.

I worked up my nerve and said, "I am Todd Crane. Number two million, nine-hundred ninety-three thousand, six-hundred and one."

Something in the timbre of the electronic humming and moaning changed, and I heard the same background cadence I had heard that first night. Yes, there were voices back there, indecipherable, but plainly present.

Then that faux-female voice came through with startling clarity: "Three billion, six-hundred thirty-one million, one hundred thousand eight, seven hundred-sixty-one. Mark."

The deep male voice followed. "Insufficient numbers for sustainability."

The female again: "Three billion, six-hundred thirty-one million, one hundred thousand eight, seven hundred-sixty-four. Mark."

"Insufficient numbers."

"Three billion, six-hundred thirty-one million, one hundred thousand eight, seven hundred-sixty-nine. Mark."

"Insufficient numbers."

Unable to fathom the meaning of this exchange, Charles and I could only look at each other in fear and frustration. Then, with an errant glance back toward the window, I detected a vague shifting in the darkness beyond. A second later, a pair of huge glittering jewels, shifting from gold to green to amber to silver, appeared at the windowpane.

"Charles." I tapped him on the shoulder.

He turned around and saw the eyes peering into the room, directly at us. "Oh, Jesus. Oh, Jesus."

"Tell us what you want," I whispered. "We can't hurt you. Don't hurt us."

As those alien eyes burned into mine, I felt as if a blowtorch were searing some kind of pattern into my very brain cells. I believed this was to be my death. Whatever these all-but-invisible entities were, they had no use for us and so intended to destroy us.

In that moment, I felt a remarkable sense of peace. Of acceptance. Of not caring that I would never grow up to experience the things life might yet offer.

Because this wasn't horrible. I wasn't going to die screaming or as a coward. We had faced our fears and we had faced *them*. We had not defeated them; we *could* not defeat them. But somewhere inside, I felt proud.

No one else had ever died this way.

Around me, it was a cacophony of voices—deep and sonorous, soprano and lilting. All artificial. None human.

"One billion, six hundred thirty-one million—"

"Insufficient numbers."

"—one hundred thousand-eight—"

"Insufficient numbers."

"—seven hundred seventy-nine. Mark."

And then, a low, whispering voice that sounded unlike the others somehow drowned all else:

"We will return in fifty years."

Of course we didn't die. Not then.

And for half a century, I have lived with every moment of those few evenings in 1969 emblazoned more brilliantly in my memory than any other. And yet those incidents have always seemed unreal, as if they were part of a most vivid dream.

Nothing bad happened to me. I grew up, always remembering that time, yet never being affected by it. I followed in my father's footsteps and became a business executive in Research Triangle Park, North Carolina. I got married, had two kids. My dad died and then my mom.

It was life in the twentieth century and then the twenty-first. Somewhere in that long progression of days, the vague notion came to me that the events of July 1969 didn't affect me because the voices we had heard, the shadows we had seen, refused to *allow* me to be affected.

And even this barely registered in my mind until the night Charles called me.

He had never left Aiken Mill. After we graduated from high school and went our separate ways, we occasionally spoke on the phone, sent cards to each other at holidays, and invited each other to our kids' graduations, to which we both sent regrets. For many years, he had worked in cable television. That was about all I knew of him.

When he called, I understood why. I knew what was happening. And what was about to happen.

"They've come back," he said.

"You're at home?"

"Yes. Can you come?"

"I will."

Aiken Mill was a couple of hours' drive away. I knew in the time it took me to get there that Charles would be sending his wife, Ida, away, probably to her parents'. *Not for safety's sake but to say goodbye.*

He still lived in the house where he had grown up. Sure enough, when I arrived, the car—they only had one, I was told—was gone. I went inside and was overwhelmed by the scent of the place, the light and shadow effects in each room, the general quietness but for the mellow ticking of the grandfather clock in the living room; all of these things were exactly the same as when we were kids. I did notice a faint, charred odor, as if something had been left on the stove a bit too long.

"Charles?"

I went upstairs and found him. Or, rather, his clothes and the shriveled, white husk smoldering within them.

Since that last encounter in 1969, I had felt as if our strange visitors had left me with tiny, particle-like traces of their presence embedded in disparate corners of my mind. Over time, those traces had slowly converged but never fully *merged*.

Until now.

Charles and I had intercepted their transmissions, yes— not with our radios but with our *brains*. Whether it was a complete fluke, a matter of being in a certain place at a certain time, or our radio experiment in fact having drawn them to us in some way, I have no idea. However, my youthful supposition that the Apollo mission had drawn alien attention to our world was not entirely off the mark.

They came from somewhere else; not outer space but *other* space. They had been to our world before, millions of years past, when mountains in the south polar region rose almost beyond Earth's atmosphere and strange, non-human beings thrived amid gargantuan stone towers scattered across the vast plains of ice and snow. Beings that no longer existed, for these *others* had discovered them.

Subjugated and devoured them.

It is a ravenous race, and though their numbers are not prodigious, their hunger requires that they tend vast stockpiles of food. Fifty years ago, our ventures into space attracted their interest, lured them back to investigate a world they had left forever changed before our kind even existed.

They found us suitable for cultivating but too few in number to sustain them for perpetuity. However, over the last half century, humankind's numbers have burgeoned over the earth.

Our numbers are now sufficient.

Those who are too old or are unable to reproduce face the most immediate fear. Being the only living human, insofar as I know, aware of their intentions, if not the precise processes in store, perhaps there are some few souls I can help prepare for life—and death—under an entirely new planetary regime. I may be wrong, but I have come to believe their transmission of these facts to me was intentional, perhaps for the very thing I have here proposed.

For those unfortunate enough to escape the initial culling, it is clear to me that life as a human being on Earth will soon be different than it ever was before.

Very different.

Escalation

2016

Ten minutes later, his gin and tonic still hadn't arrived, which irritated him because Greg was talking, and when Greg talked, it was best to drink. The rotund woman behind the bar looked harried, though only a handful of patrons occupied the darkened lounge.

Soft jazz wafted out of the far corner, where a lone young man was playing a muted trumpet, which he held in one hand while working an electronic keyboard with the other. Pity the music didn't drown out Greg's voice.

"That detective is full of it," he was saying. "There's not a chance in hell they'll do a thing. Not unless her dead body turns up."

"It's not as if we can force them." Hager felt as frustrated as the other, but Greg's endless venting was sending his blood pressure into dangerous territory.

"Why in the hell did she come to that symposium? She's not *that* religious."

"I don't know, Greg. I guess it was just something she wanted to do."

Greg must have realized he had asked the same question no less than three times, for he fell silent long enough to take a breath.

The one-man band was playing "Tangerine," à la Herb Alpert—a mellow samba beat, wistful yet soothing. Hager saw a crystal gleam in Greg's eye and his irritation softened a little. He noticed a movement to his left: a very small Asian man in a tuxedo materializing from the shadows, tray in hand. From it, he placed two drinks on the table. "So sorry for delay," the little man said, his accent strong, his words slow and deliberate. "For your wait, I let you have a film on your television. On the house."

Greg raised a cynical eyebrow. "A film?"

The waiter placed a small paper rectangle on the table. "A movie. Order movie, enter code on receipt, and is yours for free."

Hager waved him away. "Not necessary. Really."

"No, is our pleasure." A smile split the narrow face like a gash opened by a carving knife. "Again, apologies for long wait."

Greg thrust his photo of Shelly in front of the waiter's eyes. "How about you? Have you seen this woman? She was staying in this hotel."

The smile did not waver as the eyes flicked toward the image. "A striking woman. But I think not."

"My sister," Greg said. "She went missing from here three days ago. She came for some church conference here. She checked into a room but never made it to the conference."

"Have not seen her."

Hager tapped the table with his forefinger. "If she stayed here, I guarantee you she would have visited this bar."

The waiter glanced at him, still smiling. "I am not full time here. You are husband?"

"Fiancé."

"*Ah, wakari masu.* I wish for you happiness."

"What's your name?"

"John."

Greg rolled his eyes, then leaned toward Hager. "Maybe we should offer 'John' some money to jog his memory."

"No, no." John held up a hand in protest. "Is not necessary. I can show photo to others here, if you please."

"We've shown it to the bartender, the manager, the concierge, the maître d', most of the housekeeping staff. For a 'striking' woman, she apparently escaped anyone's notice here."

"Is regrettable."

"Is that."

"May I ask her name, please?"

"Shelly Reid," Hager said. "From Midland, Michigan."

"I ask other staff for you. I will."

"Thank you, John."

The overdressed waiter offered them a curt bow and vanished into the shadows. Hager had just taken a long swallow of his drink when the portly barmaid approached carrying two glasses on a tray. When she saw the drinks John had delivered, one eyebrow arched up to meet her hairline.

"Where did you get those?"

"That Japanese fellow—John—brought them to us," Greg said.

"A Japanese fellow named John?"

"That's right."

"Mister, no Japanese fellow named John works here."

"Well, he brought us these. He was wearing a tuxedo." Greg pointed to the receipt with the movie code printed on it. "And he gave us this."

She glanced at the paper and shook her head. "I don't even know what that is. But I'm the only one on duty tonight, and I didn't make those drinks."

"Maybe he uses his real Japanese name here?"

She sent him a sharp "buddy, you're an idiot" glare. "I'm telling you no Japanese man works in the bar. At all." Then she turned and clomped away, carrying the two gin and tonics with her.

Greg's eyes turned to Hager. "Well, shit."

Hager turned the detective's card over in his hands as if, somewhere on it, God might have scrawled His counsel either for or against calling the number printed on it. Nope; nothing on it but the detective's name and contact information: Lt. Ingram Trotter, Chicago Police Department, 18th District.

Trotter *had* urged them to call if they learned anything about Shelly's disappearance. They might not have learned anything, but someone who didn't work for the hotel bringing them drinks out of the blue sure seemed suspect to him.

No, that was ridiculous. In a single Chicago city block, there were more strange, disturbed, or simply eccentric individuals than in the entire town of Midland. Encountering one of them in the same hotel from which Shelly had vanished hardly established a connection.

No doubt, Detective Trotter would dismiss the incident as irrelevant. As it was, his demeanor had suggested he would rather be fishing in the River Styx than spending a moment of his time investigating Shelly Reid's disappearance.

Cold-hearted bastard.

It was hard enough holding himself together without having to deal with a cop who showed so little regard for someone in need. Not to mention having to endure Shelly's temperamental older brother in the bargain.

It was uncanny how two siblings could be so different. Shelly was energetic, affable, and even-tempered, whereas her brother had to be the most irritable, highly strung human being he had ever known. Hager had met Shelly three years ago, when they both worked at Dow Chemical. Since then, he had interacted with Greg three, maybe four times. Those encounters had hardly been any more pleasant than this one, but now, the two of them had more in common than he cared to think about.

Their twelfth-story window overlooked North Wabash Avenue, now all but bereft of traffic and pedestrians. A light coating of snow covered the streets. He turned from the window and saw Greg propped on the far bed, fiddling with the television remote. He had tuned the TV to the pay-per-view channel, and a grimace of vexation had replaced his everyday grimace of disdain for the world.

"There's no list of movies here," he said. "It just tells me to input the code."

"So input the code. Maybe then it'll give you a list."

Greg shook his head. "That doesn't make any sense. What if I didn't have a code to begin with?"

"Then you'd be shit out of luck. You really want to watch a movie?"

"No, I just want to figure out what's up with this code."

"Only one way to find out."

Greg sighed and punched the digits on the remote. On the TV screen, the number 0023 appeared and then dissolved to a view of the Rochefort Hotel's gray stone façade. The date January 20 appeared above it.

"What does that mean?" Greg said. "That's three days ago."

"The day Shelly went missing."

The image changed to a field of pulsating blue blobs with flickering bright nuclei, and a low noise—something between a hum and a hiss—issued from the speakers. The shapes on the screen shifted and sharpened until they created a brand new image: a long corridor with doors visible on either side. A hotel hallway. The camera's eye drifted with an erratic loping motion toward the far end of the corridor, only to turn and proceed down a new passage.

The view settled at a particular door, and Hager caught a brief glimpse of its number—1205.

Their room.

It had been *her* room.

The door swung open, revealing only darkness. But within the black field, something took shape—a person— and as the disembodied eye pulled back, Hager could see her clearly.

Shelly. Dressed only in her nightgown, auburn hair disheveled, eyes distant and unfocused. She took no notice of the camera or videographer, who had to have been standing only a couple of feet in front of her.

"That waiter sure as hell *does* know something about her," Greg said, his eyes blazing at a thousand lumens.

A coil of grief, rage, and longing tightened around Hager's heart. This was proof positive the phony waiter had been party to Shelly's disappearance. And now he had targeted Hager and Greg—and somehow set up this video, presumably for their eyes only.

Shelly, now only a dark silhouette, ambled away from them, toward the far end of the gloomy hallway, her attention fixed on something they could not see. The camera followed several feet behind. At the end of the hallway, she turned right and stepped into a dark, rectangular portal, which closed immediately behind her.

An elevator.

Then a voice—low, whispery, of indeterminate gender—said, "Twenty-three."

The soundtrack went silent and the pay-per-view menu reappeared on the screen.

After a long silence, Greg said, "There's only one bank of elevators in this building, isn't there?"

"I think so."

"The one she got on was in the opposite direction."

"Service elevator, maybe?"

"I don't know. But I want to check it out."

"Yes, let's."

They headed out of the room and down the long corridor of lush crimson-and-cream patterned wallpaper, past a seemingly endless number of dark mahogany doors. As they neared the far end, Hager detected a faint charred odor in the air—a sharp, electrical smell.

Please tell me this damned building isn't going to burn down.

Finally, the hallway turned to the right, and there it was, a short distance ahead: an elevator.

The elevator.

As they approached it, they saw a numbered keypad on the wall to the right of the burnished copper doors.

"What do you think?" Greg asked.

"What was the code on your receipt?"

"Zero-zero-two-three." With a shrug, he punched 0-0-2-3 on the keypad.

The elevator doors slid open, revealing paneled walls the same dark color as the guestroom doors.

Greg stepped in. After hesitating a moment, Hager followed.

Inside, there were only two buttons—one for up and one for down. None for individual floors.

The doors slid shut. The car did not move.

"Well?" Greg said. "There's no buttons to open or close the door, either."

Hager glanced up, saw no floor indicator above the door. He pushed the up button.

With a smooth whir, the car slid into motion, and Hager felt his stomach lurch. They were going up, all right. And fast.

"How many floors are in this hotel?"

"I'm not sure. Twenty, maybe."

"Or maybe twenty-three?"

And on and on they went.

"Jesus," Greg said, "we're really moving."

The car kept going, and Hager felt his knees going wobbly.

"How the hell high can this thing go?"

"I've been to the top of the Sears Tower, the Empire State Building, Peachtree Plaza. They're nothing like this."

"We can't be moving as fast as it feels."

"No," Greg said, his eyes wide behind his thick glasses. "But we are. We *are.*"

"This is fucked up."

The car kept going.

There was no handrail or any other surface to hold on to, and Hager found himself pressed against the wall, his hands desperate to grab on to something, *anything.*

After some time, he sensed a subtle change in the car's momentum, and he heard a low, deepening rumble, no doubt the elevator's drive mechanism. His throat was so dry he doubted he could speak.

The car jerked to a stop and the doors slid open. Before them, a shadowy corridor with no doors led into almost total darkness. Through a tinny ringing in his ears, he could hear what sounded like the throb of distant music.

Greg stumbled out first. Hager followed, his head whirling, his feet seeming to hover above the floor.

"That's got to be some kind of sensory illusion," Greg said. "We couldn't have gone as high as it felt like we did."

"We'd be in the stratosphere."

With every step he took Hager felt as if gravity was losing its hold on him. After walking a short distance, Hager pointed to a turn ahead. "That should go to the left, but it doesn't. How can it do that?"

"The floors must not be laid out the same."

"I have an idea." Hager reached into his back pocket for his phone and opened the GPS map, which would indicate their approximate location inside the building. The app thought for a few moments but then closed down. He tried again, with the same result. "How about you?" he asked.

Greg already had his phone in hand. "The same," he said with a deep sigh.

The faint music beckoned them. They continued down the hallway, turned right where they should have turned left, and came to a closed, solid wooden door. The music emanated from the other side—a slow, heavy bass beat behind an ethereal, sorrowful melody played by woodwinds and strings.

Or an electronic reproduction of those instruments. The musician from the downstairs bar?

Hager tried the handle and found it unlocked. He shoved the door open and stepped through, with Greg close on his heels.

A wave of sound crashed over him, chilling and soul-wrenching. The intensity of the music nearly drove him to his knees, the sweet, wistful tones gripping his heart and squeezing. How could something so mellow and lyrical— so haunting—be so driving, so *potent*?

He recognized the tune: "The Shadow of Your Smile."

He felt Greg's hand clutch his shoulder. "What the hell is this?" His voice came from many miles away.

They stood inside a huge ballroom, lit with shifting, lurid hues of red, gold, and blue. There must have been a hundred people dancing—at least he *thought* they were dancing. Somehow, they were jumping, spinning, *jitterbugging*, moving in bizarre slow-motion, keeping perfect time with the music. There were men and women of all ages, some dressed in tuxedos and evening gowns, others in wholly inappropriate tourist attire—Hawaiian shirts, Bermuda shorts, flip-flops—and some in beggars' rags.

"Your drinks, gentlemen."

Hager turned and saw the false waiter, "John," standing next to him, bearing a tray with two glasses.

"Gin and tonics for you."

"What's going on here? Who the hell are you?"

"I am John, your host." He picked up one of the glasses and held it out to Hager. "Your drink, sir."

Hager batted the glass out of his hand. It went tumbling through the air, the contents spraying the nearest dancers, who took no notice. The glass shattered on the copper-colored tile floor, the sparkling fragments splashing into invisibility. "I asked you a question."

A sudden, high-pitched ringing in his ears drowned out the music. A moment later, Greg's voice broke through the cacophony. "Bill."

He looked at Greg, who was pointing into the crowd of dancers.

Pointing at Shelly.

She was dancing with a man he knew. A man from Midland, a young man, probably ten years her junior. Hager recognized him from the church she went to.

Darby. That was his name. Darby Ashworth, if he remembered right.

They were both completely naked.

"Oh—oh, Jesus." Greg's voice broke. "What the hell is she doing?"

"This isn't possible," Hager whispered. He took a few steps forward, willing Shelly's eyes to turn toward his.

Insanity, all of this. Shelly loved him, he knew it, and he loved her. They trusted each other; they had *always* trusted each other. She *could not* have come for some depraved purpose to this nightmarish, unreal place.

She looked radiant in her nakedness, lithe, younger than her thirty-six years, her flowing auburn hair brilliant as fire under the streamers of light from above. Her eyes were closed as she leaped and whirled in defiance of gravity, so she did not see him. He found himself aroused by this unnatural manifestation of her beauty, and despite the ghastliness about it all, he loved her, desired her, now more than ever.

The young man, Darby, moved in perfect sync with her, one hand holding hers as she spun, shimmied, and swirled in bizarre slow motion.

"This is obscene," Greg said, his eyes blazing behind his thick glasses.

"Yes," Hager said. "Obscene."

"Your drink, sir." Once again, John was standing there, smiling, holding out a new glass of gin.

This time Hager took it. With the first sip—it was delicious—he felt the music starting to wend its way into his core, enticing him to move. To *dance.*

"No," he said, drawing a deep breath and wrenching back control of his muscles. "No, I won't."

John turned to Greg, his wide shark's mouth smiling. "Sir, a drink for you."

"Get away from me," Greg said, his voice a canine growl.

Hager had never seen Greg so distraught, so visibly near emotional collapse. Jewels of sweat beaded his brow, and the hair on the back of his neck looked like sharp black quills. His fingers clenched and unclenched in time with the music.

Hager took another sip of his gin and tonic, and a warm sense of well-being swelled in his body. It was false, he knew, yet somewhere inside he felt that if he denied himself this balm, his reactions would mirror Greg's, and he needed to maintain control. He needed to reach Shelly, bring her back to reality, and get the hell out of this madhouse before it swallowed them.

When he looked around, John had vanished. Greg's lips arched in a wolf-like snarl.

"Easy," Hager said, reaching out to clasp his shoulder. "I don't know what's happening, but we've got to stay calm. Neither of us can lose it now. All right?"

"That's my sister," Greg said, his voice barely audible.

At last, Shelly had opened her eyes. She now appeared cognizant of her surroundings. Her gaze took in the dancers closest to her, swept outward, brushed Hager, and then moved on. Swung back to him. At first she registered only confusion. Then recognition.

Her mouth formed his name: "Bill."

Her eyes flicked toward Greg, betrayed no emotion whatsoever, and then returned to Hager.

She smiled at him. A very wrong, very crooked, very *mocking* smile.

She turned to her partner, took the young man in an embrace of ardent desire, and pressed her lips against his, her hands stroking and exploring his body like pale, roving spiders. His dark eyes burned into hers. One of his hands slid down her abdomen, over her hips, and into the tight, shadowy space between their bodies, out of sight. Her lips released his, and she craned her head back to breathe an unheard moan of pleasure.

"This is all a lie!" Greg tore his glasses from his face and threw them somewhere into the mass of dancers.

Hager wanted to go to her, to tear her away from the young predator devouring her with every part of his body. He felt hemmed in by walls of ice, his arms and legs frozen. His palpitating heart was going to burst.

John. He had put something in the gin. That was the only explanation.

He felt Greg's hand on his arm, and then a sharp jerk as Greg spun his body to face his glaring eyes.

"Why don't you stop her? She's your fiancée, for God's sake. *Do something!*"

"I can't move."

"What?"

Hager shook his head. Now he couldn't even breathe.

He was going to die here, inept, helpless. Impotent.

"If you don't, I will!"

Shelly's head angled toward him for just a moment. Her eyes sparkled with derision.

A shadow materialized before them, moved toward Greg. Hager saw only a wide, smiling shark's mouth.

John.

"I have your order, sir."

John lifted a long dagger, bowed his head, and presented it to Greg as if it were a sacred object. Greg stared at it, mouth agape, before finally taking it in his right hand. He held it up to Hager's eyes.

"Do you want this?"

Hager shook his head.

John gave them a curt bow. "Is on the house."

Then he was gone.

Without a word, Greg strode toward his sister and the young man holding her, both still in the throes of ecstasy, oblivious to his approach. The colored lights shifted in an endless cycle, turning the dancers' bodies electric blue, molten gold, liquid crimson. The blade in Greg's hand gleamed silver.

At last Darby Ashworth opened his eyes and registered Greg's presence. He must have seen the dagger, Hager thought, but he smiled. The naked little bastard just *smiled*.

With his free hand, Greg grabbed Darby's shoulder and tore him away from his sister. Unable to move, assist, or intervene, Hager waited for Greg to attack the younger man.

He turned on Shelly.

"No, Greg, no!" Hager's inner voice cried out but his mouth uttered no word.

Shelly did not look at her brother but swiveled her head toward Hager, her eyes still mocking, now as if to deride his inaction. When Greg thrust the dagger forward, penetrating her abdomen just below the sternum, she flinched only a little.

Her eyes showed mild curiosity, as if she had suffered a bee sting. But when he gathered himself and forced the blade upward, her eyes went wide, as if only then realizing what was happening. Her lips formed an O, and her head lolled backward, her expression no longer scornful but horrified.

Greg withdrew the glistening red blade.

Hager felt a scream explode from his lungs, but the hammering percussion and warbling woodwinds swallowed it. He begged his legs to propel him forward, but they had become columns of stone.

She *couldn't* be dying, not Shelly. It didn't matter what she had done, he loved her, he could still make things right, it was *not too late, not too late, not too late.*

Her body slumped to the floor, and Darby Ashworth laughed. Hager heard it: a low gust of dark, heartless amusement. Then the young man turned, and with quick, catlike movements, vanished into the dancing crowd.

Greg looked down at his sister, who lay motionless at his feet. Beneath her, a pool of glossy red expanded across the gleaming copper floor. He dropped the blood-drenched dagger next to her, his face pale, his eyes no longer full of fury.

He stepped away from the lovely corpse and began to shuffle back toward Hager, his face now a mask of sorrow, his shoulders slumped as if in defeat. As he drew nearer, though, his eyes met Hager's, and dark energy again seemed to fill his body. He strode forward until they stood face to face.

"I loved her," Hager said, his voice now audible above the softening music. "Didn't you?"

Greg's eyes flared, his jaw dropped, and a rush of noxious breath swept over Hager like a torrid wind. And Greg screamed—a rising banshee wail, driving into Hager's eardrums like steel spikes.

Hager opened his mouth and screamed back. All the pain of his lifetime, every second of misery he had ever suffered came gushing forth, his voice blending in hellish harmony with Greg's, overwhelming the music and every other sound in the huge, bustling ballroom.

The multicolored lights flashed and strobed.

The dancers danced on.

"Do you understand your rights?"

"What?"

"Mr. Hager, do you understand what I'm telling you?"

Things began to take shape in the blinding void before him. He was in a small room lit by harsh white fluorescents, the walls gray and featureless but for a single door and a wide mirror on the wall opposite him. There were two other people in the room—a man and a woman.

The man's face floated a few feet from his. A black man with close-cropped, graying hair; narrow eyes; a cold, disapproving scowl.

Detective Trotter.

He didn't recognize the woman. Short brown hair; large aqua eyes; pursed, pale red lips. Her arms were crossed, her expression only marginally warmer than Detective Trotter's.

"What am I doing here?"

"You don't know where you are?"

"No, but I know what happened to her."

"Your fiancée? Shelly Reid?"

"She's dead. He killed her."

"He killed her?"

"Stabbed her. Stabbed her to death."

As if through a brilliant, faceted crystal, he saw the man and woman shoot each other questioning looks.

She spoke, her voice flat and nasal. "You said he killed her."

Hager nodded. "Her brother, Greg. He stabbed her."

She raised an eyebrow. "Shelly Reid's brother, Greg. *He* killed your fiancée?"

Trotter leaned close to him. "Greg Reid?"

"Yes. Sir."

"Can you tell me where this happened?"

"A ballroom. In the Rochefort Hotel. Where we were staying." His whirling mind began to slow a little. He could breathe a little easier. But he didn't know how he had gotten here—wherever *here* was.

He had some vague recollection of dancers; of music; of brilliant, shifting colors.

Of going up and up and up. Farther than he had ever gone before.

He and Greg had watched a video. Of Shelly, walking down a long corridor to an elevator. They had followed her footsteps, which led them to that impossible ballroom.

"For God's sake, Lieutenant, you know the place, you investigated." He gripped the edge of the table before him. "Look, I think I was drugged. I'm having a hard time here."

"You want a glass of water?"

"Please."

Trotter rose from his seat and went to a far corner of the room, to a table with a pitcher of water and some Styrofoam cups.

The woman touched his hand. "Mr. Hager. Would you describe the man who killed your fiancée, please?"

"He's her brother. He's thirty-nine, forty, maybe—a couple of years younger than me. Dark hair, glasses. For God's sake, he's her brother. You can look him up. I don't know where he is, where he went—afterward."

Detective Trotter returned to the table and set the cup of water in front of him. "Mr. Hager, Shelly Reid didn't have a brother."

Hager nearly exploded into laughter. "Don't be an asshole, Detective. I'm really not up for that right now."

"You seem to think we're not serious," the woman said.

"What's your name?"

"I'm Lieutenant Stanton. Remember?"

"No. But I suppose you're also going to tell me that Shelly didn't have a brother. I don't know why you're doing this, but I think I'd rather see a doctor than you two. No, I don't know where I am, or how I got here, and I think I should."

Shelly was laughing at him.

"Do you understand your rights? You need to answer yes or no."

"I don't understand shit right now, Detective Trotter, and thank you very much."

"I'll take that as a 'no,'" Trotter said.

"Now, look here. Greg Reid is Shelly's older brother. He's a manager at the Wolverine Bank in Midland, Michigan. Shelly and I have been engaged for a year, and we're going to be married in April. I asked him if he wanted to be a groomsman, and he said no because he's basically an asshole. And he, Detective Trotter, Lieutenant Stanton, *he* killed my fiancée, his sister. He stabbed her with a fucking knife."

She was kissing Darby Ashworth.

The two of them were dancing naked.

He felt hot tears brimming in his eyes. She wasn't really gone, was she? She *couldn't* be gone.

Greg. Greg was the one who should die.

Every couple had problems. He and Shelly could have made it right again.

He did love her so.

Detective Trotter glowered at him. "You don't remember going to the Rochefort Hotel, meeting Shelly Reid and the man she was with at a private party, and stabbing her to death in front of a hundred witnesses?"

Hager gaped at him. "You're no goddamn cop. You're a sadistic bastard. Why are you doing this? Why the blue fuck are you doing this?"

Trotter and Stanton exchanged glances and stood up. "If you'll excuse us," Stanton said, "we'll be back in a few minutes."

They went out through the door and pulled it partially shut, though he could still hear them speaking to each other.

"I think he believes what he's saying."

"He's either a hell of a liar or he's got issues like nobody I've ever seen."

"My god, that poor woman. What he did to her."

"Crimes of passion, don't you know."

Wait, what? They actually thought he killed Shelly?

"Are you mad?" he said to the door. "I loved her. *I LOVED HER.*"

The two detectives must have stepped away, for he could hear nothing further. He realized the mirror in the wall was two-way glass. Someone he could not see might yet be watching him from the other side. What kind of monsters would do this to him? Jesus God, thinking *he* could have killed the only woman he had ever loved?

Well, who would think that a young woman's own brother would stab her to death?

Someone—something—was moving beyond the glass. If he focused his eyes just right, he could detect shapes just beyond his own reflection. Yes, someone was watching him. Just on the other side of that dark, reflective surface.

Lord, his face looked haggard and wan. But right now, he didn't care what he looked like.

An acrid stench wafted to his nostrils. A sharp, electrical smell. Jesus, he was trapped in this room.

Please tell me this place isn't about to burn down.

Something pale was forming in the glass, right next to his face, as if it were pressing against his cheek, intimately, insidiously.

"Who are you?" he whispered.

He saw a narrow, bony face, framed with black hair, dark, almond-shaped eyes glaring back at him. A wide gash of a mouth, like a shark's.

Somewhere in the distance, a voice whispered, "Twenty-three."

"Why do you go to that church?" Hager asked. "I mean, they're really not about God and Jesus, are they? Not like your traditional church."

Shelly laughed, a light, tinkling sound. "Oh, come on. You've always hated traditional services."

"I don't hate them. They just bore me."

"I think you should go to church with me."

"No."

"You're incorrigible."

"You're hot."

"I'm trying to be serious here."

"I'm serious, you're hot."

"Well, you're cute."

"That's all?"

"That's all."

"So what's this conference in Chicago?"

"It's a symposium—'The Role of Christianity in a Post-Modern Society.' Lots of different denominations show up. Catholics, Protestants, conservatives, liberals, you name it. It's not just lectures. They have panel discussions, interactive stuff. And there's music, refreshments, you know—things that would appeal to your hedonistic nature. You'd probably enjoy it."

"No, I would not."

"Atheists and agnostics are welcome. I think you qualify."

"I'd just go the bar and drink, and I'd never see you."

"Speaking of. Here you go." She handed him a gin and tonic and gave him a light peck on the cheek. He slipped an arm around her shoulder and allowed his hand to move down her back toward the alluring curve of her ass. Her nearness, the comfortable evening breeze, and the smoky aroma of steaks cooking on the grill invigorated his senses. He didn't recall having felt this good in a long, long time. It didn't get any better than autumn in Midland. When the two of them got married, there would be many nights like this, not just weekends.

He hated she was going away next weekend because they would have to miss *this*.

"How many of you are going to this thing?"

"There were four of us—but Jan Colter and Andy Horne can't make it, so it's just Darby Ashworth and me."

"He's gay right?"

She laughed. "You know, our church recognizes gay marriage. Don't you think that's a positive thing?"

"Is he married?"

"No."

"You sure he's gay?"

"What difference does it make? Wait, you're not jealous, are you?"

"Why would I be jealous?"

"You mean you're not jealous? How disappointing."

"I don't know why I put up with you."

"Because you love me."

"Intensely."

He lifted the cover of the Weber grill and poked the ribeye steaks with his fork. "Two minutes."

"I'll get the salad out of the fridge."

With a tantalizing little sashay, she disappeared through the screen door to the kitchen.

Damn—something smelled weird. Smoky, but not like the smoldering charcoal. Something electrical.

After a moment, it faded. He breathed a little sigh of relief. The last thing he needed was some problem with the house, which he'd only lived in for three months. He and Shelly had picked out the place together, and he couldn't wait until she joined him here, in just a few months.

He heard a wistful tune playing, and he realized it was Shelly's phone going off. Her ringtone was a techno version of "The Shadow of Your Smile."

He glanced toward the kitchen door. She was holding the phone to her ear, an angelic smile on her face. "Oh, hi, Darby," she said. "Yes, I'm looking forward to it."

"'Oh, hi, Darby,'" he muttered to himself. Every now and then, he had to admit that her friendliness with, well, just about every male of the species jabbed at his ego, even if just a little bit. Nothing to worry about, he knew. Just about everyone in Midland knew that Darby Ashworth had as much interest in women as Hager had in pygmy goats.

Damn, there was that smell again.

He took a few steps down the driveway and found the odor seemed stronger away from the house. A good thing, he supposed, but it was strong, and very unpleasant.

A movement at the corner of his eye caught his attention, and when he looked around, he felt a sharp stab of surprise and—something else—something *awful*, though he couldn't identify the sensation. A kind of dark familiarity, a sense that nothing in the world was actually all right.

And he didn't know why, because, really, the sight was pretty fucking funny.

It was a little Asian man wearing a tuxedo, out in the middle of the cul-de-sac—probably one of the new people who had moved in recently—and he was dancing.

Jitterbugging. All by himself.

The little man noticed him and raised a hand in greeting.

In his head, Hager heard weird, electronic music with a heavy beat. Probably just some mental echo of the tune from Shelly's phone.

The Asian man danced closer to him, and he felt his heart sink. He had no interest in interacting with a man who might be just a little deranged.

"Good evening, sir," the man said. "My name is John."

Sure thing, "John."

"Bill," Hager said. "You live around here?"

"Just down the way. Number twenty-three."

"You seem very happy."

"I have much to look forward to."

"So do I."

"Yes," John said, his wide mouth opening in quite the grotesque smile. The little bastard's face resembled nothing so much as a shark. "I know you do."

All right, everything about this exchange was making Hager feel uncomfortable, and it was best ended right now.

"Well, John, I hope you stay this happy for the rest of your evening."

"Thank you, sir. I will see you again soon."

Hager turned away and started back up the driveway.

I hope not. I so hope not.

In the kitchen, Shelly was still on the phone, and she was giggling.

Pons Devana

2018

The governor leaned close and glared at Quintus Marcius, his unblinking blue eyes brighter than sapphires in the noonday sun. "I need to know what Titus Fabius is doing in Pons Devana. Do you understand me?"

"Clearly, Consul." Marcius liked Septimus Nerva Laurentius about as much as he liked the adders that lurked in the wildlands of Britannia, and he actually welcomed the prospect of leaving the relative comfort of Viroconium for Pons Devana, some twenty leagues to the west.

"You know Titus Fabius well, do you not?"

"He was centurion before me in Valeria Victrix. But I have not seen him in over fifteen years—not since Boudicca's rebellion."

Consul Laurentius clasped his hands behind his back and scowled. "As provincial prefect, Titus Fabius reports to me. Contacts from him have been sporadic at best, and confounding, to say the least. He has dismissed his staff. Two days ago, my agent returned from Pons Devana claiming that Fabius refused to see him. I believe Fabius has established a rule there that is not for the glory of Rome or Emperor Vespasian, but for himself." The blue eyes caught the sun's rays and froze them. "This will not do."

"I understand, Consul."

"I can spare you only a small detachment. But you *will* see him, Quintus Marcius, and report to me everything you learn. I expect reliable information so I may determine the appropriate action. You and two men will leave tomorrow at dawn."

"Yes, Consul."

"Questions?"

Marcius gave the governor an earnest look. "Do you believe Titus Fabius has gone mad?"

The governor sighed, his stern countenance softening. "It is a lonely and curious country there, Marcius. I have passed through it but once, and I have no desire to return."

"He has been there for some time. Perhaps it has affected him adversely."

"That is for you to determine. Whatever his circumstances, a provincial prefect must not be given to mad whims."

"I agree, Consul. I will not disappoint you."

"No, Marcius. You will not."

A lonely and curious country indeed.

Marcius and his two men had ridden out of Viroconium early the previous morning, the first dozen or so miles through civilized lands but increasingly into wilder and more desolate surroundings. Still, the wide, well-maintained road they traveled would have been no more than a goat path if not for the Legionaries' engineering expertise.

The road had wound up, down, and around rolling, grassy hills; along tranquil, gurgling streams; and now, through dark stands of towering trees among which no wildlife appeared to dwell. Apart from the clip-clopping of the horses' hooves and the low moaning of a restless, intermittent breeze, the chilly spring air carried no other sound, not even a distant, lonely bird call or the rustle and scurry of the red squirrels so ubiquitous in other regions.

His two companions, typical of Valeria Victrix cavalrymen, rode in solemn silence, as alert as greyhounds on the hunt. Lucius Horatius, the senior of the two, stout and bristling with thick brown hair, resembled nothing so much as a bear atop his steed, his aspect powerful if ungainly. However, while less agile than his smaller counterpart, in a conflict, he could shock an enemy with the speed and ferocity of his attack, and his first strike with sword, lance, or fist usually ended it.

The other cavalryman, Ennius Junius, appeared small and mousy in comparison, but he was the best archer in the century, and he could handle a blade with such dexterity that an opponent would often be dead before his first glimpse of steel.

The two accompanied him more as bodyguards than enforcers. They had strict orders not to interfere once Marcius began his parley with Titus Fabius unless circumstances dictated it, and he could scarcely imagine a more unlikely situation. In those long-ago years, he and Fabius had been closer than brothers, and no matter the events in the interim, only madness beyond madness might spur his old comrade to attempt violence against him.

Just past midday, the trees thinned, and in the distance, beyond an arched stone bridge—Roman-built—Marcius could see a few mud and thatch structures nestled at the edge of a forest even denser and more expansive than the one they had passed through. This had to be Pons Devana, the village Titus Fabius had claimed as his keep in the region known locally as Lloigola.

Officially, Fabius had intended to transform the remote, lonely province into a bustling commercial hub, yet even Marcius recognized the absurdity of such an aspiration.

The nearest well-traveled road lay a dozen miles to the east, and the population of the region, while not overtly hostile, expressed no appreciation for Rome's progressive influence.

"Centurion." Ennius Junius pointed to a location to their right, where tall, narrow trees rose like spear-wielding sentries against a cerulean sky. "I saw a strange light."

Marcius drew his Libyan stallion to a halt and peered in the direction Junius indicated. Beyond the palisade of trees, numerous arrays of intricate stone cairns rose from a field of ragged, dun-tinged grass. Some of the constructs appeared so precarious a mere breeze might topple them. At the farthest end of the field, around the base of a circular hillock, a dozen large, asymmetrical panels, evidently made of metal, appeared at regular intervals.

Mausoleums.

"Burial ground," Horatius said. "Not Roman."

"So it appears." He glanced at Junius. "This light. Where from?"

The young soldier's eyes scanned the necropolis. "I don't see it now. It was odd—first bright blue and then amber, it seemed. Down by those crypts."

"Sunlight reflecting on stone or metal."

"No. More like lightning, only not in the sky. And not so much a flash as a brief waxing and waning."

Marcius turned to Lucius Horatius. "Stay here. Hold anyone who passes on the road until I return. Junius, with me."

He spurred his horse forward and rode into the expanse of grass and stone, Junius close behind. These cairns, he saw, were remarkable in design. Large, jagged blocks balanced atop smaller, rounded stones, defying the earth's draw. Rows of sharp-tipped obelisks pointed like talon-tipped fingers to the sun. Towering spirals of smooth, flat stones sprang from arid ground like the questing tentacles of unfathomable sea-beasts.

Before the semicircle of sealed tombs, Marcius dismounted. To Junius, he said, "The light came from here?"

"Here or very nearby."

The strange, asymmetrical doors, each twice the height of a man, bore unique, serpentine handles and fit snuggly into frames sculpted from the living rock of the hillside. He took hold of an ornate handle and tugged. The door did not budge.

Then, off to his left, a flare of brilliant light caught his notice, but by the time his eyes found their focus, all trace of it was gone, and his scan of the surroundings revealed no discernible source.

But no. Some hundred yards away, one of the tomb doors hung partially open and was slowly swinging shut. A distant *thump-clack* resounded as it came to rest in its frame.

Just beyond the door, a dark figure, which had not been there moments before, was ambling away from them, seemingly unaware of their presence.

"You!" Marcius called. "Halt!"

He kicked his steed, and the horse bolted into a gallop, crossing the intervening space in a matter of seconds. He circled about and reined the stallion to a halt in front of the tall figure, who wore the most peculiar suit of armor he had ever seen, in battle or otherwise.

An outfit of leather and iron, its chest plate adorned with a spiraling pattern so intricate his eyes could not follow its contours. From the stranger's waist, long, broad tassets extended like a skirt over his legs, and his tall leather boots were braced with crisscrossing bands of iron.

The man wore a grotesque helmet bearing curling metal horns that resembled a ram's, and the visor covering the man's eyes appeared to be made of some faceted, blood-red crystal, like a cut ruby, glowing as if lit by fire from within.

"Identify yourself!"

The figure's gloved hands rose, unfastened a clasp at the back of his neck, and lifted the helmet to reveal a weathered, wrinkled face with wide, amber-brown eyes; a narrow, slightly bent hawk nose; and thin lips drawn into a derisive sneer. Thin, gold-gray hair swept back in waves from his prominent forehead. His lips spread in a wry smile, and Marcius saw that the sneer came from a row of oversized, crooked teeth, with incisors that protruded almost like a rat's. A homely, yet somehow stately countenance.

A familiar yet *changed* countenance.

"Titus. You *are* Titus Antonius Fabius."

"And you are Quintus Festus Marcius."

"I am."

"My old *optio*, now a centurion. So many years since our paths have crossed. I welcome you to the land of Lloigola."

With a sharp clopping of hooves, Ennius Junius's horse appeared behind Fabius. The young rider brandished his sword, but Marcius waved for him to stand down. To Fabius, he said, "You appear dressed for battle. Is there some skirmish in progress I should know about?"

"Strictly ceremonial, I assure you. An entombment."

"Are you alone?"

"For the moment."

Marcius pointed to the necropolis. "All this is peculiar to me. As is your remarkable armor. It is not proper Roman attire."

Fabius's chuckle sounded like a low, canine growl. "There is much in this place that is beyond your experience, Marcius. To establish and maintain the peace, I have had to take extraordinary measures, many of which might fly in the face of convention. But I assure you, what I have done here is for the sake of Rome."

"You turned away the consul's agent."

"Ah, the consul. Septimus Nerva Laurentius is but one of Caesar's nut-gathering squirrels who lacks both understanding and initiative." Fabius smiled, revealing again his malformed teeth. "Your expression implies agreement."

"My feelings are irrelevant. In this country, Septimus Laurentius speaks for Rome."

Fabius said nothing more, but his glare intensified, and Marcius felt a sudden deepening of the silence around them, as if the air itself had been siphoned away. Then he perceived a faint vibration, first in his feet, then in every nerve in his body, until the vibration became a sound: a deep, multilayered bass tone, like an ensemble of gigantic horns blowing a long, extended note, which rose louder and louder, as if each trumpeter possessed infinite lung capacity.

The sound swirled around him like a cyclone, yet there was no source, no living soul apart from the three Romans anywhere within view.

The tombs.

Yes, the sound *was* reverberating from those sealed tombs, as if the metal doors themselves were somehow producing or amplifying it. Marcius looked to his former centurion, but even Fabius appeared shaken by the phenomenon.

At length, the booming sound quieted, and silence again settled over the necropolis.

Fabius's former assurance reasserted itself. "Now, Marcius. Gather your men and follow me, that I may introduce you to Pons Devana. Come."

By early evening, a thick mist had begun to spread over the landscape, its ghostly fingers curling and questing among the trees and hovels. Pungent smells of smoke and cooking meat wafted through the village, dulling an almost tangible malevolence that pervaded the atmosphere. Occasional low voices and subtle sounds of movement infused some semblance of life into the still silent forest.

Fabius had offered a small bunkhouse to Marcius's two companions where they might be comfortable while he led Marcius through the village. Pons Devana, he found, was a squalid cluster of teetering hovels and ramshackle barns, its streets little more than rutted mud paths, all twisting and turning to form a bizarre, complex maze.

Clearly, the Roman engineers had halted their work at the village borders, for these streets had been designed by drunkards or lunatics. The few villagers he saw appeared wary or furtive, most lurking in the shadows, unwilling to make eye contact with him. He could scarcely believe Fabius would have settled in this place, much less entertained notions of developing it into a commercial center.

Fabius's villa, situated in a glade at the edge of the forest, comprised a house that in other provinces would be considered modest, though it was built of stone and brick, with a tile roof and columned terrace, a smaller outbuilding for staff and servants, and a stable that accommodated a half-dozen horses. Fabius escorted Marcius through a candlelit atrium to his office, where a low fire provided some small illumination and warmth.

With a metal striker, Fabius lit an oil lamp that turned the pale plaster walls flickering gold. He sat down at a disproportionately large writing desk and gestured for Marcius to sit across from him.

"Something strange abides in this land, Quintus." The chamber's high, domed ceiling amplified Fabius's low voice so that it rang sharply. "It creates. It builds. This place—" he made a sweeping gesture—"is not the work of man. Oh, the wood, the brick, the stone, men have placed these things, but there's something more here. Underneath them. *Beyond* them."

"You should know me well enough to understand that I do not appreciate riddles."

"So you don't." Fabius's wide eyes appeared dark liquid pools in the lambent light. His face, so familiar but so *changed*, bore shadows of deep concern. No, it was something else. *Fear?* "I realize that you, an outsider—a civilized man—must think I have become unhinged. I assure you, I have not. Over time, I have gained what I can only call *sight*."

"Perhaps it is fair to say you see things differently than I do."

"Very diplomatic. You don't need to be diplomatic."

Marcius leaned toward him. "What did we hear, Titus? Out there, in your boneyard. What was that sound?"

The glow on Fabius's face dimmed. "That is a question, isn't it? Quintus, what you heard was something that came from within a dream."

"A dream." Marcius drew a deep breath to help quell his rising impatience. "Titus, you and I both heard the sound. So did Horatius and Junius. None of us were asleep and dreaming."

"I did not say *we* were dreaming."

"Yet more riddles."

Once again, something that might have been apprehension crossed Fabius's features. His eyes flicked to the farthest corners of the room before focusing on Marcius again. "Have you noticed the buildings here? Not this one, it's *our* work, but the old ones, the originals. The roads? The necropolis? Does anything about them stand out to you?"

"They are not what I would call conventional. Or orderly."

Fabius's lips spread in a grotesque smile. "My friend, they *are* orderly. They are exquisitely orderly. Everything here is part of something larger, something intricate beyond measure. From where you stand, you see but a single tile in vast mosaic. Those stones near the tombs, remember? Each of them has a purpose. And every one of those arrangements is but a stone in a larger, yet more complex arrangement. Do you understand, Quintus?"

"I wish I did."

From the shadows of a far corner, a soft scratching sound caught his attention. He glanced in that direction but saw nothing.

"Rats?"

Fabius appeared uncomfortable. "Occasionally, there are rats in this place. I may need to take steps."

"Who did you bury today, Titus?"

"It was a—" Fabius's eyes flicked toward something behind Marcius, and his voice caught. "It was a youth from the village."

Marcius sensed a new presence in the room, and a low, husky voice said, "Excuse me." The sound of it raised the hair on the back of his neck, for it struck him as somehow wrong. *Unearthly.*

He looked around and saw a willowy silhouette standing in the doorway to the atrium. The figure took a few steps into the lamplight, which revealed a slender young woman with dark flowing hair and luminous blue eyes.

Marcius rose from his seat and gave the woman a curt bow.

"Quintus, this is my wife, whom I call Iuliana. You could not pronounce her actual name. She is from here in Lloigola. Iuliana, this is Quintus Festus Marcius, who served with me in Valeria Victrix. He is now centurion, as I was then."

"It is my pleasure," the woman said, or so he thought. Her voice somehow sounded both coarse and ethereal.

But when she spoke, her lips did not move.

It seemed he had somehow apprehended her very thoughts.

"Would you care for refreshment?" Her eyes penetrated his like sapphire blades.

"Forgive me, Quintus, I should have already offered you a drink," Fabius said. "I fear our stock of Roman wine is all but depleted. The ale they make here is tolerable, at least."

"Nothing, thank you."

Iuliana was not tall, but she carried herself with a regal air, her posture almost unnaturally erect but for a slight bulge between her shoulders that hinted at an arched spine. From each temple, streaks of silver gray cut their way through her sienna tresses. Despite these apparent traits of age, Marcius would have put her at no more than twenty years old.

"Iuliana has been invaluable in helping me understand the people here, the culture. In your eyes, they might appear unsophisticated, even primitive, but they possess a magnificent understanding of mathematics and science. I have studied their beliefs, their rituals. They are of an immensely strong stock. They could be far more valuable to Rome than anyone knows. But Rome cannot receive the best from these people by simply conquering and assimilating them." He leaned forward and lowered to his voice to a near-whisper. "Marcius, they—certain of them—have seen what lies beyond life itself."

"My husband does not tell you all." Iuliana's voice drifted from some unfathomable distance. "He himself has crossed the threshold of death and returned. Titus Fabius and I both have walked together down corridors that lead from this world to others beyond."

By the woman's tone, she might have announcing an imminent rainfall.

Or had she spoken at all?

He turned to face her, certain now that his hosts were deluded—or worse, mad. "Forgive me for my bluntness, but it sounds as if you both have experienced remarkably vivid dreams. Waking dreams, perhaps."

"Quintus, what you heard was something that came from within a dream."

Iuliana's lips spread in a smile, which remained fixed for so long her face became a grotesque mask. At last, she said,

"Experiences such as these might be called the ultimate dream."

Her lips did not move at all.

"In fact, my husband and I met inside a dream. I need him. I will always need him."

Not a candid statement of love or desire. More a declaration of possession.

Once again, Marcius heard a low scrabbling in the room's darkest corner. A rat *must* have made its way inside, but he could discern no movement in the shadows. When he looked back to Iuliana, she was gone.

His heart slammed against the walls of his chest. She could *not* have left the room so abruptly. It was not possible.

Fabius was staring at him. "You seemed dazed, Quintus. I was afraid I might need to snap you out of it."

"Your wife left so suddenly."

The older man glanced toward the door, and as on several previous occasions, he appeared wary, uneasy. "When you did not speak for some time she took her leave."

"It was only for a moment."

It was only a moment.

"You are exhausted from your journey, my friend. There will be time tomorrow to discuss our affairs. Allow me to show you to a comfortable suite where you may relax. I will have food and drink sent to you, though I'm afraid you may find our fare meager compared to what you are accustomed to."

"I am most accustomed to meager." Marcius looked back at the door, half-expecting to see Iuliana standing there, or just outside. No. She was gone. Fatigue *must* have gotten the better of him. And something about Fabius's cagy manner suggested he did not wish to remain in Marcius's company any longer than necessary. "Very well, Titus, we shall meet again tomorrow."

As he rose from his seat, he heard another scrabbling sound in the far dark corner. As before, he saw nothing there to make the noise. But as he followed Fabius from the chamber, a strange, bluish pulse of light from beyond the window drew his eye. A light such as Ennius Junius had earlier described.

He paused at the window and gazed into the night for several moments, but the light did not reappear.

As he turned from the window, something outside scuttled away in the darkness.

His "suite" was small, scarcely larger than a child's room in an average tradesman's house in Rome. Having departed his host, he felt less weary but more troubled by Titus Fabius's behavior and peculiar convictions. Contrary to the consul's suspicions, Fabius displayed no intention of establishing himself as a rogue sovereign.

If anything, he appeared devoted to acquiring intimate knowledge of the lore and practices of the region's people, perhaps even integrating himself into their social framework. Yet, while Fabius made a show of personal strength, it was a thin and brittle façade.

And this delusion of having traveled beyond death's door.

Had Titus Fabius gone mad?

But his wife. Her almost ghostly aspect, her uncanny manner of speaking. To Marcius, Iuliana Fabius was a mystery beyond all mysteries.

He was on the verge of shedding his clothes to retire for the night when a low scrabbling sound crept into his chamber from somewhere nearby—at the door to the hall, he thought. There was something just outside.

Another rat?

The provincial governor's villa should not be infested with rats.

His sword and dagger hung in their scabbards next to his bed on a tall metal stand that resembled a serpent balanced on its tail. Instinct prompted him to draw the dagger before moving to the door to listen. For some long spell, he heard nothing further, but then came a dull scraping, like a heavy stone on the marble floor.

He pulled the door open, dagger at the ready, but found only a dark, empty hallway. And to his left, a closed door, which he knew opened to the small, central courtyard. To his right, around a corner, another corridor led to the atrium.

He detected a low vibration, which struck a familiar chord. Then, as he had experienced in the old graveyard earlier today, the vibration became a deep bass tone, distant but still powerful enough to make the skin on his arms creep. After several seconds, the noise ceased.

Then it came again, long and deep, like numerous powerful brass instruments sounding simultaneously.

He stepped into the hall, turned the corner, and entered the domed atrium, eyes roving the shadows for any sign of movement, human or otherwise. Focusing his attention on the darkness beyond the windows, he at first discerned nothing beyond the dim terrace, but then he realized the nearest tree branches were limned in pale blue. When the sound of heavy brass again reverberated from the distance, the blue intensified, then faded again as the sound diminished.

The sound and the light, both coming from the boneyard.

He went out to the terrace and made his way down the cobbled walk toward the rings of trees that surrounded the villa. Each successive flare penetrated the woods enough for him to see the path ahead. He considered going back for his sword, but the light and sound drew him as a lodestone drew steel.

To his left, he saw a small outbuilding with a thatched roof, where Ennius Junius and Lucius Horatius were quartered. No light showed in its single window, but he would expect them both to investigate this occurrence. Perhaps they were already making their ways toward its source.

Once through the woods, he made out the palisade of trees that ringed the burial ground, and indeed it was there the light and sound originated. The brass-like tones now thundered across the open space, surely loud enough to wake everyone in the village, yet he appeared to be the only soul intruding on the night.

No, he was wrong. At the corner of his eye, he detected movement, and then he saw two figures making their way through the trees from the village. Titus Fabius, again dressed in his peculiar armor, the crystal visor gleaming red as if lit by fire from within. And Iuliana, his wife, gliding like a wraith next to him.

Fabius was carrying something in his arms: a small bundle, but Marcius could not say for certain whether it was what it appeared to be. He held back as the two figures passed through the palisade and vanished in the boneyard.

At that moment, both the pulsing light and blaring brass ceased.

Something malevolent hung in the air, as perceptible as the stench of sulfur. He started forward again, dagger at the ready, regretting he had not retrieved his sword. In the new silence, his footsteps in the brittle grass and leaves seemed as loud as the bursts of brass, and he felt an air of profound disquiet, a sensation he associated with only the rarest of nightmares.

"It came from within a dream."

As he passed through the palisade of conifers, he saw a new, bluish glow, which emanated from a gaping maw in the hillside beyond the arrays of rock cairns. He realized one of the huge mausoleum doors hung open.

Two figures stood in silhouette before the radiance, and as Marcius watched from the edge of the trees, another appeared in the opening: a tall, spindly shape that *might* have been a man, black and featureless against the glow. A pair of long, spidery arms rose as if in welcome.

As the pair passed through the portal, he could see that the gangling being stood at least three heads taller than Titus Fabius. The elongated, oblong head turned toward Marcius, and unseen eyes seemed to peer into the trees where he stood.

He doubted those eyes could see him, but he barely suppressed a shudder at the thing's unnatural appearance. After a long moment, with a jerky, awkward motion, as if its limbs bent in *wrong* directions, the ghastly figure retreated into the depths of the tomb.

The blue glow faded into the darkness, leaving Marcius to stand doubting his senses.

The bundle Fabius had been carrying was a child, he knew it. And he knew that spindly figure inside the mausoleum could not have been a human being.

Clutching his dagger, he threaded his way through the intricate rock cairns, which seemed somehow sentient, aware of his every step. As he drew closer to the gaping maw through which Fabius and Iuliana had passed, he saw only darkness within, like a gullet leading into the earth's bowels.

He scanned the cairns, the nearby trees, and the shadows beyond them. No sign of his two men. Surely, they too would have heard the sounds that had drawn him here. But the night remained empty, as if these bizarre events were either commonplace or too frightening to draw anyone to investigate.

Then, from so deep inside the chamber it might have been miles away, a bluish light appeared, illuminating hewn stone walls within before again dwindling away. His every nerve compelled him to return to the villa, retrieve his sword, and bring his men that they might venture forth in strength to subdue whatever dark force held Titus Fabius in its thrall. He knew now that Titus could not be acting of his own volition. Not the Titus he had known.

He was certain of it: Titus's wife, Iuliana, must be part of the madness inherent in this strange country. Part of it, or somehow *behind* it.

Before he realized what was happening, darkness had closed around him, and he found his feet, independent of his will, leading him into the lightless abyss.

The unknown power that had taken hold of Titus now gripped him.

Leading with his dagger, he made his way farther down the endless corridor, once pausing to glance back the way he had come. The night beyond the now tiny portal appeared as bright as an afternoon in Rome compared to the dense darkness that enveloped him.

On and on he went, until another pulse of blue light bathed the stone walls ahead—now much closer and as brilliant as a burst of lightning within a black storm cloud. In that pulse, he saw something that might have been a figure: a tall, spindly parody of a human silhouette.

From its elongated head, something seemed to be extending, growing. Something that might have resembled a trumpet.

And a blast of sound swept over him like a roaring wall of noxious vapor spewed from the underworld. A chorus of deep bass trumpets, blasting, blaring, assaulting not only his eardrums but his spirit, as though the noise were a living beast rending his flesh and tearing its way through to his core. He dropped the dagger and clamped his hands over his ears, but in vain, for the horror was already inside him.

A seeming eternity of violent, screaming madness transitioned to overwhelming silence. An utter vacancy inside his skull. A void so vast that no light or sound could intrude upon it.

The void shifted and became a small chamber with wooden walls, illumined in dim blue. Or something *like* blue, perhaps; a color his brain could not grasp or define.

The chamber walls and ceiling slanted, bent, and came together in peculiar fashion, with countless corners he should not have been able to see around, yet in some directions, his view appeared limitless, while in others, the strange light ended abruptly, as if stopped by walls that did not exist.

Somewhere in the distance, he heard the wailing of an infant. A tortured, pitiful cry: the mortal screaming of one too young to have even become aware of its own existence. Then, as if some unimaginable force had ripped the very lungs from the young body, the crying ceased.

There were three figures around him now. Perhaps they had been there all along, his senses so muddled he had simply not perceived them. Titus Fabius, now stark naked; his wife, Iuliana, draped in a dark robe that bore the same spiraling pattern as Titus's armor; and the tall, almost insect-like being, the latter barely discernible within a pool of deep shadow.

Iuliana's brilliant sapphire eyes were fixed on his, her face a crystalline mask, beautiful, yet somehow hideous in its leering, *unearthly* aspect. She took a step toward him. Titus Fabius dropped to his knees, his eyes never leaving his wife's figure. Another step forward, and Iuliana's face seemed to crack, as if the mask were about to break and fall away.

Her lips did not move, but from some immeasurable distance her voice drifted to him. "You have eyes to see. Not all who look may view the ultimate truth."

Behind her, shadows fell upon Titus's bent body, which seemed to dwindle in stature with the diminishing of the light.

Iuliana's hand rose and pointed to one of the many corners of the chamber. He saw there, though he had not noticed it before, Titus's suit of armor, as if hung upon a mannequin.

"That shall be yours. It will shield you when you take your place in this domain. You will assume this mantle and shed all fear, and you will serve the Messenger, the Harbinger—the *Prefect*, to use a term you may understand—of the land between lands, of that which was and that which shall be. You, Quintus Marcius, will be my surrogate, successor to that one, who has fulfilled his role as far as it may be fulfilled." Her eyes shifted to Titus Fabius, now wholly enveloped in shadow. "His armor is stripped away, and thus he shall serve in a more appropriate form. Behold."

The shadows writhed and shifted like something alive, a thing of wavering arms and curling tendrils. Finally, like smoke dissipating on a breeze, the ghostly shadow-thing vanished, leaving behind something small and wriggling, not even as large as the infant Titus had brought into the depths as some unholy sacrifice to the spindly thing glowering in the darkness.

Iuliana stood before him, but now he had to look *down* to meet her gaze.

He saw an ancient, withered crone, her face creased and leathery, but with eyes still radiant blue. From somewhere beyond the wooden walls of the chamber, he heard voices, or so he thought, speaking in some language he did not comprehend.

One of them was repeating syllables that sounded like "Kay-zee-aah. Kay-zee-aah."

Then everything in his vision turned blood red, and he realized he was peering out from the crystal, ruby-like visor of the helmet that had belonged to Titus Fabius.

He turned away from the old woman and saw before him an endless corridor of stone: the passageway by which he had entered this place, but now, as if illuminated by amber-tinted light, the walls appeared adorned with complex geometric figures and spiraling patterns, like those on Titus's—now his—suit of armor and Iuliana's robe.

"Everything here is part of something larger, something intricate beyond measure. From where you stand, you see but a single tile in vast mosaic."

He took a single step forward, found his body almost weightless, *feathery*, as if the armor had somehow imbued his muscles with superhuman strength. He made his way into the passage and began to walk with assurance, a stride driven by purpose.

A purpose he did not understand or even care to know, yet so inevitable, so irrefutably *his*, that he could only embrace it, if for no other reason than to hold at bay his fear. A fear that, should he lose sight of his purpose, would undo him as it had undone Titus Fabius.

The governor leaned close and glared at Quintus Marcius, his unblinking blue eyes eerily similar to the those of the woman who had called herself Iuliana.

"What do you mean Titus Fabius is gone from Pons Devana? He is dead, then?"

"Missing," Marcius said. "His fate is unknown."

"So. The place has no governor. No representative of Rome whatsoever?"

"That is correct, Consul."

Septimus Nerva Laurentius gave him a long, appraising stare. "We will discuss this situation in more depth. But given your service, your history with Fabius, and your familiarity with Pons Devana, I am inclined to appoint you the new prefect." The blue eyes gleamed as if raw energy blazed inside them. "What say you, Marcius? Would you assume that duty for the glory of Rome? Without reservation?"

"If that is your pleasure, Consul."

A low scrabbling sound drew Laurentius's eyes to the shadows in the far corner of his office. His face lost a shade of its ruddiness.

"Is something wrong, Consul?"

"I ordered this place be cleared of rats," Laurentius said with a frown of something more than annoyance. "I ordered it. Ever since you returned, they—" His words trailed away, and after a moment of apparent indecision, he drew himself to his full height. "We will discuss these matters in more detail in the morning. Report here at the first hour. You are dismissed."

Marcius raised his arm in a salute, then turned to leave the Consul's chamber. Just before stepping into the evening air, he paused and glanced into the shadowed corner where he had heard the vague scrabbling.

Yes. It *was* there.

It had followed him from Lloigola and would continue to follow him. The prospect was both reassuring and chilling. He had glimpsed it only once before, just prior to leaving Pons Devana: a thing that had sprung from inside a dream.

A thing that resembled a huge rat.

A rat with a human face.

A rat with the face of Titus Antonius Fabius.

The Devil's Eye

1995

"If you know about it, it knows about you. And if you see it, it will come for you."

He had heard those words seventeen years ago, spoken by his younger brother, Ronnie. Ronnie, now dead and gone, taken away, probably ripped apart, if there was anything to the stories told.

Didn't used to think there could be any truth to them, just rural legends that had a way of cropping up in communities tucked away from the rest of developed civilization, the way Beckham was. Well, Ronnie had believed it, and he had died for his belief, just a kid of fourteen at the time. Too young to really know what it meant to believe in anything.

Now, Jack Neely believed in all kinds of things he never had as a young one, things he couldn't have imagined then and wished he couldn't now. Easy to believe in evil when your mom drinks herself into the grave at age thirty-seven, and your dad shoots himself in the head the day after she's buried.

And when you get hooked on the hard shit by the time you turn eighteen, and you spend a couple of years in the hole after getting busted, and you find the only guy in Catawba who treated you decent smashed up so he'll never walk again, just for refusing to give up a smoke to a temperamental rapist/murderer.

Yes, it was easy to believe Ronnie had been taken away by the same kind of people Jack had come to realize lived so close that you could smell them, even if you couldn't see them. Yeah, that was the scary thing. You could never see them, not until it was too late. But they were always there.

Every seventeen years it came—just like locusts, so they said—but to eat souls, not foliage. At the autumn equinox. If you saw it, you were dead. It would take you, simple as that. And Ronnie had seen it. He had believed in it. The poor kid—the poor damned, deluded kid—went out in the middle of the night and saw the wrong thing. Or the wrong people. Neely always wondered if Ronnie had smelled them before it was over for him.

Now he made movies.

It had always been a dream of his, long before his parents went dead, even before Ronnie went missing (dead). But no one from a little rural town in southwestern Virginia could ever hope to make it big in Hollywood, especially when he didn't have enough money to get across town, much less across the country.

Dreams are dreams, they'd say, all those people that slaved with him on the line at Booker Furniture, not a one of whom possessed enough gumption to put a pen to paper and come up with so much as a witty line or a vivid scene or a pretty musical note or anything that might draw upon their latent right-brain energy. The most right-braining any of them had ever done was conjuring up the Fugue Devil, way back when.

But while going to Hollywood was out of the question, an enterprising and determined soul could still take a dream and make it real if he cared enough to really try. And Neely was quick to realize that the booming film industry down in North Carolina could mean that his neck of the woods wasn't as close to nowhere as it had always seemed.

He picked up Carolina and Virginia Film Industry directories and started writing letters. Although not much of a reader, over the course of his life, Neely had checked out just about everything ever written on the subject of making movies. He could converse with reasonable intelligence about cameras, lighting, sound, even a little about screenwriting.

He figured if he could get a position even as lowly as a grip with some studio, that would be his ticket in. He received a few callbacks, but nothing that held any promise—until he hooked up with a man who went by the name of Running Bear.

Said Bear had owned an independent studio in Wilmington that had gone bust since its listing in the Carolina directory. Green Abbey, as the studio was called, had once contracted with Ted Turner on a TV project, but long-term success had managed to elude it.

Running Bear was in the process of finding investors to get the company back on its feet, and he seemed happy enough to send letters back and forth with Neely, if for nothing more than to talk shop with an interested party. And Neely reckoned that it never hurt to get in good with anybody in the business, especially if the break Running Bear needed actually happened to come his way.

But what had sewn up their relationship was the Fugue Devil, which Neely mentioned while explaining briefly how his brother had disappeared when he was a kid. Running Bear bit down on that like a grizzly on raw meat. Something about the story appeared to inflame certain Native American nerves.

Green Abbey found some money very shortly thereafter. And word arrived that Running Bear was coming to

Beckham. His intent? To film the very thing that had supposedly killed the younger Neely on the night of the autumn equinox seventeen years before.

Every seventeen years it came. Like the locusts.

Green Abbey Studios, Beckham, was a pair of old passenger train cars parked side by side, their facing doors connected to each other by sheet metal and planking, situated where the old train station had been before it was torn down in the late 60s. The town rented the cars out to whatever business might want to use them, short or long term, didn't matter, as long as $400 a month came in on time.

For that, you got the cars. They were hooked up for running water, electricity, hot and cold air, and there was garbage pickup once a week, but you had to pay for these extras yourself.

Prior to Green Abbey, the cars had temporarily housed a lawyer's office while a permanent building was erected on Beckham's main street. Before that, the local RE/MAX agency had occupied it to show off its creative use of real estate.

Running Bear didn't look like an Indian, except for a slightly dark complexion and high cheekbones. His hair was sandy brown, his eyes blue. Native American ancestry definitely, but mixed with plenty of Anglo. He also had a regular English name, but preferred the Indian moniker for professional and social purposes.

The first thing Running Bear did was provide Neely with the appropriate government forms, a contract, and a pair of safety shoes. Thus, it was official: Jack Neely's working hours belonged to Green Abbey Studios, a real live movie company, and within an hour of signing on, he signed off at Booker Furniture, Inc. Permanently.

His title was Executive Producer, though it didn't entail putting up any dollars. What it did mean was that he would receive a percentage of the profits and a point on the gross of whatever product evolved from the footage of the Fugue Devil that Running Bear intended to capture.

The fact that the whole thing belonged to rural legend daunted neither of them.

Neely received his orientation two days before the equinox, during which they talked of death.

"Tell me more about your brother," Running Bear said, seated at his desk—a pair of card tables in one of the plywood-partitioned "rooms" of the train car, already outfitted with computer, fax, darkroom facilities, sound mixing boards, editing equipment, a couple of couches and a refrigerator.

"Ronnie was fourteen," Neely said, picturing his brother's face, his straw-colored hair, his lanky physique. "He heard the stories. I heard them when I was in school too. But it's all pretty much forgotten. Times change. People aren't so afraid of what's in the dark anymore unless it's your neighbor."

"You've never heard the scream of the Wampus Cat or seen the black Big Head rolling through the forest beneath a full moon. You've never seen the Birds of Fire light up the sky like fireflies, trailing smoke and crying out like angry children. You don't believe in these things, I know. But you lost your brother to one of their kin."

"My brother Ronnie got on the bad side of one of the local rednecks. Maybe came upon moonshiners when he was out looking for his monster. They'll kill your ass for sniffing the breeze if you're anywhere around their still. They don't care that you're just a kid."

"If that were true, I would never have wasted the time and money to come here. And I know there is something inside you that grasps the truth, though you yourself do not realize it."

"How do you know?"

"It was in your letters, beneath your words. You know, many more worlds exist than those you can see or touch. And there are places in this world where the boundary that separates us from them is very thin. This is one of those places. I knew it the first time I heard from you. And I felt it the moment I arrived here."

"So you just believe unquestioningly that what I told you really happened?"

"Unquestioningly? No. Your disbelief, for one thing, is supporting evidence for the existence of some great power here." He waved away Neely's look of indignation. "Don't get me wrong. People whose beings have been shaped solely by their physical senses seldom see or hear those things across the threshold, simply because their spirits are unprepared. Many, like you, are brushed by them, and even then shut them out, perhaps for fear of what their existence actually means."

Neely almost cringed under the intense scrutiny of Running Bear's bright blue eyes. "Well, I've known people who believed wholeheartedly in the thing," he said softly. "There was a man, a blind man. He claimed to have lost his eyes from seeing the thing. And there were deaths attributed to it, most before my lifetime. But the same night Ronnie disappeared, there were others...."

"And despite your prevailing sense of reason, that is why, deep in your heart, the Fugue Devil is real to you. I will want to hear all the stories you know. To prepare."

"And you actually mean to film it?"

Running Bear's eyes focused on something far away. "Remember how primitives used to believe that if you photographed someone you stole a part of his soul? Well, imagine actually capturing the image of this ancient spirit. No, the emulsion of film or the magnetic particles of a tape do not literally capture the spirit itself. But the power— think of the power I will steal simply by imprinting its visual likeness on physical media as it crosses from its territory into ours. The opportunity is unimaginable."

"Let's say you're able to do this. Don't you think there's terrible danger?"

Running Bear did not immediately answer. A moment later, he said, "Tell me—do you know how the Fugue Devil got its name?"

"Well, as the story goes, there was a man from Beckham, back in the twenties, who learned how to summon spirits by playing music. One night he stood on the summit of Copper Peak and played his violin. And called down the Fugue Devil, which took him away."

"Tell me again the rules that govern its existence."

"The Fugue Devil appears every seventeen years on the night of the autumn equinox. If you know about it, it knows about you. And if you see it, it will come for you."

"Well, you and I already know of it. And in order to photograph it, one would reasonably expect to have to see it, right? To survive that, my friend, is the challenge before us."

Green Abbey Studios employed a staff of about a dozen, but Running Bear had brought only a single assistant with him. This gentleman, name of Hugo Eckert, acted as cameraman, sound engineer, editor—whatever the needs of the moment, he was the man.

In the past, he and Running Bear had put together a couple of biker-from-hell flicks for direct-to-video release, and Eckert looked like he could have played the biker himself: mountainous body, with little excess fat; crinkly black hair in a ponytail; earrings; leather; tattoos on both arms and probably elsewhere.

And a more soft-spoken man Neely had never heard. Not an effeminate voice, but a quiet and unassuming tenor with a gentle, erudite quality that one would more likely associate with a timid, bookwormish man. But he had been in the navy, seen the world, heard lots of stories. Neely's Fugue Devil didn't seem much of a stretch for him. In fact, Neely suspected that Eckert shared some of Running Bear's apparent reverence for the mystical.

The morning before the equinox, the company went scouting for locations in the official Green Abbey van, with

Eckert playing chauffeur and Neely as tour guide. Beckham nestled in a hollow at the foot of Copper Peak, home to about a thousand souls, except during school months when the college added another thousand to the population.

The one main street included a few shops, a gas station, a bank, and a couple of restaurants; nearer to the college, a tavern and a bookstore overlooked the road from a tall, tree-girdled mound, and beyond this, the local post office—a trailer painted red, white and blue—huddled beneath a stand of tall, ancient white pines.

Just beyond, the road curved to the left, leading around the base of Copper Peak until it reached Aiken Mill, a somewhat larger town in the next valley over. To the right, overhanging tree limbs formed a dark canopy above a narrow, crudely patched blacktop road.

"I used to live out this way," Neely said, pointing down the little road. "My mom and dad and Ronnie and me."

"Where was the last place anyone saw your brother alive?" Running Bear asked.

"He was at some friend's house, on this road. He left there that night and never got home."

Neely found his nerves jangling as Eckert turned the van onto the rougher pavement. The only reason he ever came back this way was to pick up moonshine now and again from Bill Miller when he didn't feel like drinking legal spirits. And he had to admit the memories of his old home life were still vivid and painful.

"Is your brother's friend still alive?"

"No idea. I know he was alive after that night. But I don't know whatever came of him."

A couple of miles farther on, off to the left, they saw a wide field of tall, dried grass that belonged to old Mr. Miller.

"Slow down," Running Bear said. "It started around here." Then softly, mostly to himself: "I knew this was the right place."

"How did you know that?"

"As I told you, the boundary between the worlds is thin here. Your brother saw it around this place."

Eckert parked the van beside the road, and the three of them stepped out to a thunderous screeching and squawking of birds that congregated in the trees in advance of heading south. In the background, a low wind droned through the forest, but none of the nearby trees so much as rustled. A strange air of expectancy seemed to prevail in the late morning sun, which each of them felt, Neely not the least of them.

"There," Running Bear said, pointing to the turtle shell hump of Copper Peak. "Up there. That is where it first appeared to the boys. We will place the cameras here."

Eckert held up a Canon High 8 video camera and looked through the viewfinder at the mountain. "I can set up a digital beta cam with night lenses in the field. But there may be some diffused light from that farmhouse," he said, pointing to the Miller place, which peeked surreptitiously through the tall grasses at the far end of the field. "The 35 millimeter will give us twelve minutes. Video will give us two hours."

"Save the 35 for close up," Running Bear said.

Neely couldn't help shuddering. To think his brother might have stood in this very place the night he was killed, peering up at the mountaintop for the first sign of—something. What had he *really* seen?

"Jack," Running Bear said. "I have a lot of work to do this afternoon. Much to prepare for. Hugo will go over the operation of the equipment with you at the train cars. I'm most interested in you learning how to edit. Sound okay?"

"Sure, sounds good," Neely said, relieved to be focusing on the more comfortable subject of moviemaking.

As they returned to the van, Running Bear took a long last look at the mountaintop, and Neely noticed that he bowed his head as if in reverence. Odd man, this half-breed; almost as if he were trying to make himself out to be more Indian than he really was. What if all this turned out to be some misguided venture, born of Running Bear's peculiar fixation? Surely, it would be the last nail in the coffin for Green Abbey Studios, and the death knell for Jack Neely's only shot at a career in the movies.

No, he couldn't afford to think that way. In fact, it was better not to think at all of what they were doing. If they were successful in securing the footage they sought, it could mean that Neely would end up meeting his brother again very soon indeed.

Neely spent that afternoon with Eckert learning firsthand what he'd seen many times in his books—how to thread film through the editing machine, how to make cuts and splices using the digital film counter, how to match the soundtrack to the visual images. A crash course, superficial at that, but enough for Neely to get an idea of what it was like to physically put together a work print.

As practice, he spent some time cutting and splicing footage from an as-yet-unreleased soft-core porn flick that Eckert and Running Bear had made before Green Abbey's first incarnation turned completely red. Eckert happily told him that, when completed, *Cherokee Cherry* would be the first movie to boast Jack Neely's name in the credits.

"How come you guys make these kinds of movies?" Neely asked. "You're obviously capable of much better."

Eckert chuckled. "We were hoping to make some quick dollars to finance our more ambitious projects. It had just begun to work, too. You know, we had half a dozen features go straight to video, and we got the contract with Turner to work the second unit on a made-for-TNT movie. But our stuff ran into lots of distribution problems. Companies wouldn't pay on time, or wouldn't pay at all. Lots of assholes in this business, let me tell you. And once you start getting in with the big studios, your problems multiply by a factor of ten. We learned a lot of lessons the hard way, some of them too late. But if we can get this project off, I think we'll be back in the money."

"I hope so." He paused. "Hugo—do you really believe in this thing? That the Fugue Devil is real?"

"Don't you?"

"I don't want to."

"Listen, my friend. I've been with Running Bear for a long time. He's got his quirks, make no mistake. But he is a man of conviction. You saw him out there today. He knows things. He feels things. I trust his instincts. And mine. I know I feel something very strange in this place. I believe in it."

Neely nodded, gazing past Eckert to a day seventeen years ago, to a young Ronnie Neely bursting with excitement at the idea of something wondrous and spectacular so close to home. If only he'd had the slightest idea of what he would actually find.

"You're thinking about your brother, eh?"

"It shows? Yeah. He was a good kid. I still miss him an awful lot. If he'd grown up, he'd have been a lot less fucked up than me."

Eckert clapped Neely on the shoulder. "You're going to be all right. Yeah."

Neely smiled, until he saw something way back in Eckert's eyes.

Fear.

Running Bear returned to the train cars at twilight.

"I spent the afternoon at the college," he said. "Interesting place. I was surprised to find no one who could tell me more about the Fugue Devil. It's the sort of legend to intoxicate your average college student. Most places they would turn out in droves to watch for it when the time is right. Like when there's an eclipse. But not in Beckham."

"The night my brother disappeared, so did some kids from the college. Some of them probably know about the stories. But they've never been widespread."

"All the more reason to understand that there is a special power here," Running Bear said. "Imagine, if the existence of something such as the Fugue Devil was common knowledge—a novelty—it would become impotent. Suppose hundreds saw it. Would it destroy each and every one of them? Does it have that kind of power? Its real power lies in its ability to freeze tongues. To hold dominion by fear over the select few who do know of it."

"Then, you consider that it has a weakness?"

"That is what tonight will prove."

Eckert nodded. "Since it's getting dark, I'm going to go set up the beta cams. I don't think we'll have to worry about anyone messing with them."

"No," said Running Bear. "Nothing to worry about there." He turned to Neely. "Let's you and I have a good dinner and talk business. We need to come to an agreement about your position once we go back to Wilmington. You'll need a place to live. I know some good apartments near the studio that aren't too expensive. I want to hear your ideas. I want to know what interests you most."

"This is a lot to think about," Neely said, not sure the whole situation had yet sunk in. "It's happening so fast."

Running Bear chuckled. "I know it is. But I could tell from your letters that you are a serious man. You have a deep desire to achieve your goals. You're creative—I can see this by the steps you've taken to understand all you can about the business. You learn fast. Your ability and enthusiasm are more important to me than your experience. You're exactly the kind of man I want to work with me."

"Well, thanks."

"Now. Your first and foremost task is to guide us to some palatable food. Can it be found in this town?"

They ate pizza and drank beer at The House restaurant, considered by most to offer Beckham's finest cuisine. It was an old southern mansion that had been turned into an eating establishment, which, in its forty-year history, had been owned by about every businessman to pass through Beckham. Neely was more than satisfied, and even Running Bear seemed pleased.

As the hour grew late, Neely realized that anxiety had crept up stealthily on him, and by eleven, his heart was racing—less from a sense of danger than from the memories of his little brother that relentlessly flooded his mind. Eckert had closed himself in the editing room to

338

finish up some work on *Cherokee Cherry*, and Running Bear was in his office doing paperwork.

Neely had been trying to keep his mind on the spec book for the 35 mm camera, unsuccessfully, and jumped up, startled, when a firm knock sounded at the train car door.

Running Bear emerged from his office and waved Neely down. "I'll get it."

He opened the door and, with a cheerful greeting, admitted two young couples, obviously of college age, quite attractive and neatly dressed. Neely stood up and Running Bear introduced him as "Executive Producer Jack Neely."

They each shook his hand, imparting considerably more respect than he was accustomed to. "Now let's see if I can get this right," Running Bear said. "This is Rob Armstrong and his girlfriend, Jenny Barrow. And you are—" he paused, holding up a finger as if searching his memory, "—Jay Strand and Heather Wiedemann."

"You got it," said the first one, the one named Armstrong, obviously pleased to have made an impression in the director's memory.

"They're members of the college drama club. They have kindly agreed to help us out as extras on the set tonight," Running Bear said.

"What?" Neely blurted, but found himself at a loss for words. He looked warily at each of the young people, who seemed a bit puzzled—and obviously afraid that they might have gotten into the middle of some creative dispute among the filmmakers.

With a reassuring look at Neely, Running Bear said, "We'll be setting things up shortly and will start shooting right about midnight. The location is not far from here, just a short distance out from town. It's on an isolated road, but there will be studio lights, so don't worry about being in an unsafe place."

"No worries," Jenny Barrow laughed. "This is Beckham."

"Good. Now, let's step into my office; we'll take care of some very quick paperwork. That way I can issue you checks as soon as we've wrapped tonight. Is that okay by you?"

"Sure," they agreed, and as Running Bear led them back through the car to his partitioned office, Neely heard him say, "Now, the scenario concerns an old legend, in which an ancient spirit is summoned from the sky by a mad musician. It is called the Fugue Devil, and it appears only at certain times every few years."

A chill shot up Neely's spine. "Wait!" he called after them, his lower lip quivering. "But it's real. It's real!"

The youths laughed, no doubt figuring the producer was trying to get them into the proper frame of mind for the night's shooting.

Running Bear waved them inside and gave Neely a broad smile.

"You see," he said softly. "You believe. You do believe."

Neely rode with Eckert in their rented car, while Running Bear and the four students went in the van. As they turned onto the dark road where he and his family used to live, Neely found himself trembling.

"I don't like it, Hugo. This is wrong."

"Jack, settle down. Let's just get out here, do our jobs and go. You said before it was just a legend. Now, is it or isn't it?"

"I don't know. I don't *know*."

"Look. All you have to do is help me set up the lighting. That's all. We'll be out in no time. Even if it's real, it can't harm you, man."

"But those people! You mean to sacrifice them? They're just kids!"

"Now look. If you're not up for this, just say so, and you can stay in the car. But consider our priorities. We came here with a job to do. And that's exactly what we're going to do."

"They'll die."

"Okay, Jack. Let's suppose you go up and tell them they have to leave because at midnight the Fugue Devil comes down from the sky to kill them. They're city kids. What are they going to do, Jack? They'll believe you're making fun of them. Or worse—they'll think you're a lunatic."

Eckert was right. There was no way he'd be able to stop what was about to happen. No way.

"You were chosen for this, Jack. Running Bear chose you. Don't let him down."

"Before I wrote to him, he didn't even know about the Fugue Devil."

"He knew, Jack. Not in any way you or I understand. But he knew."

Ahead, Running Bear stopped the van on a stretch of road short of Mr. Miller's field where no lights polluted the darkness. A chill wind had begun to blow down from Copper Peak.

"Keep it cool and let's just do our jobs, Jack. We're going to put the lights up just like I say, right off the road over here. You all right, man?"

Neely nodded reluctantly. "I'm okay."

"Be sure."

They got out of the car to an excited flurry of voices from the students. Neely tried to swallow his apprehension, told himself they couldn't really be in any danger. The worst that could happen was that they wouldn't get the footage Running Bear wanted so badly.

And Neely would have to call off going to Wilmington. He'd be stuck here—without even his job at Booker to go back to.

What had he done?

"Okay," Running Bear said, taking the students off the road into a reasonably clear area among the brush. "This is where we're going to set up the action. All you have to do is stand around chatting, waiting. You know that at midnight, something's going to happen. I'm not going to tell you what, because I want your reactions to be completely authentic. And afterward, just stay put. The camera's going to keep rolling because I want to get as much natural footage as possible. I can edit the parts I need afterward. So don't worry if nothing happens for several minutes. Okay?"

"Sounds fine," one of them said. The kids gabbed excitedly among themselves, out of Neely's earshot.

"Jack, you know how to set these lights up," Eckert was telling him. "Get yours set up there at a forty-five degree angle to the marks. Focus them slightly downwards, so there's no direct lighting above their heads. I'm going to put some indirect tints on the field. Got that?"

"Got it." Neely set to work as Eckert had shown him, concentrating only on the job. Only on the job. No way the thing that had killed Ronnie could so much as touch any of them. They were working. This was their job.

It was just after 11:30.

A bunch of rednecks had killed Ronnie.

Running Bear himself mounted the 35 mm camera on its dolly about twenty feet from the clearing and focused it on the gathered students. Neely could hear snippets of their conversation.

"Wonder if we'll get free copies on tape?"

"A hundred dollars each is pretty good money for standing around, huh"

"This can lead to more pictures, Jenny, no shit. We've got credits now!"

"I want my mom and dad to see this. They'll be really proud."

Ronnie came across a still in the woods. There were so many in these mountains.

Eckert came to check his work. Clapped him on the back and nodded his approval. "Good deal."

They don't care that you're just a kid.

Running Bear came up to him and looked him squarely in the eyes. "You'll be all right, Jack. Everything's going to be fine. Trust me. Don't you trust me?"

"I guess so."

"Good. Come here. Get a look through the camera. Let's see what you think of the lighting. Okay?"

He knew Running Bear was patronizing him, but he couldn't bring himself to object. "Okay."

He looked through the viewfinder at the tableau before him. It was an expert job: long shadows behind the students, atmospheric, half-seen scrub behind them disappearing into green shadows tinged with red. In the distance, an onyx mountain cutting into a midnight blue sky. He could even see the glittering stars.

"That's a hell of a good camera."

"We got this from Jim Cameron's studio. No shit. Used it in *The Abyss*. After one movie, they often sell the cameras cheap. You know how much this thing is new?"

"About five or six hundred grand, I'd say."

"Closer to a million. I paid just over a hundred thousand."

"Wow."

Eckert was setting up the mike booms just above visual range of the camera. *This* was moviemaking. Neely had always dreamed of this.

"Almost done," Running Bear said to his cast. "Now, what we're going to do is drive a short distance down the road. The camera's going to run automatically. I don't want there to be any presence on this set other than yours, and that includes crew. During the shooting, you just act natural. That's all. I want every reaction to what you see to be completely genuine. At ten minutes past midnight, we'll be back to break down. You get paid and you go back to campus. Couldn't be simpler."

"So, you got a special effects crew working or something?" asked the young man named Strand.

Running Bear laughed. "I hope you'll be impressed by what we've devised."

The group laughed as well. To Neely's surprise, Running Bear then went to the van and pulled a small cooler from the back. He opened it and took it to the kids, passing it around so each could grab a beer.

"Hey, thanks!"

"You might as well enjoy yourself while you're working." He handed one to Jack. "Drink up, my friend. You deserve it."

Jack took one, comforted by the familiar, cold metal of the can. He popped the top and guzzled hard. It was almost midnight.

"Okay, ladies and gentlemen," Running Bear said. "Very shortly, I'm going to start the camera rolling. There's twelve minutes of film in here, and I mean to use every second of it. Jack, let's be sure we've got everything squared away."

A couple of minutes later, all was ready. Running Bear told Eckert and Jack to go on and he'd join them back at the train cars. Neely nodded and turned toward the dark path to the road after giving the college kids a long last look. One of them waved to him. He got into the back seat as Eckert slid behind the wheel.

A minute later, Running Bear leaned inside. "Hugo, keep your eyes only on the road. Do not look at the sky. Do not look at the mountain. You look only at the road. Got it?"

"Got it."

Eckert shoved the car into gear, and Neely glanced back at the little island of light amid the great sea of dark brush.

"You too, Jack," Eckert said. "Keep your eyes down. If you don't look out there, you've got nothing to worry about."

"I know."

"We'll be back to pick up the equipment tomorrow at sunup. Not one minute before."

They drove back down the dark road at high speed. Eckert kept his eyes locked on the road directly ahead. Jack tried to hold his gaze on his feet, despite the constant temptation to look out at the sky.

He couldn't do that. He *couldn't.*

"It's midnight," Eckert said. "It's time. I hope the beta cam at Miller's field picks it up."

A heavy lump in Neely's throat threatened to choke him. Finally, he just closed his eyes to shut out everything until they arrived back at the cars. When the rumble of the engine died and the front door opened, he remained in his seat, and only moved when he heard Eckert unlock the train car door and call his name.

"Better hurry, Jack. I don't think you want to be out here all by yourself."

With that, Neely scrambled from his seat and practically leaped up the short stairs into the cozy warmth of the car's anteroom. He tried to compose himself, to keep from looking like a fool, though he figured it was all too late for that. Eckert went through both cars making sure all the windows were covered.

Running Bear arrived moments later in the van. He brought Jack another beer. "You're scared out of your skin, my friend. You don't need to feel bad. I understand completely."

"I'm sorry, man. This is just too crazy. All these memories, these feelings that this is the wrong thing to do."

"I know. It's going to work out. Tomorrow, we're going to be looking at serious opportunity. Lots of money. No worries."

"It's those kids. Why didn't you tell me?"

"I didn't know for sure how I was going to work things until the opportunity arose. And this was the only thing to do."

"Cheer up," said Eckert as he came back through the door to the connecting car. "There's always the chance nothing's going to show up tonight."

"There is that chance," Running Bear said with a grim nod.

Neely swigged his beer and shrugged. "Let's say it does, and you get its picture. You don't suppose seeing it on film will draw it to you, just like if you saw it for real?"

"Well, assuming the rule that 'if one sees the Fugue Devil it will come' is true, I believe it's because the eyes themselves are the link. Eye contact builds a bridge between the individual and the demon. On film, the connection cannot be made, for awareness only passes one way—us to it. It's missing half of the equation. That is what will save us. But at the same time, our ability to duplicate the medium will actually serve to diminish the long-term power of the Fugue Devil. This is because, should knowledge of its existence become widespread, it would be forced to act against a prohibitive number of individuals. I say prohibitive because it appears bound by the physical laws of this universe. In essence, its power to even come forth would be compromised."

"This is all just a theory, right? You could be wrong."

Running Bear bit his lip and nodded. "I could be wrong."

"What if you are?"

"Then we may die. But I am certain I am correct. Do not fear. And do not look out the window. The greatest danger to ourselves is that we do know of it, and very likely it will come near us intending to show itself. Hugo, what time is it?"

"Ten after."

"Well. In all likelihood, our footage has been captured. And I would be very much surprised if there is a living human being left at our set."

Neely's stomach lurched into his throat. Running Bear was so calm, so calculating. You didn't want to cross this man. That he could so carelessly throw away human lives...

With Jack Neely as an accomplice.

"What do we do now?"

"We wait."

And so they did, for better than an hour without hearing so much as a sound from the outdoors. No night birds. No crickets. No distant traffic or trains. No whisper of wind. Neely drank beer while Hugo again fiddled in the editing room and Running Bear disappeared into his office.

At one-thirty a.m., Neely heard a scuffling sound outside the car, and sat up quickly, all his senses alert. A couple of low voices. There were people outside!

"Running Bear," he called. "Company!"

"What?"

A sudden furious knocking on the door nearly startled Neely half out of his wits. And an angry young voice cried, "Hey, in there! What the hell's going on?"

"Jesus, it's them!" Neely whispered hoarsely. "It didn't come!"

Running Bear hesitated a moment before opening the door. Then Rob Armstrong stalked inside, puffing heavily.

"What the hell did you leave us out there for? Is this some kind of scam or something?"

"I am so sorry," Running Bear said earnestly. "I was beeped and had to come back for a critical phone call. We've been tied up in a conference with one of our producers in Wilmington and we only just got done. This is terrible, just terrible. Come in, and I'll cut checks for each of you. I am really sorry. Shit like this is always happening in this business."

"After midnight?"

"My friend, it comes at all hours. You have no idea how many times I've been called out of bed in the middle of the night for some piddling technical problem."

"Did you walk all the way back here?" Neely asked, barely keeping his voice from breaking.

"You're damn right we walked."

"I-I should have gotten away and come to pick you up. This was wrong, really wrong. I'm sorry."

Armstrong's expression softened a bit, but his girlfriend Jenny Barrow gave Neely an icy stare that didn't warm even when Running Bear said he'd give them each an extra twenty dollars for their trouble.

The other young man, the one named Strand, lifted his eyes to meet Neely's, as if to gauge his sincerity. No doubt they smelled something fishy in all this, and Neely didn't know if he could play along with Running Bear convincingly.

"Did—did anything happen out there?" he stammered.

"You mean the fireworks that came off the mountain? That was it? There was a light that shot out across the sky, and it was gone. That what you're talking about?"

"You saw what?"

"Was that what we were supposed to see?"

"I—I think so." Neely felt the blood drain from his face, and for the first time he saw Running Bear look as if he might lose his composure.

"I will write these for you and then you can be on your way. Won't take a second. Just a quick second," he said and rushed back toward his office.

"Hey," Strand said. "These checks are going to be good, right?"

"Of course," Neely said, voice coarse and dry. "I promise they're just fine."

"You're not looking too good, man."

"It was—it was not good news in Wilmington. Personnel problems."

Another scuffling sound came from outside. A soft, short intake of breath. Strand turned to the door, apparently surprised to find Heather Wiedeman no longer behind him.

"Hey, where'd you go?"

He stepped outside to look for his girlfriend. Running Bear appeared a moment later carrying four signed checks. "Okay, we're all set. I still have some problems to attend to here, though. We'll have to get out to pick up the equipment later."

"You're going to give us a ride back to the campus, right?"

Eckert appeared in the office door. "It's not far to the college. You guys walked over here earlier, right?"

Armstrong gave Eckert a piercing stare. "Not after walking three miles from your 'location,' freezing our asses off. It's getting fucking cold out there!"

Running Bear noticed the open door. "Where are your friends?"

Jenny Barrow turned around—just in time to hear a shrill, masculine scream erupt from just beyond the door. She cried out in surprise and leaped to Armstrong's side, nearly pushing him off balance. A writhing shadow briefly appeared in the doorway, and a second later, a wet ripping sound silenced the screaming.

A spray of blood suddenly covered the train car door, and Neely himself let out a high-pitched shriek.

It was here.

"Oh God, Running Bear! You said we were safe!"

The four slips of paper dropped from Running Bear's hand. And he slowly turned away, brought his hands up to cover his eyes, and began to hum in low tones.

"Christ!" exclaimed Eckert, face now as pale as Neely's own. "Okay, out," he said to Armstrong. "Get out. You can't stay here."

"What? What the fuck are you talking about, man? What the hell is that?"

A low buzzing sound drifted in from the darkness beyond the door; a heavy, rhythmic sound, almost like deep breathing.

Neely heard Running Bear softly say, "Whatever you do, Jack, do not look at it."

Eckert rushed forward, very near panicking. He pushed at Armstrong's back. "Come on, move. Out of here. Get out of here right now!"

"No, don't," Neely said, knowing it was futile. But Eckert *had* to get them out. They'd seen the thing, and if they stayed inside, it would come in after them.

Running Bear's voice then rose above the others, and the two students paused when they heard him call their names. "You may leave now," he said. "After all—it's just movie magic!"

As if hypnotized, Armstrong and his girlfriend obediently turned toward the exit. But they stopped in their tracks when they again saw the blood streaming down the door.

"No way—that can't be real," Jenny Barrow whimpered. "It's not real, it's not!"

Eckert took the opportunity to grab both of them by the arms and use his overbearing bulk to push them along. "I'm sorry," he said. "You cannot stay here." He shoved Armstrong straight toward the exit.

Then he stopped, peering in slack-jawed wonder into the darkness. "Oh, Christ," he whispered. "Oh fucking Christ."

Armstrong, balanced precariously at the top step of the car, stumbled forward and his momentum carried him out, one hand still gripping his girlfriend's. A second later, both of them were gone. Eckert slammed the door behind them and bolted it.

He turned away from the door, and his expression nearly caused Neely to scream again. Eckert's face had drained of blood. Bone white it was, the flesh drawn tight over his skull, his eyes blazing from within deep, dark hollows. A series of tremors wracked his entire body.

"You saw it," Neely croaked. "Oh, Jesus, he saw it. Now it's going to come in!"

"Hugo," Running Bear said softly. "I'm afraid I'm going to have to ask you to leave."

"God—no! I can't go out there! I can't!"

"You can't stay in here. Don't you understand that, my friend? You don't wish to endanger both of us, do you? You know what you have to do."

From without, Neely heard the sounds of a struggle: a low, frantic moaning. Heavy thumping against the side of the train car. A scream, quickly stifled. Then the window nearest Neely shattered, and something burst through the drawn shades, showering him with warm, red liquid. The object bounced off the far wall and rolled to a stop just shy of his feet.

Jay Strand's head, torn from his shoulders, muscle and tissue hanging from the ruined neck.

A pool of blood spread slowly over the floor where it lay. And Neely's voice no longer worked. All that came out was a muted hiss, which died when the remaining glass in the window clattered to the floor as something in the darkness beyond pounded against the train car wall.

"Hugo, it's coming for you," Running Bear said, voice tremulous. "Please do us the favor of departing. Now. The keys to the van are on my desk. Take them. Take the van and flee. You may yet have a chance if you can avoid it until daybreak."

Eckert gaped at his partner, face still bloodless, eyes as bright as train lanterns. "I—I can't move. I can't move!"

Neely summoned what little nerve he had remaining and sprang toward Running Bear's office door. He saw the keys on the desk, grabbed them and rushed them back to Eckert. "Take them, man. For God's sake, don't bring this thing in on us."

He dropped the keys into Eckert's palm. The big man nearly dropped them, but he managed to snag them before they fell. At last, as if he had resolved his inner struggle, his jaw firmed, and a tinge of color rushed to his cheeks. "You're right. I can't let it come in." He gave Neely a wild, frightened glance. "But how can I go out there?"

Running Bear said, "It's between the train cars right now. It won't see you if you go through to the other car and out its rear door. Then head for the van. That will give you a head start—maybe enough to get away. Go, Hugo. You have to go now."

The car shook again, and the wall beneath the shattered window began to bulge inward.

"If it comes in, you'll have blown all our chances, including yours. Go, Hugo. Go."

Taking a deep, quavering breath, Eckert nodded, and after a brief hesitation, leaped with surprising speed for the door that led to the adjacent car. Simultaneously, Neely heaved a deep sigh of relief. "It'll go now, won't it? I mean, it won't come back for us, right?"

"I don't know," Running Bear whispered.

Suddenly, the sound of tearing metal screeched in Neely's ears. More glass shattered, and then the lights went out.

But he could still see Running Bear, bathed in the beam of a streetlight—from outside. The thing had ripped out a portion of the train car wall. Without thinking, Neely leaped after Eckert and dashed through the partitioned corridor to the passage to the companion car. Somehow he managed to avoid looking back, swung into the six-foot-long wood and metal connector, and barreled toward the rear door, which he could see hanging open. Eckert had gotten out, all right.

Neely feared now that the sounds of the assault on the car would abate as the demon turned its attention to him or Eckert, but they did not. It seemed that its focus was not on Hugo at all, but on Running Bear.

He saw Eckert's bulky figure behind the wheel of the van and heard the engine crank to life. With a desperate lunge, he grabbed for the passenger door handle, found it, and pulled so hard he nearly ripped the door off. The van was moving as he clambered inside, and Eckert cast him a shocked glance. "What the fuck are you doing here?"

"It's after him. *Him!*"

"You sure?"

"I think so."

The van's tires kicked up gravel as Eckert sped out of the unpaved turnaround in front of the train cars. But before they reached the paved road, with a squealing of tires, the van slammed to stop. "Jesus Christ!" Eckert shouted.

He had barely avoided running over the girl, Jenny Barrow, who appeared frozen in the headlights like a mesmerized deer, her eyes blazing with terror, black hair so wild she might have been an inmate escaped from Catawba Sanitarium. Neely reached to open the rear passenger door, but with a curse, Eckert hit the accelerator and spun the wheel to go around her.

"What the hell? Aren't you going to...?"

"No way. I saw—behind—"

Before Neely could grasp his meaning, he looked back and saw Jenny break into a sprint after the van, hands reaching out for the van's rear door. But then, as if her trailing hair had been snagged by a rope at the end of its slack, she was jerked backwards—and *up*—by something unseen.

Neely heard her panicked screams, and saw her hair and scalp brutally ripped from her skull; then the horror was swallowed by the darkness—which was all that prevented him glimpsing the thing that had apparently resumed its rightful quest: the elimination of those unfortunate enough to have laid eyes upon it.

Which meant that Neely had foolishly placed himself in exactly the wrong place if he hoped to survive the rest of the night.

Unable to think of anything else, he bowed his head and covered his eyes, praying Eckert could make the van move faster than its pursuer. "Where is it, Hugo? Is it coming?" he moaned.

"I don't know. I can't see it!"

"We've got to get away from here. Where can we go?"

"I'm heading for the main highway. At least there will be other cars. Other people."

But as the van rounded a curve, Neely heard a panicked cry and nearly flew from his seat as Eckert spun the wheel. The vehicle skidded, thumped roughly over gravel, then tilted wildly as it slid down the shallow embankment off the edge of the road. A second later, the bole of a huge tree materialized in the headlights. Neely heard a terrific crash—and his head slammed into the dashboard.

Stars swirled before his eyes, and his thudding heartbeat drowned the fading echoes of the collision. He shook his head, trying to regain equilibrium, and saw Eckert already fumbling at his seatbelt, eyes bulging grotesquely from a chalky mask. In an instant, Neely was doing the same, caring not a whit if he'd sustained any injuries. If he lived through the night, whiplash or a concussion would be a blessing.

Eckert opened his door, started to climb out—and screamed a shrill scream as something plucked him out of the car like an apple from a basket. Neely locked his eyes on the ground, slid out of the van and began to run, gripped by the thrilling knowledge that he had somehow, again, avoided seeing the demon, even at such proximity.

Tree limbs whipped at his face and thick brush entangled his legs, but he blazed through the dark woods, guided only by instinct, for all rational thought had evaporated in a sizzling rush of terror. Behind him, on the road, he could hear keening, high-pitched screams as the Fugue Devil pulled Eckert apart a bit at a time. In a brief flash of clarity, he realized now how wrong he had been about what had really killed his brother.

He nearly pitched headlong as his legs found a path clear of obstruction. He had come out on the railroad tracks that led from the train cars around the base of the mountain to Aiken Mill. Once he regained his balance, he paused only long enough to draw a few deep breaths and then bounded down the tracks, which disappeared into a tunnel of darkness beneath the towering trees. Eckert's screams had faded into distance or death, and now he heard only a mad chorus of night creatures mocking him from the darkness.

After a while, his muscles all but out of steam, he slowed to an unsteady trot, lungs heaving, heart ready to burst. He had been heading away from town, following an unconscious drive to put distance between the Fugue Devil and himself. But now he realized he was a good ten miles from Aiken Mill.

Between here and there lay only deep woods, except for a few stretches where the tracks paralleled the main road. And there wasn't much on that road; a couple of gas stations, a car dealer, a little grocery store. But those would all be closed, and even if he made it to any of the homes in the vicinity, no one would ever let him inside.

Still, he knew he could not go back toward Beckham and his own place. Only by the grace of God had he avoided laying eyes on that hellish apparition. His only comfort was the knowledge he still bore no death mark—not like poor Eckert or those kids.

Those kids he himself helped lead to their doom.

At the memory of that horrible slaughter, tears pooled in his eyes. How could he have allowed himself to be manipulated by an evil man who sought only his own gain, regardless of the cost? A cost to be paid by others, at that! No, Neely had been too dazzled by the possibility of his dream coming true to care.

Even now, he doubted Running Bear was dead. Somehow, that clever bastard would have found a way to avoid sight of the monster, even as it tore its way through the train car to get at him. Maybe Running Bear had even managed to get out to the location and pick up his equipment, and would end up achieving his goal of exposing the demon.

Yet somehow, deep down, Neely knew better. No matter how much the egotistical Running Bear thought he could gain, Neely knew the Fugue Devil would eventually win out. To believe a mere camera could hold dominion over such an eldritch force! It was lunacy.

Pure, unmitigated—fatal—lunacy.

Once his inner heat began to wane, the chill night air began working its way through his clothes, into his flesh. His neck and head hurt from the van's collision with the tree, but he didn't think there was any serious injury. He had been lucky. The crash itself could have killed them even if the Fugue Devil hadn't been there to dole out its own brand of death.

Out here, where he could barely see his hand in front of his face, he began to feel a strange peace, a harmony with the night, as if leaving Beckham behind in some way cleansed him of the evil he had wrought. He knew he could never atone for the blood on his hands, but if he could just stay alive long enough to see daybreak, he could begin some kind of healing.

And he would do what he could to set things right. Expose Running Bear as a fraud—and a murderer. Whatever it took.

When a black shadow briefly blocked the stars overhead, the terror did not immediately strike him. A stray cloud drifting on the breeze, or a tree swaying lazily over the tracks. Even the deep buzzing noise that rose around him did not fill him with panic—until he recognized it as the *breathing* of something huge.

Something nearby.

Before him, a massive black figure materialized and towered over him. A figure whose weight splintered the wooden crossties and sent a ringing tone up and down the metal rails. Neely smelled something hot and sulfurous. High above, a pair of vast wings—wings composed entirely of shadow—unfurled before his shocked eyes.

He looked up...and up...and up.

"Oh, my God."

Amid the starfield, two glittering jewels shone down at him. Jewels that had depth, an inner brilliance the color of the blood in which he had soaked his hands.

"I see you." He sang the words like a dirge. "I really do.

"I see you."

About the Author

The writer is *not* the infamous Stephen King antihero Mort Rainey, but the far more nefarious author of the novels *Dark Shadows: Dreams of the Dark* (with Elizabeth Massie), *Balak*, *The Lebo Coven*, *The Nightmare Frontier*, *Blue Devil Island*, *The Monarchs*, *Young Blood* (with Mat & Myron Smith), several novels in Elizabeth Massie's *Ameri-Scares* series for young readers; five previous short story collections; and 200-some published works of short fiction.

Those with long memories may recall that Mark, as he is known to most, edited *Deathrealm* magazine from 1987 to 1997. In its decade-long history, *Deathrealm* won a bunch of nice awards and featured hundreds of short stories, poems, and essays by authors ranging from the most established professionals to young, aspiring first-timers, many of whom proceeded to carve out names for themselves in the horror/dark fantasy field.

After *Deathrealm's* passing, Mark edited an anthology for Delirium Books—titled *Deathrealms*, believe it or not—which featured a selection of short stories from the magazine. He has edited a couple of other anthologies as well: *The Song of Cthulhu* (Chaosium, 2001), which features 20 stories of Lovecraftian horror, and *Evermore* (with James Robert Smith, Arkham House, 2006), which is a volume of short stories about Edgar Allan Poe, many featuring him as a character.

Mark lives in Greensboro, North Carolina, with his wife, Kimberly, and a passel of housecats. He is an avid geocacher and, whenever he can get away with it, poses as a musician, actor, and graphic artist.

**BLACK
RAVEN
BOOKS**